Charlie Chaplin's Uncle

OR

THE ENGINE DRIVER'S TALE

IAN OKELL

Published in 2012 by FeedARead.com Publishing –
Arts Council funded

A CIP catalogue record for this title is available from
the British Library.

Dedicated to my wife Margaret, who
suggested the book be called
'Euston - We Have a Problem'.

Acknowledgements:

*I wish to thank the following for their
help: Matthew Ellis and Peter Thorpe at
the National Rail Museum, Clive Goult at
the North Yorkshire Moors Railway, Ben
Smith and Carys Lewis at Finsbury
Library Historical Research Centre, John
Green of the Library of Freemasonry at
the United Grand Lodge of England, and
the most friendly and helpful staff of the
Whitby Museum Reference Library. And
finally to Cate Howell for discreet
personal services. I might as well also
acknowledge that I have knowingly
tinkered with the founding date of the
Navy Lodge, but it really was necessary to
the plot.*

*Given enough time and a following wind, I
should be able to blame any of my
mistakes on one of that lot.*

Meanwhile,
the newspapers reported . . .

The newspaper excerpts quoted between chapters have absolutely no connection with the story and may, if you wish, be ignored. Their purpose is simply to give a feel for the atmosphere of the time. They are taken from a variety of North London publications, and have been edited for the sake of brevity.

They are all from Oct. – Dec. 1892.

<u>ONE</u>

<u>London – December – 1892</u>

"Look, it's just for two weeks, and you know I'll never get a chance like this again."

"Hannah, it makes no difference, I'm not going to do it."

"Why not? It's not as if you've got any kids of your own to look after."

"It's nothing to do with that, I still have my own life to lead, my own husband to look after and my own job to do."

"Your job – what's that worth? You spend your time doing la-di-da Clara bloody Griffiths' donkey work, that's not a job that's skivvying. This could be my breakthrough to the West End – and you're just jealous, as usual."

"As it happens I earn more in a week as House Manager than you do in a month as Lily Harley, and what's more I'm working every week - whereas you're lucky to get three months a year."

"I was right when I said you were jealous, it's not about the money - you're scared of standing up in front of an audience. You'd just hate to see me succeed, doing something you can't. It was the same when we were kids; it was always me that helped Mum and Dad with the act. They said then that I'd make it big one day, and they were right."

"Oh for God's sake, you were seven years old and winsome, now you're 27 years old and drunk – and you still can't sing in tune. They were just being nice to a stage struck kid, it's what parents do."

"Just two weeks, that's all I'm asking. I'll never get another chance to be on the Alhambra bill, and I promise the boys won't be any trouble at all. Please – just this one last favour."

"All Weinberg wants you for is to keep his bed warm. You'll get one song in the first half and the back row in the finale, you'll be cheaper than having to pay for a tart – which is what he usually has to do. Besides, he only wants you on stage to help make the proper singers sound good."

"It's not like that; you know it's not like that, he's going to help me with my career."

"Hannah, you don't have a career, first because you don't have the talent and second, because you're not prepared to do the hard work. Weinberg just thinks you're a gullible push over, and so do I. They're your boys Hannah – you look after them."

*****

Chalk would seem to be more closely related to cheese than the two Hill girls to each other. Although it's true that, to the best of my knowledge, they share the same parents and are thus biological sisters, and it's also true they're both good looking – but that's where it ends.

Ruth, my Ruth, has taken the attributes she was born with and worked with them. Half the reason I love the woman is the rare and remarkable fact that, in an unequal world, she doesn't have to rely on anyone, not even me, to make her way in life. She

8

earns almost as much from her work as I do from mine and, though not extravagantly wealthy, I would have to admit to being well paid for doing a job I would happily do for nothing.

In contrast, her sister Hannah has specialised in the less demanding pastime of dropping her drawers, and she's not even very good at that. Ruth's position in life, apart from being my wife, is that of House Manager at the Sadler's Wells music hall. Hannah's position is most frequently on her back. Some women can take this natural inclination and turn it into a paying proposition, and although I would never for a moment condone immorality, I sometimes think it a shame that Hannah isn't one of them.

It's not that I wish to see my wife's sister on the streets, that would be unthinkable, but it remains a fact that most professional married men keep a mistress and, at the risk of levity, it occurs to me that there must be an opening there. It might not be the most respectable of positions, but it would at least bring some stability to the exercise of her only known talent.

She passes through life endlessly hoping that if she gives it away sufficiently often, someone will stay long enough to be her friend. The reality is that she gets pregnant and deserted in roughly equal quantities. At the age of 27 she has had three children that we know about, all from different fathers, and two other suspected pregnancies that she doesn't wish to acknowledge. We don't know how they ended, but I can take an unhappy guess.

Even as recently as the infant Charlie, the one before last, she could still have rescued the situation. Charlie senior, despite being another theatrical and a

9

boozer with it, had actually done the decent thing and married her, calmly accepting the presence of an earlier bastard. But good fortune is never quite good enough for Hannah, and last August she gave birth to another child, George, openly admitting that her new husband was not the father. Charlie need never have known and would probably have learned to live with any suspicion. If the stupid girl can't keep her legs together she could at least learn how to keep her mouth shut.

The deeply unsatisfactory, though wholly predictable, result was that Charlie senior packed his bags and left. What on earth did she think he would do with the news?

The latest addition, the baby George, has now been taken to live with his father, leaving Hannah to raise Sydney and Charlie junior. Despite Charlie senior's departure she still calls herself Mrs. Chaplin, though I don't know why she bothers – there's not a lot of point in being a Mrs. if you don't have a Mr. And there's not much call for any appearance of respectability in her profession.

All of which means that in order for her to continue her lacklustre and faltering career as Lily Harley, horizontal chanteuse, she has to either save enough from her small income, before it goes on booze, to pay for a child minder, or turn to her sister.

Ruth calls it being cruel to be kind, saying that every time we accede to her desperate pleas for help we are simply encouraging her to further folly. And she's right, none of the help we have ever provided has resulted in any improvement in her behaviour, and none of the cash we have ever 'lent' her has gone anywhere but across the nearest taproom bar. Her behaviour is not so much ill intentioned, as weakly and predictably inadequate. The current compromise is that we, or more frequently just Ruth, look after Sydney and Charlie, the two remaining boys, for one night a week, and turn deaf ears to all other entreaties – no matter how colourful the accompanying pack of lies.

There is, as you might have guessed, also a deeper and more personal reason for our intransigence, in the eight years of our marriage Ruth and I have yet to be blessed with children of our own. Wanting children is one thing, but for that want to be used as the reason for dumping Hannah's feckless fecundity on us, comes close to rubbing our noses in it. I honestly hope this doesn't sound callous, but don't really mind if it does.

The only fly in the ointment of our determination in this matter, and there was bound to be one, is the fact that we have become very fond of the two remaining boys. We would be distraught if Hannah were to disappear with them into that unsavoury world where the lower end of the stage merges into prostitution.

It would hardly be a surprising end for her; in fact it sometimes seems inevitable. But it would be heartbreaking to think of the boys abandoned and starving in some unheated garret, whilst she frittered away the rest of her life debauched and drunk.

Our struggle now is to avoid this growing affection becoming known to Hannah, who would immediately use it to blackmail us into further concessions. Even for an ex sailor like me, these are very muddy waters to navigate safely. If only our troubles had ended there.

*****

11

Social class in this country was once thought to depend exclusively on birth and to be fixed forever; but throughout the nineteenth century, especially in the long years since the Queen's accession, a reforming wind has blown away many such prejudices. The House of Lords, once packed with nothing but Bishops and the descendants of Norman landowners, now sports almost as many industrialists, some from very humble origins. Though one can scarcely imagine them ever being joined by those who tread the boards.

Ruth and I have bought a pleasant suburban villa off Clerkenwell Green, a comfortable middle class area, and once that would have defined us – but now? Ruth works in a music hall and is the daughter of music hall performers, which would suggest a position very close to the bottom of society's pyramid. To set against that is the fact that her intellect and natural bearing are perhaps superior to my own, and yet I was for a while a commissioned naval officer, albeit quite junior, which makes me almost a gentleman.

This seems to make our station in life something of a moveable feast, so it's probably fortunate that neither of us really gives a damn. And anyway, as I shall come to explain, my own station in life is usually with the Great Northern Railway at King's Cross.

Ruth's position, whilst well remunerated, is somewhat less straightforward. Despite being a famous theatrical location, Sadler's Wells theatre is a commercial lame dog. Not since the days of Mrs. Bateman, and her successor Phelps, has anyone managed to make any serious money with the place.

The premises have been bought and sold, let and re-let and even for a period run by an actor's cooperative, the best that any of them managed was to break even – and that not for long. Ultimate ownership of the site is presently held by absentee interests, and all dealings are with a lady acting on their behalf called Clara Griffiths. However, she cares little for the daily running of the theatre and is rarely seen on site, preferring instead to work through a trusted intermediary: Ruth.

In view of this uncertainty it has recently been the fashion at the Wells for the producers of visiting companies to style themselves as Theatre Managers for the duration of their run. Hence the use of the term House Manager to describe Ruth's role in things; basically nothing happens on site without her approval. The circumstances of the arrangement are far too volatile for this to be regarded as a long term position, but for now she finds the work interesting and is perfectly content to let the overall finances of the place resolve themselves as they will. As I might get round to explaining, we have sufficient funds to remove us from any pressing concerns on that score.

The most recent development has been the decision, last month, by the London County Council to refuse to renew the Wells' license for music and dancing. The current front of house Managers, Wilmot and Freeman, campaigned vigorously in the area, even raising a petition of 5,000 signatures in support of the renewal.

But ultimately a small group of local clergymen, led by that poisonous bigot the Reverend Ross, managed to persuade the Council against it. Apart from anything else this has resulted in me being banned from attending any further services in St.

James's, a thing I had previously enjoyed, if only for the hymn singing reminder of my naval days. I do sometimes wonder if I shouldn't be more assertive in my own household.

However, following on in a long tradition of theatrical ducking and diving, Ruth and the two other Managers have now fallen back on a strategy of producing straight plays, which require no such license, and simply inserting solo acts at intervals throughout the drama. They're currently presenting Henry VIII, complete with singers, jugglers, comedians and Clarence the Clairvoyant Pig. It's an artistic delight.

Despite the shaky underpinnings of her job and the uncertainty of our position in the social order, from time to time both Ruth and I seem to find ourselves having occasional brushes with the Royal Family. The Prince of Wales, universally known as Bertie, despite being the outward epitome of marital respectability and having recently celebrated his 51st. birthday, is a not infrequent visitor to the rather questionable entertainment on offer at Sadler's Wells.

It has become an accepted convention that the staff should pretend not to recognise what is undoubtedly the best known face in England, if not all Europe, as he blandly introduces himself to everyone as Mr. Mountfast. The lack of subtlety in his deception giving some clue to his character: larger than life, but essentially honest.

One of the front of house Managers always finds a decent box for him and his two or three companions and then makes sure to keep the champagne flowing. If nothing else the convenient fiction saves an awful lot of bowing and scraping, and the staff are always happy with a good tipper, under any name.

That particular evening as he appeared in the box, a voice called out from the circle, 'Hats off boys – the guv'nor's here', followed by a good-natured cheer, all of which he acknowledged with a smiling bow. The star turn was the latest young sensation, Marie Lloyd, around whose appearance the underlying drama would be summarily suspended for the duration. She could always guarantee a full house and was probably the reason for his presence.

The girl was a truly gifted performer, but also a shameless trollop, a winning combination. When reprimanded by some zealous local Watch Committee for the crudity of her song 'I Sits Among the Cabbages and Peas' she obliged them by changing it to 'I Sits Among the Cabbages and Leeks'. It brought the house down and heaped ridicule on the Watch Committee.

Sure enough, on the night of the Royal visit she milked the occasion for all it was worth, particularly during her current big number; 'The Boy I Love Is Up In The Gallery'.

She aimed the whole song directly at the box containing Bertie and his friends and was rewarded by a standing ovation from them when she finished. It was an open secret, that she was not only married and had a child, but that she and her husband were currently estranged, I certainly never heard of him attending any of her performances at the Wells. This gave Bertie more than enough reason to try his luck, and as soon as her part of the performance ended, his portly figure was to be seen gliding unstoppably through her dressing room door.

Unfortunately for him, Ruth, despite running a fairly louche establishment, put her friendship with the various performing Lloyd sisters before pandering to royalty. Marie had a tight schedule that evening and was due to appear in three more venues before the night was out, and although not averse to the pleasures of illicit encounters, she had no time for them that night.

Holding his hat and cane in one hand and stroking his moustache with the other, his diamond cravat pin glinting in the lamp light, this exotically elegant figure seemed surprised to see Ruth.

"And you are?"

"Ruth sir," she replied, resisting the urge to curtsy, "The House Manager."

"Well Ruth, absolute charmer though you clearly are, it was actually Miss Lloyd that I came to see, so perhaps if you could go and do whatever it is that one does when managing houses, then she and I can have our little chat."

From behind his back Marie could be seen making a face and shaking her head.

"I'm awfully sorry Mr. Mountfast but Miss Lloyd suffers from *Regalis Nervosa*, and people who look as much like the Prince of Wales as you, tend to bring her out in spots, spots in very delicate places. So I'm afraid that my place will have to be by her side." This delivered with a polite but flat certainty.

"My dear Ruth, what an attractively firm young lady you are, and how drawn I am to firm and attractive young ladies. Are you perhaps free for a spot of supper yourself, or are you another martyr to – what did you say – *Regalis Nervosa*?"

"Ooh sir, I'm afraid she is," said Marie, "She must have caught it from me."

Unlike Hannah Chaplin, the Prince of Wales knew exactly when he was wasting his time. "Well Ruth, as House Manager I would imagine that you're here most nights, so I'm quite sure you and I will meet again." Then with a movement too quick to be objected to, patted her firmly on the bottom and bade them both good night.

*****

As I seem to have started this account with a long recital of domestic matters it is perhaps time that I told you something of myself, and how I came to occupy my present position. My original career was in the Royal Navy, where I began life as a gunner. Despite the service's reputation for sodomy and the lash, by the time I joined, the lash had disappeared and the sodomy become optional. I found that, without those two requirements, life in the service suited me and I enjoyed the close comradeship and occasional bursts of action.

The happy chance of being in the right place at the right time meant that I found myself leading boat parties on two highly successful cutting out expeditions, one against Chinese pirates and one against an over eager foreign navy. In reality it might be fair to ascribe my success as much to luck as my own natural genius, but that wasn't how it looked to the Navy Board. As a result my shipboard promotion to Acting Lieutenant was confirmed and made permanent and, in order to use my case as an example to encourage further recruitment, they even sent me to Buckingham Palace to be given a large and shiny medal.

A flurry of flattering, though usually inaccurate, newspaper stories completed my rise to brief public attention. In short I was a made man and both I and the large shiny medal were all set to pursue a long and glittering naval career, but within a year of me joining the wardroom, disaster struck.

My elder brother, Alfred, was killed by being thrown from his horse and shortly after that my father died of a seizure, whether brought about by my brother's death or not, I cannot say. Alf and my father had run The Moon in View, a large and prosperous public house, between them, and all our family's money was tied up in the business. They had developed the place into the best known meeting place in Clerkenwell; the bars were crowded and the restaurant always busy. The large upstairs meeting rooms were equally successful, being filled with wedding receptions, birthday parties, Masonic Lodge meetings, even Mr. Marx and his society of Communists were made welcome - as long as they paid their bills and didn't break too many glasses.

The business was too profitable to be abandoned, and nor could it be sold for a song to the vultures who clustered round after the funerals, it needed to be kept on as a going concern. Unfortunately, there was no hope of my mother managing on her own and Alf's widow had no head for business. I was left with little option but to resign my hard won commission and roll up my sleeves.

Inn keeping was never going to be my life's work, and so after managing it for a year with the help of my mother, and without any outright disasters, I managed to find a suitable buyer willing to pay a decent price. It was during this year that I met Ruth Hill, and from that day on all prospect of me ever going back into the navy was abandoned. I still didn't know what I wanted to do with the rest of my life, but at least I now knew who I wanted to make that journey with.

After the constant unfolding of new horizons offered by the navy, the prospect of settling down to a life of humdrum suburban drudgery was unappealing; but what were the alternatives? We had Ruth's wages and my own small naval pension, upon which to live modestly but comfortably, together with a considerable capital sum from my share of the family business; I was rather spoiled for choice. But whichever sort of business I contemplated would inevitably result in me being tied to one place, and turning slowly but surely into just another rabbit in the metropolitan warren.

For a while, I seriously considered farming, the outdoor life and all that, but failed to summon enough enthusiasm to make it seem sensible. I've always found turnips boring and have you ever tried talking to a cow? Ruth subsequently expressed her deep sense of relief at having avoided the farmyard, she would have come with me, had that been my choice, but was very happy that it wasn't.

Eventually, and I can't remember which of us first thought of it, the prospect of a career on the railways came up. There was an indefinable, almost gypsy like, attraction to a life on the rails, and heavy locomotives were the nearest thing to the raw power of large naval guns that I could imagine. I went to King's Cross station to speak to the Great Northern Railway, as they just happened to be the nearest to my home.

They seemed pleased with the idea of me joining them, but all the positions they offered me were managerial, even with the carrot of a guaranteed promotion after a certain period - but all of them involved working from a fixed office, which was not at all what I had in mind.

It took considerable persuasive efforts on my part to convince them of my serious interest in becoming an engine driver; there were repeated assurances that it wasn't really the type of work for a gentleman. However, as I had only been a gentleman for a comparatively short period that didn't bother me. In the end they were sufficiently keen to recruit a naval 'hero' that they fell in with my wishes.

So it was that I spent six months as a fireman and then progressed to being a local relief driver for a year, before joining the exclusive roster of long distance express drivers, and found that I loved the job.

There was a degree of resentment in some quarters at the speed of my promotion, but it soon evaporated when it became clear just how seriously I took the job and also that I wasn't, as some had feared, a management informant. The only remnant that still lingers from that time is the occasional half derisory, half respectful, nickname they gave me: the Captain. It grossly overstates my actual rank but it would be pointless to object, so I don't.

Now my work combines a welcome amount of responsibility with an even more welcome amount of travel: Durham, Newcastle, Edinburgh, there's even talk of opening a through service to Aberdeen.

My latest advance is to be selected as one of the GNR Royal Train drivers. Ruth considers it a great honour, which I suppose it is, but for me the best part is that it takes me onto an even wider variety of interesting and different routes. It doesn't pay much more but I think I must be one of a fairly small group of people to have shaken hands and chatted with both the Queen and the Prince of Wales, and very pleasant they were too. Though I'm told that I was lucky to have avoided her Majesty's former companion, Mr. John Brown, who was found by my predecessor to have been a great busybody and a sore trial.

*****

The same evening that found Ruth fending off unwanted advances at the theatre, found me attending the December meeting of my Masonic Lodge. Like many sailors and, for that matter I suppose, railwaymen I'm not an overtly religious individual and rarely bother the Almighty with my problems, on the basis that even if He didn't actually cause them Himself, He's probably already heard about them. A whispered aside from a passing Archangel about Fowler having buggered up something else, being met with a divine rolling of the eyes and a heavy sigh.

Which is, perhaps, why I found the less specific nature of Masonic moral strictures to be more in line with my natural inclinations. Their requirement that a man should simply affirm his belief in a creator, rather than specifying precisely which God he should worship; and their concentration instead on the requirement to have square and level dealings with ones neighbours, suited my generally benign outlook.

The best part of the monthly meeting was the communal meal after the ceremony, which we referred to as the Festive Board. Being a Naval Lodge we all shared a common background; though several Brothers, including myself, had now left the sea we were still welcome as Lodge members. No matter who I found myself sat next to at table, even if there was no pre existing friendship, there were always shared interests and mutual acquaintances. Somehow or other I always seemed to reach the end of the evening with a smile on my face, and an almost impossibly long list of things to tell Ruth.

However, there were dangers, particularly during the actual Masonic ceremony itself. If one were simply a seated observer of the proceedings, rather than taking an active part in the ceremony, it sometimes required significant willpower to maintain the necessary level of awareness, especially during some of the longer exhortations and charges. Public speaking is a gift given to few, and even when Lodge officers had learned their lines perfectly, a dull or monotonous delivery could rob them of their meaning.

Whilst usually avoiding the preparatory drink that some of the Brethren indulged in; the tiredness following a day's work, the unusually formal clothing and the warmth of the room, could all combine to produce an effect not unlike laudanum.

I had often found the explanation of something called the Second Degree Tracing Board to be a particular danger area. A lengthy exposition on the significance of the decorative features of the pillars in King Solomon's Temple can sometimes be a difficult thing to sit through, without what might be called a slight loss of focus.

The fatal moment, to be avoided at all costs, being the involuntary spasm when your subconscious has realised that you are about to fall off the chair and snaps you back to wakefulness. The reflex jerk from a slumped position to being fully upright, with your eyes suddenly and unnaturally wide open, is usually a giveaway to those nearby. Although if you can avoid the accompanying snort, it is sometimes worth trying to pretend that you were simply changing position.

Happily, there was no such danger this evening, for though tired from a particularly strenuous time at work, I was an active participant in events - in my role as Senior Deacon I was required to be on my feet for most of the time. It was my job to guide the candidate around the Lodge during the ceremony of his being raised to the Third Degree, the final stage in becoming a full member of the Craft.

Andrew McAllister, a naval engineer, and this evening's candidate, was not a man I cared for. My dislike of the man was too imprecise to have merited a black ball in the ballot, but I still thought he had probably joined with a view to career improvement, rather than self improvement. My opinion of him wasn't helped by the distinct curl of his lip when he learnt of my own occupation.

Following my lead, he had moved confidently enough around the floor of the Lodge, being in turn presented to the existing members, the Worshipful Master and the other senior officers.

We had now reached that part of the proceedings called The Obligation, where the Junior Deacon and I stood on each side of him as the Master dictated the words of the undertaking he was required to give. The familiar phrases rolled over us, as sentence by sentence they were given and returned.

". . . . *dispose my heart to succour his weakness and relieve his necessities, so far as may fairly be done without detriment to myself or connections: that my breast shall be the sacred repository of his*

23

secrets when entrusted to my care – murder, treason, felony, and all other offences contrary to the laws of God and the ordinances of the realm being at all times most especially excepted. And finally that I will maintain a Master Mason's honour and carefully preserve . . ."

Was it just my imagination, or was there something in his voice that sounded slightly disappointed with those words about Masonic confidences staying within the law. We did occasionally find a candidate who had ignored everything he'd been told about us, and arrived on the floor of the Lodge expecting some magical network of connections to be opened up for him. I rather hoped that McAllister might turn out to be one of them, then he'd probably be gone within the year. My mind returned to the present just in time to catch:

". . . so help me the Most High and keep me steadfast in this my solemn obligation of a Master Mason."

Unless of course it was me who'd misunderstood things, that has happened before. Perhaps there was some sub text that I should have plugged myself into, perhaps I could have been a Director of the Great Northern by now and not just one of their drivers. The problem with that scenario was that a driver was what I wanted to be, not a Director. I don't carry enough weight to look good in striped trousers and a frock coat.

The Master intoned. *"Rise newly obligated Master Mason."*

That was my next cue, so I steered him a few paces backwards into his next position, and concentrated on looking more attentive, more plugged in.

24

DISTURBANCE AT THE ISLINGTON TEMPERANCE SOCIETY

The Secretary welcomed Miss Constance LeStrange who had agreed to present her readings 'Pathetic & Humorous'. These included; The Hands of a Dying Child, The Drunkard's Dream of Home, A Maiden's Prayer, and Deny the Demon Drink Dad.

By great mischance, whilst still only part way through a Maiden's Prayer, the front portion of the stage was seen to tilt sharply forwards, causing Miss LeStrange to slide uncontrollably down onto a trestle table at the front of the hall. Preparation had already been made for refreshments, and the table was heavily laden with crockery and a tea urn. The addition of Miss LeStrange to this load proved more than the construction could bear and the table then collapsed.

Unfortunately, the Secretary's Jack Russell was at that time asleep beneath the table and was most alarmed at this turn of events. In the ensuing confusion Miss Lestrange was quite badly bitten, it is believed by the dog.

TWO

The previous night we had lain in bed talking over events at the theatre. There had been some changes in the house ensemble at Sadler's Wells, following the departure of three of their house singers to join the new Gilbert & Sullivan touring company; this had led to accusations of poaching. As Ruth was a friend of the touring company's leading man, George Grossmith, there had been suggestions that she might have been involved. However, she said that everyone had been perfectly friendly tonight, so that particular storm in a teapot had probably blown itself out. But there would be something else to fret about next week; the theatrical world was always in the grip of some sort of backbiting scandal.

That led on to a description of the events with Bertie, about which she was clearly more amused than offended. As we both led such busy and varied lives our time in bed together was precious, and anything of importance or interest was always discussed there.

Ruth sometimes quoted an actress friend of hers referring to 'The deep deep peace of the marriage bed after the hurly-burly of the chaise longue'. In fact the strength of our emotional bond was, at least to some extent, built on the success of our physical relationship, and Ruth was very direct in her willingness to address this.

No doubt as a consequence of us both having been born in the same year, 1856, the West End playwright and noted aesthete, Mr. Oscar Wilde and myself are the same age. If ever there was any shortfall in the conjugal side of our relationship, Ruth used this distinctly flimsy connection to wonder loudly if I was beginning to take after my *old friend* Oscar. Or perhaps, in view of my naval background, might it help if she dressed as a cabin boy?

I responded the last time by deploring the unfortunate blood-line of the Hill family, who had long been noted for their degenerate and lascivious tendencies. The simple use of the lip smacking phrase, *degenerate and lascivious tendencies,* had the predictable results.

Although Ruth was confident of her ability to fend off Bertie's advances, I felt the expected mix of male emotions: annoyance that someone should try to lure my wife into unfaithfulness, together with a slight and rather guilty small pleasure that her beauty had been recognised by such an authority on the subject. I finally fell asleep, unsure what I ought to be feeling.

The weather next morning, as I made my way to the station, was what one might expect for late December - cold and windswept. There was already talk of snow, and my brisk pace was as much to keep warm as to hasten my arrival. The route was along familiar streets: Farringdon Road and then cross over onto Gray's Inn Road. The dominating shape of the Lighthouse Building could be seen rising above its surroundings, to mark the location of the King's

Cross forecourt, well before the station halls came into view.

Despite the palatial modern splendours of the stations themselves, and their adjoining railway hotels, the immediate area in front of King's Cross, and its neighbour St. Pancras, was an absolute slum. There were cheap boarding houses, wretched pubs and the lowest class of whores all jostling for space. It was not a place to linger. However, if one includes the nearby Euston, then this group of stations make the busiest entry point to London, with the endless procession of carts, omnibuses and carriages testifying to that fact.

Every day brought crowds of bewildered new arrivals to feed the capital's constant need for fresh blood. At any hour of day or night groups of them could be seen standing there, delighted to have safely negotiated the train journey, but unsure what to do now. In many cases they would probably have been told to take an omnibus to wherever they were going next, but their advisor might have omitted to mention that there would be such a vast traffic jam of omnibuses, all going to different and unheard of locations.

Pickpockets and prostitutes laboured tirelessly to uphold the Protestant work ethic; even the occasional soap box preacher tried his luck at relieving them of their surplus cash.

As usual, I strode rapidly through this Sargasso Sea of human flotsam, the set of my face discouraging casual importuning. I knew exactly where I was going. Entering the working side of the station, after the surrounding mad house, was to return to a precise and well ordered world, the sort of world that suited me. There had been word the previous day that a Royal trip was in the offing, and so it was no surprise when there was a message waiting for me to report to Mr. Dolan, the General Manager.

"Ah Fowler, just the man, do come in."

Dolan was one of life's worriers, and it was fortunate for his disposition that running a railway company offered such scope for disorder, from his agitated look I assumed that he had just found some,

"This idea for the Newcastle trip is completely ridiculous, you'll have to speak to His Royal Highness, he might listen to you. God knows, he never does to me."

"I'm afraid you have the advantage of me here sir, I don't know what you're talking about."

"The Newcastle trip." He repeated with some emphasis, as though I might not have heard him the first time. "This notion that we're going to take the Count of Monte Cristo on the footplate up to Newcastle tomorrow."

"To the best of my knowledge Mr. Dolan, the Count of Monte Cristo is the title of a work of fiction by some Froggy type called Dumas."

"Well alright then, *not* the Count of Monte Cristo, but some other damned dago dignitary – who knows what his real name is, it's all supposed to be top secret."

"And he wants to travel on the footplate, with the fireman and me? Well as long as he doesn't mind getting dirty and keeps out of our way it should be no more than a passing inconvenience."

"But that's the trouble Fowler; he has no intention keeping out of your way. Apparently, whoever he is, he's some sort of demented railway enthusiast and plans to be your fireman for the trip, complete with overalls and a shovel. On top of all that, we're supposed to make sure that no one else hears about it, his identity is a state secret. It really won't do – it really won't."

"Well as neither of us knows who he is, it shouldn't be too difficult to keep his identity secret." I remarked. He shook his head, tutted loudly and drummed his fingers on the desk, in a concerted display of unhappiness.

"At all events it now seems to have been taken out of my hands; I've just had this telegram." He slid the buff rectangular Telegraph Office form across the desk to me. The heading stated that it was from Lt. Colonel the Rt.Hon. H.K. St. Aubyn-Jollie, Equerry to H.R.H. the Prince of Wales. The text was scarcely longer than his title and said; 'REGARDING TOMORROWS JOURNEY PLEASE ARRANGE FOR ROYAL TRAIN DRIVER TO BE AVAILABLE FOR BRIEFING WITH YOURSELF AT 0930 STOP ST. AUBYN JOLLIE STOP'

Dolan looked meaningfully at the large wall clock, every railway company office had one and they all kept perfect time, timekeeping being the lifeblood of our system. The minute hand clicked firmly on to 29 minutes past the hour, quivering slightly in its new position. As it did so there came a knock at the door.

"Enter."

Dolan's secretary came in followed by a thin man with grey hair. The secretary had no chance to speak before the visitor handed a card to Dolan and said "St. Aubyn-Jollie."

Dolan had risen to his feet and responded. "Henry Dolan sir, General Manager." They both turned to look at me. I smiled politely and, as neither of them had bothered, made my own introduction.

31

"Good morning sir, I'm Mr. Fowler the Royal train driver." Taking half a step forward I extended my hand to be shaken. The gesture seemed to be unexpected and the Colonel simply stared at my hand for a long moment, but as I didn't withdraw it he was eventually obliged to shake it: very cautiously.

"Yes – well - that's excellent, Fowler you say - jolly good." He cleared his throat. "The thing is Fowler that your passenger tomorrow is a very distinguished foreign visitor, a Crown Prince no less." There followed a lengthy pause, so I helpfully filled it with what struck me as a pertinent observation of my own.

"That really shouldn't be a problem Colonel, as I'm accustomed to driving her Majesty the Queen, who comfortably outranks every foreign Crown Prince that's ever been born."

Dolan had narrowed his eyes as I spoke, perhaps expecting me to be 'awkward', railwaymen are noted for it, and so occasionally am I. But that wasn't my intention I was just trying to be helpful. The Colonel pressed on anyway.

"It's Crown Prince Ferdinand of Rumania, a good friend of this country, and he will be visiting the Armstrong Mitchell shipyard on the Tyne. We expect him to place an order during the visit, for a battleship to be precise; they could do with the employment up there. Which is why we are so unusually keen to offer him every hospitality, and show just how accommodating we can be."

"Please excuse my ignorance sir, but even supposing they could afford to pay for it, their navy is strictly an inshore small boat affair and lacks the expertise to man a capital ship, and anyway who on earth would they use it against?"

"I don't think you need trouble yourself with any of that Fowler, wiser heads than ours have already decided the matter. Wiser heads than ours." He tapped his forehead as he repeated the phrase, to avoid any physiological confusion. "Your job tomorrow will be to assist in catering to this bizarre whim of the Crown Prince, and help him pretend to be a railwayman for the day." He seemed genuinely baffled that anyone could be visited by such a desire, but I was already shaking my own head in a negative manner.

"I'm afraid sir, that quite apart from any technical problems which may arise; there is a more serious issue. It is unfortunately the case that the last time I met any Rumanians I . . ." There was moment's hesitation, as I sought a less brutal way of describing the situation, but there wasn't one. "The fact is; I killed four of them." Dolan and St. Aubyn-Jollie stared at me.

"It was when a Rumanian naval patrol boat improperly detained a British freighter in international waters in the Black Sea; they had put a prize crew aboard and were taking her back to their new port of Constanta. I was responsible for re-taking the vessel and regrettably their prize crew failed to surrender in a sufficiently timely manner."

"So you killed them?"

"Well as I say, I only killed four of them personally, the rest were dealt with by my men. That's how the law works on the high seas."

His lips pursed in instinctive disapproval, his sort of war was more usually fought on horseback. "That's the trouble with you blighters in the Navy; you're all so very, what would one call it - gung ho – that's it. Well you'd better understand Fowler, there's to be no gung ho tomorrow. D'you hear me, no gung ho."

"Absolutely clear sir, no gung ho. It's just that with my unfortunate record in dealing with his fellow countrymen, might it be more tactful to use a different driver?"

"No, no, least said soonest mended Fowler, you just leave your blasted cutlass and your parrot at home and he'll never know the difference."

When we finally settled down to the practicalities of the case, it turned out that the Crown Prince was a fervent railway enthusiast, and was desperate for the chance to make a trip on the footplate of what was one of the most famous railway routes in Europe.

The ongoing speed trials from London to Newcastle and Edinburgh under the general name of 'The Race to the North' had attracted great public interest, which was of course the idea behind it. Speeds for a twelve or fifteen coach train on this route were now passing 70 mph. in places and some of the new designers were raising the possibility of fully loaded trains reaching 100 mph. It was an exciting time to be a railwayman, and his interest struck me as entirely rational.

The reasons for the secrecy were entangled in the murky world of Balkan politics. It seemed that an alliance between Bulgarian military intelligence, and a newly formed organisation known simply as the Brotherhood, was determined to remove the Rumanian ruling class, to facilitate their own takeover of the country. Apparently they preferred the certainty of the assassin's bullet to the chancier option of the ballot box.

Though the notion that we would encounter some roaming mob of murderous Bulgars in the draughty purlieus of King's Cross station, or whilst steaming at speed through Doncaster, struck me as the height of improbability. People like that might present a genuine threat in or near their own home territory, but like certain types of wine probably didn't travel too well. Nonetheless, if the Palace was paying my wages and they wanted me to take the idea seriously, then I was happy to go along with them.

Use of the word *plan* might be to overstate our arrangements. The schedule was that tomorrow's departure was take place at 9.00 that evening, and it was agreed that I would meet the Crown Prince, with him suitably dressed as a locomotive fireman, tomorrow evening at 7.30 in Mr. Dolan's office. I would then take him down to the train shed for some basic introduction to the duties of a fireman, before making our way to join the Royal train as if we were just normal crew members.

Then shortly before departure a distinguished looking figure, muffled against the cold, would arrive with a suitable official entourage and be formally seen off, as though he were the Crown Prince. The late departure time would not only mean that the replacement Crown Prince would be boarding in the dark, but once on the train he could then plead tiredness and retire to his bed for the trip, so avoiding unnecessary exposure.

It all sounded reasonably straightforward to me, though I had a strong suspicion that we were attaching rather too much significance to a very remote threat, but as I said – it was their time and their money.

That night being a Wednesday was the night we looked after the two boys; Sydney now seven and a half and young Charlie now three and a half, a time that all four of us usually enjoyed. Ruth and me, because it was almost like having our own family, and the boys because they got a lot more personal attention from us than they did at home.

Once they were ready to settle down I sat with them in the bedroom and told them another of my railway stories. I gave all the locomotives names, and this one was about Percy the big green express, all GNR engines are green, who would talk to me as we were steaming along, and who would complain if I asked him to pull too many carriages. The usual sort of bedtime stuff. Ruth said that I should write a book of these stories one day.

After they had quietened down, I told Ruth about the next day's play acting and my role as nursemaid to our important visitor. Her only comment was noticeably lacking in any fellow feeling for the Crown Prince. She looked very serious and took my hands in hers.

"If there's any trouble, that's his problem not yours. We've got enough difficulties in our own family without taking on any of his. Just remember you're married to me – not him, and I expect you back here in one piece."

"It's alright I've already promised, there'll be no gung ho."

Owing to my forthcoming overnight shift I wasn't due on duty until late afternoon, and so the next morning should have been a rare and luxurious opportunity to lie in bed. However, the two boys were shouting and running round like lunatics before

7.00 and so we all had a noisy early breakfast together.

It had been arranged that Ruth would give the boys their lunch and then Hannah would collect them around 2.00 o'clock, and so I occupied the rest of the morning taking them with me on some small errands I had about the area. It was nothing special, simply a visit to the ironmongers and returning some books to the Lending Library, but we took our time, enjoying a brief glimmer of unseasonal sunshine, chatting and pointing things out. I was relaxed and the boys seemed happy with the small change of domestic life and the different scenery.

However, Ruth was obviously unconvinced about my assurances of the trip being purely routine, because after lunch when I picked up my knapsack ready to walk up to the station, I found it unexpectedly heavy. As it should have contained nothing but a change of clothing, a book and some sandwiches I gave her a puzzled look over the boy's heads and raised my eyebrows.

"Your Webley and some spare shells." She said quietly.

"What's a Webley Aunty Ruth?" Asked Charlie.

"It's Uncle's gun, don't you know anything?" Said Sydney, getting in first.

"Be quiet the two of you and just finish your rice pudding."

I should have realised that she was likely to do something like that, but smiled at her all the same. "A wild over reaction, but I promise if anyone even looks at me the wrong way." I pointed my finger. "Bang!"

"Just you make sure you do." The four of us had a round of goodbye kisses; I swung the knapsack over my shoulder and set off. The sunshine had disappeared by now, which was to be expected at this time of year, and I found myself turning my coat collar up against a sharp north wind as I made my way up Farringdon Road to meet my new apprentice.

A MOST DISTRESSING CASE

Appearing in a breach of promise case on Friday last, before Mr. Justice Melrose, the plaintiff, Miss Eunice Havergall, stated that the defendant had repeatedly entreated her hand in matrimony, and that she had many witnesses who would testify to this, and that furthermore she had only succumbed on account of his great persistence.

The defendant, Mr. Alfred Jones, of Trevor Lane, Hackney, replied that she did not need her witnesses as he accepted her claims, in so far as they went, but was most perplexed as to why she had not told the court 'All the rest'. Defendant then claimed that the plaintiff had repeatedly rejected his proposals on the grounds that she could never contemplate life under his roof, 'As long as he kept the old b---h living with him.' Defendant further stated that he was most fond of his dog, which he had owned since it was a puppy. However, owing to the determined nature of the plaintiff's requirements he eventually took the unfortunate creature to the veterinary surgeon, where it was put to sleep.

Some days later, when the plaintiff visited the defendant at his home, he told her of his actions and hoped that this had now cleared the last obstacle to their happiness. But when the defendant's mother, who lives with him, later entered the room, the plaintiff remarked, 'You are a very silly man, the old b---h that I referred to was not your dog'. (Cries of 'Oh No' in court)

The defendant was given a glass of water to help overcome his emotions. Plaintiff said that the defendant was an evil man who only wanted to cheat her of her entitlements.

THREE

The title of Royal Train was a fairly loose one, covering many different levels of service. If Her Majesty was travelling then it was the full performance; the engine would have been specially cleaned and polished and would have swags of ribbons and garlands, it might even have a Royal crest on each side. The crew would be in new uniforms, with the driver, and occasionally even the fireman, wearing white gloves. Magnificently impractical, but then, she is the ruler of more than a quarter of the world's surface, and if she wants white gloves - then white gloves is what she gets.

Not only would the departure from London be overseen by the Station Master, but at every station en route the local station master and senior staff would be lined up on the platform, with no public access allowed. The Queen's train was even preceded by a pilot engine, running five minutes ahead to ensure that everything was exactly as it should be. It was a thoroughly impressive operation, and disaster would befall anyone who made a mess of things.

The Prince of Wales merited a slightly lower level of pomp, and had his own two special carriages. Owing to the frequency with which he had a travelling companion, other than his wife Alexandra, it was often claimed that the springs on his sleeping car had to be changed every year.

Once one stepped below that rank of seniority, in other words a visiting Crown Prince, then the level of service was that of a private train, such as may be hired by any wealthy individual. Although the very title Royal Train still ensured that we received priority routing, which ensured that whoever else was delayed by heavy traffic on the lines, it wasn't going to be us.

After a brief chat with my fireman, to confirm that everything was under control with the engine, I spent some time in the traffic office reading the Route Notifications, a collection of notices detailing work on the line and any special circumstances applying to the trip. It was all reassuringly straightforward and confirmed my feeling that this was going to be an unexceptional trip, just the sort I liked.

Surprisingly, when I arrived at Dolan's office, slightly early at 7.20, there were already four people waiting for me, probably deluded but satisfyingly punctual. As well as Dolan there was a fresh faced young man in his mid to late twenties, with a wide and extravagant moustache, he was not quite as tall as me and wearing a brown boiler suit; presumably the disguised Crown Prince. With him was what looked like another Palace equerry, the fourth person was a solidly built, overcoat wearing gentleman of the sort that Americans would describe as a *heavy.*

Dolan and I nodded to each other and the equerry made the formal introduction to the Crown Prince, I shook his hand, gave him a small dip of the head, which he could interpret as a bow if he wished, and said how pleased I was to meet him. He replied in excellent English.

"I'm sure the pleasure will be all mine today, I only hope that I don't interfere with your work too much." That was a promising start. The equerry waved a limp hand at the man in the overcoat.

"This gentleman is one of the Prince's . . er . . attendants and insists on accompanying him at all times."

I pointedly ignored the 'gentleman' in question, took a deep breath and started to make waves.

"Yesterday Colonel St. Aubyn-Jollie stressed the requirement for complete confidentiality, is that still the case?"

"Oh most certainly." Said the equerry, I ignored him and looked directly at the Crown Prince. He hesitated for a moment but then nodded his head and spoke for himself.

"Yes, there is a continuing threat to my person that requires constant vigilance."

"Well then that boiler suit will need changing, it's far too clean and appears to have been recently pressed. I'm the driver, I stay fairly clean; you're the fireman, you get dirty. And this gentlemen can go and find himself a seat in the train because he's not coming on the footplate." If we didn't get this sorted out now then we might as well all go home.

There was a barrage of what I presumed to be Rumanian from the overcoat wearer, he didn't sound happy. The Prince explained.

"Major Antonescu was sent by my uncle, King Carol, to supervise my safety and he says that he must stay with me."

"That is completely agreeable to me." I said. "Then the two of you can both find yourself seats in a carriage and I shall drive the train with my regular fireman. Because if you turn up dressed like that, accompanied by him, we might as well make a public announcement over the station loudspeaker about who you are and what you're doing."

The equerry took half a step forward, trying to work out the exact grounds for his objection to my statement, but the man in the overcoat beat him to it and launched into another incomprehensible tirade.

He was clearly a man accustomed to getting what he wanted, and to hell with anyone who got in the way. He continued to express his views, with the Crown Prince struggling to get a word in. The equerry and I exchanged glances, we were both surplus to requirements until these two made their minds up. After further furious loud and finger jabbing exchanges they lapsed into silence. Then the Crown Prince turned to me and said perfectly calmly, as though there had been no argument,

"Major Antonescu and I have discussed this matter fully and decided that we shall agree with your suggestion. The Major has decided to travel with the rest of the Rumanian security team."

"Very well, if you would be kind enough to wait here I shall go and find you a more suitable overall." When I returned, four or five minutes later with a moderately grimy boiler suit, a fireman's flat hat and an oily rag for him to hold, the four of them were still standing where I'd left them. There was a distinct feeling of unfinished business in the air. I had considered enquiring exactly what sort of a country it was that thought it a good idea to call their King, *Carol*, but in view of the atmosphere, decided not to bother.

As the Crown Prince got changed Antonescu came over and grasped my upper arm in an uncomfortably firm grip, he was an extremely powerful man and the wisdom of picking a fight with him began to seem more doubtful.

"If you responsible to spill Rumanian blood – I hunt you like mad dog."

"And if you don't let go of my arm I shall have a bruise there tomorrow."

The Crown Prince started to laugh at this small piece of stupidity, but then stifled it in the face of Antonescu's glaring hostility. I like a man who laughs at my jokes, but just hoped they never found out about those Rumanian sailors. Probably a bit late to worry about that now. Nonetheless, all I had to do was drive the train to Newcastle, then this circus troupe could disembark and get on with their Balkan intrigues, without any further assistance from me.

"Gentlemen, after the Crown Prince and I have left here, should you see him on or near the train, if you wish to preserve his anonymity you will not look at him, approach him or speak to him. And now if you would come with me sir, there's work to be done."

Without waiting for any sort of a response, I turned and walked out of the office, unsure if he was following me or not. Fortunately, he was, or I'd have looked a complete fool. Waiting until we were alone in the corridor leading to the engine sheds, I stopped and turned to him.

"You're obviously worried about death threats, and travelling in the engine will separate you from your security staff, perhaps Major Antonescu has a point. Are you quite sure you wish to go through with this? Quite apart from the security concerns it's going to be hard dirty work, it's not too late to change your mind."

"This is the first time in my life that I've ever had the chance to do something like this, and when my uncle hears about it, it will probably be the last. Thank you for standing up to Major Antonescu, people don't do that at home, but now we have got this far I wish to continue."

"Alright," I sighed, pulling from my pocket a pair of scissors that I had picked up earlier, "Stand very still whilst I trim your moustache." He recoiled slightly at this suggested assault and was about to protest, when he realised that the luxurious growth covering most of the lower half of his face would utterly ruin even the best disguise. With enormous self-control he silently stood his ground as I snipped off the carefully waxed outer ends, turning it from a regal adornment into a mundane affectation. His determination to be a railwayman was even stronger than my own.

"And from now on you will call me Mr. Fowler or even Boss, that's what any other fireman would do, and I will call you Pedro."

"Why Pedro?"

"Because even with the skeletal remains of a moustache like that you certainly don't look English, and Pedro makes you sound safely Spanish, otherwise people will look at you and wonder. We should answer their question before they ask it."

"Right oh Boss."

I nodded approvingly. "That was good."

It seemed that we were to spend our time playing a children's game of make believe, it might not have been my first choice of an activity, but it's better than getting shot at, and I should know because I've done both.

Our first stop was the engine shed where I gave him a general walk round of the various engines. It was pitch dark by now, but the King's Cross engine sheds were always busy, day and night, so there were plenty of lamps to light our way. I pointed out the significant features of various engines and at the same time tried to establish the extent of his own knowledge. Fortunately, although he had almost no practical experience, on the grounds that it was considered demeaning for him to mix with engineers, he was very widely read on the subject of steam locomotion and probably knew as much as me on subjects such as power conversion ratios.

Coming to England, with our more enlightened and relaxed views on social class, was his first chance to put on a pair of overalls and handle a shovel, and he had no intention of letting the moment pass, with or without Major Antonescu's blessing.

Having seen that he was settled into his new role, I walked him across the tracks towards the area of the public platforms. As we went he was telling me of his admiration for the Prince of Wales and how much more fun he was than his uncle, King Carol.

"It was incredible, two nights ago he even took me to a music hall to see Marie Lloyd, it was a wonderful evening. I've never seen anything like it before. We were supposed to be incognito but everyone in the audience knew him and they all cheered, it was thrilling."

"That would have been the Sadler's Wells music hall would it?"

"Yes, that's right – do you go there yourself?"

"Now and again, you know, now and again."

"During the show the Prince of Wales went to see Miss Lloyd in her dressing room, but came back saying that there was another lady with her, one of the theatre staff, who was much more beautiful. He says he's going back to see her again, what girl could possibly resist such a charming man as that?"

My comment; "We'll bloody well see about that." Produced a puzzled frown but I offered no explanation.

As we approached our engine, coming to it at ground level, rather than along the platform, it towered above us; and I was struck once again by just what an impressive piece of machinery the Stirling eight footer was. The name 'eight footer' coming from the size of its huge main drive wheels. The fully loaded engine, when coupled to the new larger tender weighed in at seventy tons. That is seventy tons of green painted, highly polished, glistening, steaming, hissing power. Pedro was duly impressed, who wouldn't be?

Climbing the three steps to the footplate I introduced him to my fireman.

"Pedro this is Stan, Stan this is Pedro. He's from Spanish Railways and he'll be joining us for the run up to Newcastle, to see how we do things. He can share the shovelling, I reckon he could do with the exercise." Stan gave him a brief, but not unfriendly, grunt of acknowledgement.

I stood for a moment, silently inspecting the cab. The shed crew would have had the fire lit at least eight hours ago, long before the journey crew made their appearance. Stan would then have spread the fire across the grate and adjusted the primary and secondary air intakes, slowly raising the pressure, preparatory to moving her round to the platform

The boiler was already up to a low working pressure, the dial settled on the 120 psi. mark, slightly below our running pressure of 140, but that would be rapidly adjusted by the final stoking and opening the dampers immediately prior to departure. The boiler water level was on the correct line, both injectors were shut, the duplex dial was showing a vacuum chamber pressure of 21 inches of mercury, the fire box door louvers were shut, the coal was trimmed, the glass in the two forward portholes spotless, everything looked clean and ship shape – exactly how it ought to be. I nodded my appreciation to Stan, who'd been standing by waiting for that.

"What sort of lamps did they give you?" Lamps weren't left on the engines, but were issued by the stores for each trip, and for an overnight trip I didn't want the old type that had to be refilled every four hours.

"No need to worry, they're all the new long burners, and I re-trimmed them myself, they'll last the trip." I was normally responsible for all this sort of preparation myself, but Stan had been warned that I wouldn't arrive until later and so had got on with the job himself. An experienced and compctent fireman could do pretty much everything a driver could.

"Have the wheels been checked?"

"Shed maintenance did the carriages before they were brought round."

Stan turned to Pedro. "You'll need to watch yourself young feller, the Captain here's a bit of a stickler, a place for everything and everything in its place."

"The Captain?" Queried Pedro.

"That's right, it's on account of him being an ex naval officer, we don't have too many of them round here."

Pedro turned to me. "You were in the Royal Navy?"

I was thinking that Stan could usefully have kept his comments to himself, but actually said. "Well if you're going to join anybody's navy, then that's the one to go for."

As a means of changing the subject, I left Stan in charge of the engine, picked up a gallon can of lube oil and took Pedro with me to start checking the engine oil reservoirs. A steam engine doesn't just use coal and water it also goes through a great deal of oil. The thinner lube oil was for moving parts and bearings, particularly the big end, where the connecting rod, running down the outside of the wheels, joined the hub of the drive wheel. Because of the higher pressure and the temperatures involved, the external cylinders used a much thicker and heavier oil, almost a grease. This personal attention to detail was absolutely basic to the good running of the engine and not the sort of thing that any responsible driver would ever dream of leaving to other hands.

We'd finished with the engine and had worked our way down the length of the train, arriving at the point where the last carriage was coupled on, and I thought it a good idea to give Pedro a closer look at the coupling itself and the brake pipe connection. These were underneath the concertina shuttering of the connecting passageway and quite difficult to get at. I explained all I could by leaning across the buffers and pointing out the various parts, but then ducked down to climb under the train to get to the items in question, beckoning Pedro to follow me.

The last two carriages were dedicated baggage cars, without seats or furnishings and equipped simply with bare wooden floor boards. As we crouched down by that last coupling, we were half underneath the front end of the last carriage and could hear voices from inside. Pedro made a shush shape with his lips and pointed up to indicate that he was listening, I joined him. The voices were those of two men speaking in low and confidential tones, unfortunately for me it wasn't in English.

I gave Pedro a quizzical look, but he put his finger to his lips and moved to get his ear closer to the floorboards above us. A look of alarm, if not horror, passed across his face. Whatever he was listening to, he wasn't enjoying the experience. Then there were some footsteps and, in what seemed to me to be mid sentence, the voices stopped for a moment before being joined by a third, this one speaking in normal tones. There was a brief exchange, followed by more footsteps as they all moved away down the carriage.

Without saying a word to me Pedro squeezed under the far set of buffers to reach the edge of the platform, where he raised his head to look down it, along the side of the train. After watching for a moment he turned back to me.

"Quickly please Mr. Fowler, we must get out of here, to where we can speak privately."

Containing my curiosity, I led him back along the tracks to stand beside the engine, next to the Stirling's huge driving wheel, where anything we said would be covered by the grumbling and hissing of the engine. I asked him what was going on.

"The first two men were talking in Rumanian, one of them said to the other that he had just been told that the operation was to go ahead as planned. He said that as soon as they had equalised the numbers they would deal with the German pig and Dettman too. The other man asked where he had received this message from, and the first man said that Number One had told him personally. He said they would telegraph Bucharest as soon as they could with news of the deaths. Then someone else arrived and asked if they had finished checking the baggage, they said that everything was fine and then walked back down the carriage together."

"What did you see when you looked along the platform?"

"I just saw a back view of three men in heavy coats, but the light was poor, they were all wearing hats and had their coat collars turned up. I couldn't say who any of them were - but they have to be members of my security team. Presumably this 'Number One' they mentioned is as well, which means that at least three out of my eight security men want me dead."

"What about the German pig and Dettman?"

"I'm afraid the German pig has to be me. My father is a German Prince and I was born and educated at Sigmaringen in southern Germany. My grandmother is your own Queen Victoria. I am Rumanian only by adoption and dynastic necessity; and Dettman is my elderly personal secretary."

We both fell silent for a moment, considering the separate ramifications for each of us. This sort of thing was going to completely ruin my scheduled running times, but there's always that old naval comment to any emergency – if you can't take a joke, you shouldn't have joined up.

"Have you any thoughts on what that comment about 'equalising the numbers' might mean?' I asked.

"Only that it sounds as if they intend to have reinforcements joining the train, so that they can outnumber the loyal members of my team and the Scotland Yard policemen."

"Then I'm afraid the answer's simple, we cancel the trip immediately and have your entire security squad arrested, particularly Antonescu. The police can then take them down to the cells and slap them around for a while, until one of them decides to talk. To do anything else what be to fall in with their plans."

"No, definitely not, we must go ahead with trip. As I said, Dettman is my personal secretary, he's been with my family since before I was born, there can be no possible doubt about his loyalty. But the fact that they mentioned killing him as well as me must mean that they don't yet know I'm going to be travelling on the engine. Which means that Antonescu can't be involved."

"No it doesn't, if Antonescu's the gang leader, then with a personality like his he won't discuss details with his juniors until he has to."

"Even so, this has to be our best chance of catching these people, they can be taken by surprise as they pursue the wrong man. For the first time we have advance information about their plans, it could be our only opportunity to trace this plot back to its source and discover who is directing these murders. "

I was beginning to get the impression that my young friend regarded all this as a sort of game. Well

I didn't. I've seen men shot dead before, and when it happens - that's the way they stay. As I had no intention of joining them it was time to inject a note of reality into the proceedings.

"Look; I'm a retired sailor with a headache, Stan's a non violent Methodist and you're the product of 500 years of inbreeding; we couldn't fight off two tired nuns with cucumbers, never mind a gang of Balkan assassins."

"I'm truly sorry Mr. Fowler, but I have decided that we shall continue with the trip and force them to reveal their hand. That is correct isn't it; *reveal their hand*?"

"Grammatically, yes – rationally, no."

"There is something else I must tell you Mr. Fowler, something of which your own police will be unaware. If these people are indeed members of the Brotherhood, who recently made an attempt on the King's life, then your own family might be in danger." The look on his face was as serious as his words.

"How exactly?"

"They kidnapped the wife and child of the Royal Chamberlain in order to make him unlock two internal doors in the palace, this allowed them to enter the King's private rooms. The attempt came very close to success."

"And were the wife and child then released?" I felt stupid even asking such a question, but I had to know.

"I'm afraid not, they had been killed as soon as they were taken. These people are utterly without pity. Are you married Mr. Fowler?"

Suddenly the Balkan game playing took on an entirely new dimension, I felt sick at the appalling prospect that had now opened up before me. Pedro said nothing as my face must have displayed the emotions I felt. I ran through the various possibilities that might secure Ruth's safety. The police wouldn't take a garbled tale like this seriously, and even if they did, the idea that a couple of Bobbies with truncheons standing at our front door would deter or even delay such people was absurd.

There was only one course of action open to me, the usual one – do it myself.

But as I was reaching this decision, a nearby crunching of the track ballast stones as footsteps approached, startled the pair of us. A tallish man with close cropped hair, a toothbrush moustache and a belligerent expression had arrived, and after looking us both up and down, he discounted Pedro and addressed me.

"Would I be correct in assuming that you are Fowler, the driver?"

"No you would not, as far as you're concerned I'm *Mr.* Fowler the driver. Who are you and what are you doing on the tracks?"

"All you need to know about me Fowler is that I am Chief Superintendant Parkinson of Scotland Yard, the senior police officer on the train. No one will be doing anything on this journey without my authorisation, and that includes you."

"Bugger off Parkinson, I'm busy." I began to turn away, but incredibly he caught hold of my arm to detain me. I seized the offending hand, deliberately crushing his fingers together to make my point, but even so I wasn't angry, he had simply failed to appreciate the underlying reality – round here I was in charge. To my surprise he felt the need to persevere.

"Fowler this train is under police control, and that means my control – you'd better get that point clear before you find yourself in serious trouble." You could see that his hand was hurting, but he'd die before admitting it.

I used my other hand to point a finger in his face. "You can give orders to as many passengers as you like Parkinson and perhaps they'll listen, but make no mistake - when this train pulls out of the station I am its Master Under God, just like on a ship. Pedro, get on the footplate." I turned to follow him.

"Get back here, I haven't finished with you yet."

"Perhaps not, but fortunately it's not your decision, and I've got better things to do." As I climbed the steps up to the engine I think he was still talking, but I'd already switched him off.

"Right Pedro you stay on the footplate and keep your face out of sight. Stan, I've got an errand to run which will take me thirty or forty minutes. Now listen carefully, this is what I want you two to be doing while I'm gone."

<u>*Meanwhile*</u>
   <u>*the newspapers reported . . .*</u>

POLISH GENTLEMAN in the fur trade, newly arrived in London, seeks friendship with lady to practise language. I am 60 yr. old widower with 2 grown up daughters and a Lurcher, but all are well disposed and most amiable, will cause no problems to any suitable lady.
Reply in confidence to Box 489

WIDOWED GENTLEMAN in Bloomsbury seeks respectable lady with view to renewal of domestic harmony. My much loved mother will complete our home, her sage advice on so many matters having proved invaluable down the years. Please contact us in strictest confidence to arrange an interview. Box 1254.

FOUR

Stepping out onto the platform I looked for a familiar face and spotted St. Aubyn-Jollie surveying the arrangements, he would do nicely. I made my way over to him, trying to behave as though casual and unhurried.

"Colonel, please try not to seem alarmed but the Crown Prince and I have just discovered the existence of a plot to kill him during the trip." One has to give the man credit, the only give away to any surprise he felt was one raised eyebrow. I took this as a sign to press on and explained the overheard conversation, and the Crown Prince's interpretation of it. His eyebrow edged fractionally higher as I did so.

"Who's going to be responsible for seeing off his stand in?" I asked.

"The Prince of Wales, he's due to arrive in half an hour or so, with the official party."

Having heard what I had to say, the Colonel readily agreed to arrange for the Royal party to be delayed out of sight, before it reached the train, and for me to have an audience with Bertie. That left me just enough time, if I ran.

And so I ran, I ran the mile and a quarter back to my house, with every step thinking: please Ruth, be in when I get there. Although dusk had brought with it a sharp crispness to the air I could still feel my own temperature rising as my boots clattered noisily against the pavement, whether this rise was due to the apprehension or the exertion wasn't clear. Ruth was in, but astonished to see me, the original schedule should have had me thundering my way north by now.

"Whatever's the matter? You look desperate, as if someone's chasing you."

I hugged and kissed her in relief, which surprised her even more. But just then I realised that young Charlie was stood in the doorway, watching these strange goings on. He was a lovely boy, but not here and not now.

"I thought Hannah was collecting both boys this afternoon, what's happened?"

"Another of her emergencies, she took Sydney to leave him at her mother's, and promised to be back here by nine to collect Charlie."

"That's no good, we don't have the time, you're going to have to come with me, we need to be out of here within the next two or three minutes. Don't ask any questions, just go and get just enough things together for a couple of nights away and put a heavy coat on. I'll get Charlie's stuff while you're doing that, and then we can drop him off at Mrs. Jackson's. I'll explain everything on the way," Despite such an injunction, anyone else would have been unable to resist bombarding me with questions, but Ruth accepted what I said without comment and hurried upstairs to get her things.

I rushed round to make arrangements with Mrs. Jackson, a short distance round the corner, but the door was locked, there were no lights on, there was nobody home. I glared at her front door, almost kicking it in exasperation – how dare she be out when I needed her in? What to do next? This wasn't the time for delays. I couldn't leave Charlie sitting alone on our doorstep on the vague chance that his errant mother would eventually turn up. Mrs. Jackson had been our only hope, there was nowhere else within reach that Charlie could be left, dithering was out of the question. There was no other option – he would have to come with us.

As I came back down the road, still sorting things out in my mind, I saw under the street lights that a Growler had pulled up outside our house, with a brightly gleaming coach light on each side. The Growler is an enclosed four seater, two horse, carriage, with the driver sitting up front. It would be a perfect vehicle in which to perform an abduction. The horses were steaming in the chill night air, so these weren't local visitors, they had come from some distance. Two men got out of it and looked around. Significantly, they left the Growler door to the pavement wide open. Such behaviour was either very careless or spoke of plans for a quick departure.

They were large and determined looking men, and from what I could see of them by the street lights they seemed more like public omnibus than private carriage trade. They weren't workmen coming to fix a gas pipe; they carried no tools, and tradesmen don't arrive by night in a carriage. They weren't residents - they didn't belong here. Their purpose was plainly to fulfil the kidnap warning Pedro had given me.

I stepped off the pavement and into the road, as though to walk around the outside of the carriage. But as I passed alongside it I drew my Webley revolver and climbed, quickly and unannounced, up onto the driver's seat. The two men on the pavement, having checked the house numbers were now starting to walk up our front path. I did say that we lived in a nice middle class area, and all the houses in our street have small front gardens, it's really quite select.

The driver turned to me in surprise. "What the bloody hell d'you think you're up to?" He demanded, raising his whip to use as a club. I poked the Webley into his side, hard, to make it felt through his coat.

The two men turned to see the cause of their driver's raised voice. "Get going, before I kill you like the rat you are." I told the driver and jammed the gun even more viciously into his fat gut. As he shook the reins, desperate to get moving before I shot him, I looked past him and called out to the two men.

"Sorry fellers, but I need to borrow your ride, you can have it back in an hour or so." Then I laughed at them, which always annoys people when you're stealing their property. To the driver I said, as harshly as possible: "Move it – now!"

Everything sprang into motion, the two horses started forward to avoid the whip, and the two men started back, to catch the means of carrying out their plan. In retrospect they would come to realise that their best bet would have been to remain calm in the face of provocation and carry on with the kidnap, they should have let me steal their carriage and to hell with me. Carriages are ten a penny, they could have hailed another, and then kicked off the driver. But it's usually a safe bet that most people will seize the obvious option, rather than engaging in analytical thought, especially when they've just been severely provoked.

It all now depended on the timing, alerting them too soon might have given them a chance to overpower me on the driver's seat, and leaving it too late might have meant they wouldn't catch us at all.

Luckily, they were just fast enough to leap desperately into the open door as we began to pick up speed down the street.

Like the bird pretending to have an injured wing to draw predators away from the nest, so I was removing the threat to my home. Fortunately for me, the type of person employed to perform abductions is not generally in possession of great ornithological knowledge, so the comparison probably didn't occur to them.

I directed the driver all the way round Clerkenwell Green at the best speed our horses were capable of, whilst the two unwilling passengers shouted at me through the side windows, threatening me with every sort of retribution. I took them up onto Corporation Row and then down the far side of the old prison site, giving them a free guided tour of the new school they're building. It's possible they might not have been interested in local development, and for as long as their attention was on me, providing we turned enough corners, they would soon lose track of our location.

After a four or five minutes of chasing round the houses, I made the driver turn into that small entry at the top end of Pear Tree Court, a singularly gloomy place after dark, which rapidly becomes too narrow for carriages. I had myself poised and ready, as we skidded to a halt, unable to go any further. I leapt down and scooted through the alley at top speed.

The passengers erupted after me, still enraged and still shouting. But they believed themselves to be several minutes' fast drive away from their target, and me to be some half witted chance thief. They had finally worked out that they had more urgent priorities to attend to, and the driver called them back, saying he needed their help to turn round.

They can't have been local, as none of them seemed to know that in our six or seven minute gallop we had done no more than take a circular tour of Clerkenwell, and that the alley I had run down led towards our own house. I ran through my front door, still gasping and wheezing.

"What was all that shouting in the street?" Asked Ruth.

"I've no idea, but this area's gone to hell in a hat box since all those blasted Italians moved in."

"You're all out of breath."

"Just keep quiet and move,"

I managed to get the three of us, and our bags, out of the front door in less than a minute, desperate to be clear of the house before they returned. I led us through the St. James's Churchyard as a short cut to the nearest place we could pick up a cab. Making our our way around the dark bulk of the church, Charlie was clasped in my arms, frightened by our own fear into an unnatural silence of his own.

As we went, I saw through the railings the Growler trotting past, the driver peering about him and a face visible at the side window - apparently still lost, but not for long. For myself I was angry, but for Ruth and Charlie I was frightened. There were three of four gas street lamps visible from where we were, but all were too far away to illuminate us, all we had to do was to stand very still and we'd be invisible. We froze, shivering slightly in the graveyard shadows. An owl hooted nearby, further away a door slammed and someone could be dimly heard shouting, we remained motionless. Eventually they passed and we continued our flight.

We sank back into the seats of the first Hansom we saw, breathing hard, hats pulled down across our faces, my revolver ready to hand, simple trickery wouldn't work twice. I turned to Ruth.

"As a general rule I don't care to have my shaves quite that close."

The Hansom took us towards King's Cross as I repeated the unlikely story, when I finished Ruth said. "Would it help if Charlie and I just stopped in a hotel until you got back? If we weren't at home they wouldn't know where to look for us."

"I don't know if we're still being followed, and we can't take that sort of chance."

"So what do we do now?" She asked.

"First we drop Hannah a line to say that you've had to go away for the night, and taken Charlie with you, and then we're all going to go for a nice train ride, Charlie'll like that."

*****

Considering the apparent disparity of our social standing, my relationship with the Prince of Wales was perhaps rather unexpected, but our common ground was one where outside rank didn't seem to have quite its usual importance. For Bertie was, like myself, 'On the Square'. That is to say we were both Freemasons, although of markedly different rank.

He was Grand Master of the Craft throughout Britain and I just a junior officer in one of three Navy Lodges currently in existence. However, as well as his exalted position in our order nationally, Bertie was also a member of the same Navy Lodge as myself and attended our meetings on a reasonably regular basis. Though he seemed to have been otherwise engaged during the last one.

Freemasons make a particular point of saying that their ranks are open to, and in fact already contain, people from every section of society, and this is undoubtedly an estimable aim. However, as with all human institutions, the reality falls somewhat short of the ideal. If you wished, for example, to encounter a stevedore or a rat catcher you might be better advised to visit the nearest public house, than attend one of our meetings. Yet despite this rather obvious fact, it is still the case that my own Lodge spans a range from the heir to the throne to an engine driver.

My father had been a Mason and had invited me to join his own Lodge, but I hadn't felt ready, and a life afloat didn't seem to lend itself to a regular attendance at meetings. He had told me that whilst there were undoubtedly some self-serving scoundrels to be found in Freemasonry, such people were, he said, noticeably thinner on the ground in the Lodge than in the rest of society. After my promotion to Lieutenant I had been invited to join the Navy Lodge, and with my family background it had seemed wholly natural to do so.

Since joining their ranks my own experience has shown that my father was right, and although not opening any otherwise locked doors, the Craft has remained a welcome element of my life.

During our occasional brief encounters on the Royal train, this connection had never been alluded to, not, I suspect, from any sense of secrecy, but more because it wasn't relevant to the occasion. Despite this there could be no doubt that he knew exactly who I was, and I wondered if this might prompt him at least to listen to my concerns, rather than simply brushing them off.

I had only just arrived in Dolan's office, having concealed Ruth and Charlie in a disused storeroom, when The Prince of Wales arrived. From the unusually serious look on his face I assumed he'd heard there was trouble.

"Ah Fowler, Jollie here tells me you've got wind of some damned anarchist plot."

I explained the circumstances and the Crown Prince's determination to go ahead with the trip, in the hope of catching the plotters.

"I knew it." He said almost triumphantly. "Didn't I tell you Jollie, absolutely sound that boy, absolutely sound. That's exactly the right tactics; hold your nerve and lure them out, that's the way to do it."

"But sir, there's no way that Crown Prince Ferdinand and I can fight off an armed attack. I really do feel that this would be a most ill advised risk to his life." Not to mention my own.

Bertie drew closer and lowered his voice slightly. "The thing is my dear Fowler, although we couldn't tell you earlier, matters are already well in hand. In fact we have made allowances for exactly this sort of occurrence. It might have seemed to you that our plan consisted entirely of a dozen of Scotland Yard's finest, plus eight or nine Rumanians, looking after our decoy Prince, whilst you kept the real one hidden. But there's another layer you see - as you railway chappies would say, wheels within wheels," He looked pleased with the slight witticism.

"In conditions of deepest secrecy we have arranged for the finest consulting detective in Europe, together with his assistant, to be part of the train staff. Even I don't know what identity he's using – but I do know that he's never been known to fail."

I breathed an inward sigh of relief, my concerns had been valid and I was right to raise them, but I should have had more faith in the establishment's ability to cope. You don't build the biggest empire the world has ever seen by being anything other than sharp, extremely sharp.

"Thank you sir, that's helped to set my mind at rest, does this detective know the Crown Prince's actual whereabouts on the train?"

"Yes, but apart from the Rumanian Chief of Staff, he's the only one. All the police officers believe the decoy to be real."

Then turning to St. Aubyn-Jollie he said. "This is the fellow I was telling you about Jollie, an ex tar, now a railwayman who's on the square. Always good to have some variety in the Lodge, nothing duller than a roomful of blasted admirals. He's just been made up to Senior Deacon in the Navy Lodge – been told he did sterling work in a third degree ceremony the other night. Taken to it like a duck to water he has. I shall be watching his progress with interest." Jollie received the news with a raise of the same eyebrow as before.

This turn of the conversation to Masonic affairs made me wonder if this would be a good time for me to draw the Prince's attention to that part of the Third Degree Obligation which spoke of the requirement to respect the chastity of a Brother's wife, especially mine. Perhaps when it came to it I lacked the nerve, at all events I failed to act quickly enough and the moment passed; no doubt Ruth could take care of herself, she usually did.

Unaware of my thoughts, His Royal Highness turned back to me. "All ship shape now Fowler and ready to cast off – eh?"

"Certainly sir, just one more question if I may, who is the consulting detective?"

"Ah yes, of course, it's Mr. Sherlock Holmes and his companion Doctor Watson."

A weary wave of déjà vu swept over me, first the Count of Monte Cristo and now Sherlock Holmes, somebody in this operation was losing touch with reality and I hoped it wasn't me. I looked at both men's faces, there was no trace of humour or sarcasm.

"Sherlock Holmes is a fictional character sir, I've read his stories myself and they're very entertaining – but not real. He's a product of the author's imagination."

Bertie laughed. "Exactly my dear boy, that's just what you're supposed to think, it gives him more room to manoeuvre if everyone thinks he doesn't exist. I'm told it's what they call a double bluff. Damned clever if you ask me."

With that, he turned to leave, pausing at the door for a final comment. "Time for action stations now Fowler, all of us to our positions and full steam ahead."

I wasn't sure if that last steaming comment had been a naval allusion or a railway one, but I knew that if I just waited for a while, Father Christmas would pop his head round the door and perhaps he would explain it all. Short of walking out of the station and taking the Crown Prince with me, to get drunk in the nearest pub, there seemed to be no alternative to going ahead with the trip.

The Prince of Wales was in almost every respect a splendid fellow and would, in due course, make an excellent King – just as long as he could keep his hands off my wife. But as far as today was concerned, my best hope was that the opposition shared his level of gullibility.

The formal send off, when it came, was most impressive and would certainly have fooled me. A military band played jaunty airs in the background as the Royal party alighted from their horse drawn landaus directly onto the platform. The steam rising from the horses almost matching that from the train. The Prince of Wales, now wrapped in a heavy astrakhan coat and a Homburg, shook hands with two well muffled gentleman, one of whom appeared to possess a moustache.

The idea was that our decoy should avoid being spotted as an imposter by promptly retiring to his sleeping car, pleading exhaustion from trying to keep up with Bertie's social schedule, and not be seen again until Newcastle, and it was an excellent one. The essence of a good plan should always be simplicity, and that was about as simple as they come.

The carriage doors along the train banged shut, one after the other, the guard blew his whistle and waved his flag, it was time to leave.

Over on the left hand side of the cab, Stan pulled back the cylinder drain cock lever, to purge the system of standing water for the first three or four revolutions. Whilst I used both hands to grasp the heavy reverser lever, on its huge ratcheted quadrant along the right hand side of the cab. Despite its name, this controlled the engine's movement in both directions, I swung my body weight behind it to push it fully forwards, our direction of travel. Then I released the vacuum brakes and slowly pulled out the regulator lever, and with a hammer blow succession of pressurised whoomphs from the funnel, the eight foot driving wheels began to roll us forward.

Starting us on our journey, either to Newcastle or violent death.

REVD. JEREMIAH HARKER IN THE CASE OF FELONIOUS AGGRAVATION

Numerous residents of Tavistock St. had testified to having been visited that evening by this wandering evangelist. It had been his habit to rap firmly upon each door and then kneel down to shout through the letterbox, that all inside were sinners who would soon surely die and be cast into everlasting torment. Many of the affected householders declared themselves to have been seriously disturbed by these events.

However, on reaching No. 72, the home of Mr. Francis Cross (known in the area as Two Fisted Frankie) events took a sharply different turn, for most unusually the door of that house opened outwards. Mr. Cross, having been alerted by the approaching commotion, flung his door violently open as soon as the rapping commenced. This action caused the Revd. Harker to be projected backwards and down the front steps. His arrival upon the road surface causing bruising to a part of his person.

Upon hearing of the Revd. Harker's intention to pursue a counter action for said bruising and the soiling of his britches, Mr. Groom, the magistrate, declared himself baffled as to who was the aggrieved party.

FIVE

I had warned Ruth to stay hidden in the tender with Charlie until we reached open country, there were too many signal boxes around London. She looked fetching in her regulation brown boiler suit, her hair carefully tucked under a flat hat. Charlie thought it was the biggest adventure he'd ever had and couldn't wait to tell his big brother all about it.

After leaving the meeting in Dolan's office I had kitted Ruth out with the same sort of clothing I'd given Pedro. I had then taken her and Charlie through the staff entrance to the outer end of the adjoining empty platform, where I sat them both on a baggage cart, with boxes stacked around them. I then wheeled the cart to the side of the engine and as Pedro and I ostentatiously moved boxes around, the two stowaways slipped onto the footplate and through into the tender. I was as sure as I could be that they had not been seen.

Worryingly, Pedro was as excited as Charlie by all the subterfuge. I had the unhappy feeling that he would be almost disappointed if nothing happened; but then people who have never seen action can't be expected to understand the terror of it.

Fortunately, for the purposes of concealment, we were using one of the new larger, Mark Five, high sided tenders, which had a compartment for storing tools opening straight onto the footplate. During my absence Stan and Pedro had cleaned this out, stacking the tools and spare shovels on top of the water tank. It was very small and would be claustrophobic, but it was just big enough for Ruth and Charlie and their small bag to squeeze into. It would be noisy and frightening at the en route stops, as ton upon ton of coal cascaded into the tender, but should be secure.

As long as we kept Charlie out of sight, and a maximum of three people visible on the footplate whilst passing signal boxes, particularly the low level Battle Bridge Road box by the station entrance, we should be safe.

King's Cross station is in many respects a splendid piece of railway engineering, and the pleasing proportions of the two great train halls are a lasting tribute to the unerring eye of its designer, Mr. Cubitt. Its functional simplicity even holds its own against the showier attractions of the larger St. Pancras station, next door. Unfortunately, however, no one has ever successfully explained why in heaven's name it was situated *where* it is.

True, it was a successor to a temporary structure built to deal with passenger traffic to the Great Exhibition, but that alone should never have encouraged anyone to make the mistake permanent. The Regent's Canal is situated right across the only way in and out of the site, and within 200 yards of leaving the station an engine must either go over or under the water – and as railway engines dislike inclines either one of these options forms a serious impediment. In matrimonial terms it would have been enough to call off the union.

The decision was taken to tunnel under the canal, in what we call the Gas Works tunnel. No sooner had it been built than it was found to be insufficient, and plans were made for a second tunnel. As is the way of these things no sooner had the second tunnel been eventually finished than that too was found to be inadequate. A third Gas Works tunnel has just been opened and should there come word of plans for a fourth it would cause no surprise at all.

Leaving the lights of the station approach we plunged into the deeper darkness of the tunnel, breathing unpleasant amounts of soot and smoke as we did so, and suddenly deafened by the increased noise. Our head lights showed the curved and soot blackened brickwork all around us. The downward slope to pass under the canal helped our acceleration for a while, but it was nowhere near enough to power us up the far side, and by the time we emerged into the clean night air the regulator was almost fully out, blasting huge quantities of steam into the cylinders.

The incline, or 'bank' as railwaymen call it, continued through the Copenhagen tunnel, a total distance of over a mile. There followed a brief spell on level ground through Holloway and Wood Green, before the next climb, the so called Northern Heights. It was a testing stretch for any locomotive, and for their crews but Stan and I made a good team, we could cope.

Stan had moved Pedro to one side and was shovelling coal as fast as he could, this wasn't a good moment to introduce a newcomer. The primary air damper in the base of the firebox was fully open and so were the firebox door louvers, which provided what we call the secondary air. As we left the Gas Works tunnel I applied the blower to inject waste steam into the exhaust flow, and create a partial

77

vacuum that would draw the fire even more strongly. This made the thumping noise that everyone recognises as typical of an engine under pressure. The engine thundered onwards, Stan and I could get blood out of a stone with this machine.

A railwayman's view of life is often one of back yards, back gardens, back bedrooms, and washing lines, and in daylight the occasional waving child. I usually waved back, I'm a friendly enough sort, when not dealing with the Rumanian security services. Apart from the regular tunnels, this endless succession of lit up back windows was our landscape as we headed north, clattering and rocking across every one of the thousand points and junctions that made up the first ten miles of track, before finally clearing London.

It had been almost ten o'clock by the time we eventually pulled out of King's Cross, with a 300 mile run ahead of us. On speed trials, especially with a train as light as this, we could do that in four and a half hours, the eight carriage set up we were hauling today was less than half our normal load. Royal trains usually run slower than other expresses, especially at night, the better to look after their delicate passengers – but on a trip like this I could safely take us up to 45 mph. without anyone complaining. So allowing for the coaling and water stops I had scheduled our arrival time in Newcastle for 6.00 a.m. Depending on our progress up the country I could speed up or slow down, as required, to maintain the ETA.

As for my crew: it's not true what you sometimes hear said of Methodists, about them all being gloomy puritans, I think that's just Church of England sour grapes. Give them some down trodden workers to evangelise or just a good hymn to sing, and they're fine. Of course you have to remember not to blaspheme in front of them and try to keep the booze out of sight, but it has to be said that as religious groups go, they have an excellent record for not burning people at the stake. Stan, my regular fireman, was a fair example of the type.

He was always slightly reserved with strangers, but believing Pedro to be a visiting Spanish engineer, and impressed by his grasp of English, had extended him a professional welcome. However, the arrival of Ruth and Charlie had completely upset his notions of how a railroad ought to be run.

There was usually a sense of release at the start of a long run, it meant that we'd finished with the tedious performance of checking and organising everything and were finally free to settle into our routine and let the locomotive do what it was built for.

This was often a cue for Stan to treat the passing countryside to one of Charles Wesley's compositions, in a surprisingly good baritone. Well known constituents of the Methodist and Anglican Hymnals such as Love Divine or Lo, He Comes With Clouds Descending, being favourites of both of us. I usually joined in, after childhood Sunday school and ten years of weekly divine service in the navy, I knew most of the words. But the unexplained disruption to our day's routine, and the increasing numbers crowding onto the engine had managed to silence him.

Although not wishing to involve him in a danger he hadn't volunteered for, I felt that under the circumstances it would be unfair and pointless to continue lying to him. Besides if he knew what was going on he was more likely to be useful. I took a moment to nudge the regulator a little further open, to take our speed up to 35 mph, told Pedro to keep shovelling and began to tell the story once again.

The revelation of Pedro's identity and rank had made little impression on my fireman's Methodist view of life. After all, they had founded their church on the abolition of Bishops, against which, a disguised sprig of minor Balkan Royalty was no great cause for excitement.

To Stan the most shocking part of the story was the fact that there were people about who would attempt to kidnap, and probably kill, Ruth and Charlie. This was an unprovoked and brutal attempt on the lives of people he knew, not some distant collection of feuding Europeans. As was sometimes the case he sought to express himself in biblical terms.

"It says in Peter's first Epistle; 'The devil like a roaring lion seeking whom he may devour'."

He apparently thought that dealt with the matter, but I wasn't taking that as an easy answer.

"Don't talk rubbish, they aren't devils, they're people, and we'll deal with them as people. You quoting carefully selected bits of the bible is just trying to avoid the fact that some people are plain nasty." I would have left it at that but his pursed lips and doubtful look demanded more detail.

"The devil isn't some cartoon creature from the inferno, with two horns and a spiked tail; the devil is someone well known to you, someone you trust. The devil is a friend, a close friend, who stabs you in the back."

He smiled at my intensity. "You might be right, I'm just pleased to find an ex sailor having thoughts beyond liquor and women, I'll get you to join me in chapel one day." I ignored the comment and continued to explain our improbable circumstances.

"So all we know," he said, when I'd finished the tale, "Is that at least three people on the train, all probably members of the Crown Prince's – sorry, I should say Pedro's - body guard are planning to try and kill him somewhere between here and Newcastle, is that right?"

"That's about it."

"Well then why don't we simply tell the Scotland Yard detectives and let them take care of it?"

"Because we don't know for sure that one or more of *them* aren't involved, and in order for them to be of any assistance we would have to tell them that Pedro the fireman is actually the Crown Prince; and concealing that piece of information is currently our trump card. If we let the plotters show their hand by attacking the wrong man it will reveal exactly who they are, and then perhaps the police officers can do something about it."

Stan nodded his understanding but still looked pensive. "This is playing fast and loose with the lives of the two decoys isn't it?"

"That is a worry." I agreed, vaguely aware of, and uncomfortable at my lack of honest concern.

"What do we do if someone tries to reach the engine by climbing over the tender?"

"Discourage them – chucking lumps of coal at them might be a start."

"Or I could get the rabbit gun down." He said, looking up to the battered old rifle held on clips just under the cab roof. I'd forgotten all about that, like a lot of train crews we kept a rifle or a shot gun in the

81

cab for potting the odd rabbit when stopped in the country, we even had an equally battered stew pan somewhere.

"Is it loaded?" I asked

"Yes, I did it last week, five shots."

"But would you actually fire it at someone, I'd always thought your lot were a bit fussy about killing people."

"Just as any Christian man should be, or do you Freemasons think it acceptable to take human life?" We'd had this sort of conversation before, and both rather enjoyed baiting the other, knowing from experience just how far to push it. Unlike some engine crews, once we were out of the station and on our way, there was a complete equality between us. Unfortunately, it seemed to take Pedro by surprise, as he stopped shovelling and looked at me in astonishment.

"You are a Freemason – and you admit the fact?"

It was my turn to be surprised. "Why shouldn't I?" Stan and I forgot our casual bickering and both stared at him.

"Well the sacrilege involved, the denial of our Lord and the worship of Satan."

"You're gibbering man. What on earth are you talking about?"

But it was Stan who answered. "He's a Papist, you can spot them a mile off."

"No he's not, aren't they all Orthodox in Rumania?" I asked, slightly unsure of my facts.

"I don't know about the rest of them, but this one sounds like a Papist to me, if you take a look you'll find he's got a picture of the Virgin in his pocket."

"Well coming from Cardiff, I'm not sure how you'd recognise one of them."

It must have been a considerable novelty for the Crown Prince to find himself the subject of this sort of casual chat amongst commoners, but calling him Pedro seemed to make it alright, and he was hardly in a position to pull rank.

We both turned back to look at him again, awaiting clarification.

"It's true that the King and most of the other members of the Royal family are of the Orthodox faith, however, I was born and raised in the Holy Mother Church, which is still my position."

The look on Stan's face was unusually smug, though he wisely resisted the urge to put the feeling into words. But Pedro had a question of his own.

"It is a well known fact that the members of the Bulgarian Brotherhood are Freemasons, how can I know that you are not one of them?"

"If I ever meet any of them in a social setting then I promise I'll ask. But when it comes to Bulgarian assassins, it's become the subject of regular comment how very few of them we have in my Lodge, even Jack the Ripper wasn't a member – at least we don't think he was."

"You treat this matter as though it were of little consequence, but the murder of our country's leaders will have international significance,"

"Pedro, when you stood up to Antonescu at the station it showed nerve and independence of outlook on your part, I admired that. You should try making a habit of it, because if you think that I have any connection with this nonsense then ask yourself why my wife and small nephew have been forced to run for their lives." This man's cloistered upbringing and

83

naive outlook had left him need of some basic home truths.

"And just you remember that Stan, a man whose opinion I value highly, thinks the same sort of thing about Catholics that you do about Freemasons – the main difference being that he's probably got some justification. Now will you pick that bloody shovel up, your Royal Highness, or shall I stick it . . ."

Then I realised that Stan was already tutting at the 'bloody', before I'd even reached a destination for the shovel, so I thought it best to let it go, but Pedro wasn't finished.

"When you spoke to that detective earlier and said that on the train your were the Master Under God, is that correct?"

"Absolutely, for just as long as I can get away with it, then it's correct. But I wouldn't care to rely on it in court."

Meanwhile,
   The newspapers reported . . .

APPLICATION FOR RETURN OF FEE
The plaintiff, Mrs. Ellen Jackson, was applying for the return of money she had paid to Mrs. Vera Lowe, for the purposes of communicating with her father. The plaintiff had asked Mrs. Lowe if it would be possible to make such communication, and the plaintiff had replied that she could do that. At a séance the following afternoon the plaintiff claimed that she had made contact with the gentleman through her 'Spirit Guide' Grey Eagle.
Judge – 'Are you telling the court that you were speaking to a dead man?'
The defendant – 'Yes sir, this is the normal course of my profession, I also give Tarot readings.' The plaintiff interrupted, shouting aggressively, 'She was no more speaking to my dad than she was to my dog. She didn't even know his name. I told her he was called Norman just to test her, and she said that he answered to that – which was never his name. She is no more than a criminal deceiver.'
The defendant – 'She said she wanted me to speak to a recently passed spirit called Norman and I did that. I cannot be blamed

if she does not even know her own father's name. Perhaps her mother did not know it either.' (Loud exclamations from gallery)

Defendant – 'That is a terrible lie, I was very close to my father and she has no right to blacken his name. She should not be allowed   to say these things.'

Plaintiff – 'I did not say it before, but her father said that he had never thought very highly of her.' (More exclamations)

Judge – 'That is quite enough of that sort of talk.'

SIX

Ruth's delight at her and Charlie's release from the cramped hiding place lightened the mood and temporarily suspended hostilities on the footplate. It wasn't possible to continue sniping at each other with Charlie in such a state of excitement, this was a treat to dwarf any other wish he'd ever had, and his face positively glowed with the wonder of it all.

The noise, which any regular railwayman took for granted seemed to be the biggest surprise to our three passengers. The roaring of the firebox draught, the regular scraping of the shovel, the clanging and slamming of the fire box door, overlaid by the thumping sound of the cylinders and drive rods, and the clackety clack of steel wheels on steel rails. Behind all that there was the constant rocking and the non-stop rush of air past the open sides of the cab, I hadn't noticed any of it for years, until I saw how overwhelmed the others were.

Fortunately the height of our funnel and the speed of our travel made it unusual for us to get smoke and cinders in the cab. For me this combination of factors represented exactly the joy of life on the open track that I had hoped for when I applied for the job.

I held Charlie up to let him pull the steam whistle lanyard; even I still liked doing that. Ruth enquired after Aggie, Stan's wife and fellow devout

Methodist. Aggie was fine, thank you for asking, and how are you, and how's Hannah? The usual to and fro of civilised society, only exceptional because of our location.

At this stage Stan and Pedro were noticeably under employed, there wasn't enough shovelling to keep them both busy. At the start of a trip, with the coal filled right up to the front of the tender, the work was relatively easy. You could almost complete the cycle of filling your shovel and swinging round to the firebox in one movement, but as the trip proceeded the work grew harder. Most people seem to imagine that the tender is filled to the brim with coal, when in fact most of the space is taken up by the massive water tank, but as the coal sits on top of that, then it's the coal that you see.

With our present tender the front part of the coal area is angled downwards to help slide the coal forwards, which certainly helps, but even so there is a constant need to climb in and help matters along. This is the time when a fireman begins to earn his money.

But for now, whichever of them wasn't shovelling held Charlie up to one of the portholes, to look forward along the side of the engine and watch the regular green lights of the all clear signals rolling past us, and the red hot sparks coming out of the funnel.

Ruth put her arm round me for a while, was it a sense of danger, or a sense of excitement? Perhaps a bit of both, I'm not sure, but I understood the need for contact. Turning her face to mine, to be heard without shouting, she said, "This is the first time I've really understood what you see in this life."

It sometimes seems that the sheer size and population of London, all those people and all those fires, must produce its own small climatic zone. It was so often the case, and today was no exception, that when you finally cleared the Metropolis there was an apparent drop in the temperature. I noticed it again today as we headed the thirty odd miles up to Hitchin, not a stopping place, but the first of our running time checks.

The outside air thermometer was giving a reading of 32 degrees Fahrenheit, exactly freezing point, which meant there was a danger of ice on the rails. That could ruin any calculations of braking distance. The darkness surrounded us, but the occasional glow of light from passing towns and villages didn't have far to travel before it was reflected back from the low cloud base.

This morning's weather report, telegraphed down from York, had said they were already getting some occasional light snow. From the looks of it that position might worsen, but it still wouldn't affect us, it takes an awful lot of snow to inconvenience a modern train. In emergency there were steam snow ploughs at Doncaster, though they probably wouldn't be necessary, bad weather might slow us down but it wasn't going to stop us.

Despite the strangeness of our manning arrangements, I had never seen four adults and child on the engine before, we settled into an easy routine. If Charlie wasn't being held by Pedro or Stan than he had to hold Ruth's hand, this would be a lethal place for a child to be unsupervised. The firebox door was red hot, the sides of the cab were open and then there was the constantly moving joint between the footplate and the tender; it was too narrow to trap an

89

adult, but the side of a three and a half year old's shoe might just be caught. It was the middle of the night and he should have been tired, but the excitement was too much.

The first of our two scheduled coal and water stops was at Grantham, 105 miles from King's Cross. At our relatively unhurried speed that was going to take two and half hours, which would put us there about twenty minutes after midnight. Ruth and I had discussed the possibility of her leaving the train there, to find accommodation for them both in the town, and await my return trip the next day. By that time my involvement in trying to foil any sort of skulduggery would be over, one way or another.

The trouble was that getting the two of them off the train unseen would be almost impossible. My ploy of getting them aboard at London had only worked with the aid of a baggage trolley and the fact that there was a perfect hiding place for them in the tender storage locker. There was going to be no baggage trolley on an isolated coal siding, and nowhere to hide them if they did get off. That had been very much a one-way trick, especially since my new best friend Chief Superintendant Parkinson was taking such a close interest in me and my doings. All things considered, the safest, though not very satisfactory, option seemed to be for them to stay where they were.

It was close to midnight and we were steaming across that dull flat countryside between Peterborough and Grantham, with scarcely a light visible in any direction - they're all farmers round here and they'd all gone to bed. We had been lulled into relaxation by the near normality of our routine, when there was a jerk, a hesitation in our forward motion, as if the brakes had been briefly applied.

My eyes went immediately to the vacuum gauge, there had been a drop of four inches of mercury in the train pipe, enough to cause the brakes to move slightly but not enough to apply them fully. The vacuum chamber pressure would equalise that and the air pump would have everything back to normal in minutes. I didn't think there was much doubt about what had caused it.

"You were right." Said Stan looking at me, but offering no further explanation.

"Right about what?" Asked Ruth.

After a pause to see which of us would answer, Stan replied. "He said that somebody would try to stop the train with the communication cord, so we disabled the system before we left King's Cross."

Ruth clearly felt this an inadequate response and looked to me for more detail.

"When Pedro and I heard the plotters, they said that they were going to equalise the numbers, in other words get assistance in order to outnumber the police and security men. The most probable way of doing that would be for them to stop the train somewhere using the communication cord, if they did this in a place where they had enough accomplices waiting they could simply overwhelm us ."

"But could they stop the train wherever they wanted, don't you have to do that?"

I explained that for the last three years it had been a legal requirement that pulling the cord automatically operated the vacuum brakes. There had been *'Yet Another Dastardly Railway Murder'* to shock, horrify and thrill the newspaper reading public, and Parliament had felt prompted to try and calm public fears by passing a law that anyone being done to death on a train could now bring the whole thing to a halt. Whether or not that would be the slightest use in reality was open to question, but it made it seem as though something was being done.

However, I had arranged for a spanner to be put in the works. After my first encounter with Parkinson, when I had rushed away to collect Ruth and Charlie, Stan, acting on my instructions, had systematically gone along knocking wooden wedges into the butterfly valves on the end of every carriage. Nobody seeing him, who was not themselves a railway engineer, would have any idea what he was doing, but with the valves wedged shut the emergency braking system was out of action.

I intended that full control of this train should remain in my hands, and a passenger operated braking system didn't fit in with that idea. So now anyone pulling the cord would get a satisfied feeling, but that was all, for the brakes to work I had to operate them.

"We'll be in Grantham in five minutes, and as long as I've got the Crown Prince where I can keep an eye on him, then whatever's going on back there doesn't affect us."

As a precaution I told Ruth to hide herself and Charlie back in the cramped little locker. We could see no signs of anything unusual down each side of the train, and a few minutes later we pulled into the Grantham coal siding.

If we had been carrying Her Majesty we would have uncoupled the carriages two or three hundred yards away before taking on coal, even at the age of 73 the Queen was likely to be extremely forthright in her opinion of having her carriage covered in coal dust. However, with today's arrangements I didn't bother, the less time we spent shunting around at low speed the less time there was for anyone to start looking too closely at the engine crew.

As soon as we pulled into the siding, before the coal chute was rigged or the water pipe connected, Antonescu appeared - striding towards the engine, determination written all over him.

Even before he reached us he was shouting instructions to the coaling crew that had been stood waiting for us. From his tone of voice and dismissive arm movements he seemed to be telling them to either go away or wait till he'd finished. This was another piece of impertinence that needed nipping in the bud, I jumped down and strode over. Away from the heat of the firebox the cold was breathtaking, it was like plunging into icy water.

"Mister Antonescu, shut up!" He could start demanding his military rank when he found his manners. "You men," I said to the coaling crew, "carry on with your work. The only person who gives orders on this train is the driver – and as you're all well aware that's me."

Swinging back to Antonescu I continued. "And you'd better explain yourself, what do you think you're doing?"

He pushed himself forward, so that our faces were inches apart, an effect that was spoiled by the fact that although he was a much broader and more powerful man than me, he was also two inches shorter.

"You say me in London that my man not possible on the engine - because peoples will see.

Here there are no peoples, so my man go on engine, now, and stop there. He watch what you do."

"Not in a thousand years. Get back to your carriage or I will leave the train here and it will go nowhere."

"That good, my man he drive train. Nobody need you for driving engine. My man he train driver from Bucharest."

"Well you tell him to bugger off back to Bucharest, because he's not touching my engine. This train doesn't move an inch without me."

Without bothering to reply he pushed past me and started shouting up at Pedro, in Rumanian. This time Pedro took a firmer tone and even included some gestures to reinforce whatever his points were. As he was doing this a tall figure with close cropped hair strode into the argument. This time Parkinson was accompanied by a thin, worried looking, colleague.

"Major Antonescu, you will be so kind as to leave this matter in my hands." This was said in tones no friendlier than mine, but this time Antonescu obliged, by closing his mouth and taking a couple of paces back. Parkinson planted himself in front of me, clearly in no mood to trouble himself with pleasantries.

"What the devil happened to the brakes Fowler? It might have escaped your notice, but there's an Act of Parliament which says they must come on immediately the communication cord is pulled."

"I have absolutely no idea what's going on Superintendant, did someone pull the communication cord? Perhaps there's a fault in the vacuum braking system, which is why we also have manually controlled mechanical brakes."

"It's *Chief* Superintendant, and don't you forget it Fowler. And just so that we understand each other, I don't believe for a minute that there's anything wrong with the brakes, I think that you've got a hand in this somewhere – but not for long, believe you me."

"If you pulled the cord Parkinson, then you better have had some good reason for doing so, because the very same Act of Parliament you mentioned makes it an offence to operate the communication cord without just cause. What precisely was the nature of your emergency?"

Parkinson hesitated before replying, only for a second, but it was enough to tell me that whatever he said next would be a lie, or a concealment.

"That's none of your business Fowler, you just see if you can manage to drive the train properly and leave me to worry about the security."

"I'm afraid that's not good enough. The legal responsibility for the safe operation of this train rests on my shoulders, and it is my decision as to whether or not a problem is serious enough to affect its running. So I'll ask you again, and this time I want an answer, what was the emergency?"

Clearly reluctant, but feeling obliged to provide an answer, he finally came up with what was probably the truth. "There was no emergency, I simply wished to test the system, and it seems just as well that I did as you clearly hadn't bothered to check it properly before we left."

"And you, Mr. Parkinson, should remember what happened to the little boy who cried wolf – he got eaten."

As if acting on a theatrical cue, there came the sound of dogs barking from somewhere nearby, half my conscious mind said that a pack of dogs in the middle of a large area of railway sidings was unusual. The rest of my mind carried on with the argument.

"You'd be better employed dealing with Major Antonescu and his merry men, a gang of gun wielding Bulgarians, apparently answerable to no one."

"Rumanians, not Bulgarians." Said Parkinson's previously silent companion, with a prim schoolmasterly air.

"Oh of course, Rumanians, did I say Bulgarians? How silly of me. And who are you?"

"Inspector Scroop, Carlton Scroop of Scotland Yard."

"Carlton Scroop?"

"That's correct."

"Carlton Scroop, like the village in Lincolnshire?"

"Indeed, it was named after my great grandfather, an earlier Carlton Scroop."

"An earlier Carlton Scroop." I repeated the phrase, rolling it around my mouth, and savouring it as one might the taste of cognac. Unfortunately, I have only limited patience with bad jokes, particularly from people claiming to be called Scroop, and was unable resist a cheap rejoinder.

"I must remember to introduce you to an old girl friend of mine called Betsy; Betsy Coed".

But Parkinson wasn't interested in any comments of mine, he was here to instruct rather than listen. "You can complain all you like Fowler, but one of the Rumanians is coming on the footplate for the rest of the trip, it was agreed with St. Aubyn-Jollie before we left London. And if you don't want to drive then I shall simply take another GNR driver off one of the Grantham trains. You're not irreplaceable, so don't think you are."

Then turning directly to Antonescu he said: "Go and fetch one of your men to put on the engine." Antonescu gave me a triumphant and disdainful sneer before striding back down the train to instruct his man.

Parkinson had called my bluff, and he knew it, he just didn't know how important it was. As far as I knew he still believed that the decoy Crown Prince was the real thing. I couldn't allow Ruth and Charlie to be discovered, that could be literally a matter of life and death, but how this could be avoided was unclear. Quite apart from the threat to my family, there was also the possibility that the man chosen could be one of the conspirators and simply want to use the privacy of the footplate for the planned assassination.

There was an answer out there somewhere, but I couldn't see it. Then Stan, who must have heard everything from the footplate called down. "Beggin' you pardon Captain, but that man of the Major's, he'll be no problem. It'll be no different from that extra passenger we picked up at Selby." He didn't give me any sort of meaningful glance or over emphasise his words, he sounded completely natural, like a man who simply wished to be helpful. And he had been, I knew exactly what he meant.

Parkinson meanwhile was telling Scroop to go and make sure that Sergeant Jones understood he only had another few minutes left with the hounds, Scroop turned and left.

"Hounds? You planning to flush the odd fox are you Parkinson, got your horse in the baggage van perhaps?

Parkinson's face darkened with anger and he drew closer. "I'm going to flush whatever there is to be flushed on this damn train Fowler, something round here smells to me and I'm going to get to the bottom of it. Which is why I telegraphed ahead, to have the local dog handler waiting for us. And as for our friends and allies the Rumanians, you can set your mind at rest on that point. I have formally enrolled the Major and his men as Special Constables, so now they'll do as they're told - or face the consequences. Just like you."

"Is that legal, having Special Constables who are not only foreign nationals but don't even speak our language?"

"Whatever I choose to do is lawful, they speak quite enough English to follow my clear instructions and know exactly who's in charge around here. Which is, apparently, more than can be said for you." Turning away from me he bellowed, "Sergeant." A voice from the far side of the train replied, "Yes sir."

"Have the dogs finished in the carriages yet?"

"Yes sir, but no results so far, we're moving on to do the engine and tender next."

"Do what to the engine?" I asked, feeling a horrible knot of fear in my stomach.

"Check it for foreign scents, check it for what shouldn't be there, that's what – just like you should have checked the brakes."

This was going to be a disaster. But then a new voice joined in.

"There will be no need for that Chief Superintendant."

Ruth was standing in the open entrance to the engine cab, looking down on the pair of us with a noticeably haughty air, she was good at haughty. Parkinson and I were both astonished; me because she was supposed to be in hiding but had somehow cleaned herself up and changed into a dress; and Parkinson because he had no idea what was going on. I kept my mouth shut, this was clearly Ruth's show. After a brief and obviously baffled pause Parkinson recovered sufficiently to demand.

"And who exactly might you be madam, and what are you doing on that locomotive?"

"Who *exactly* I am is something that you will need to take up with the Prince of Wales, you may address me as Mrs. Castlemaine, and I am here at the direct instruction of His Royal Highness."

"With what end in view, might I enquire?"

"To observe and comment on the efficacy of your arrangements. Foremost among such observations being the length of time it has taken you to conduct a proper search of the train." Then turning around she addressed someone, presumably the dog handler, who was visible to her on the far side of the engine.

"Those are fine looking hounds Sergeant, they do you credit, but they won't be needed any further as I have already searched the engine and tender." Her tone invited no discussion on the issue. The reply was drowned by the yelping of the hounds, but it must have been in the affirmative as their noise began to recede.

Parkinson managed to produce an outraged, "Madam!" but it failed to register, and still with her back to us, she addressed to two men on the footplate.

"Thank you for your assistance gentlemen, you have been most helpful, a fact which shall be noted." With that she turned and, firmly grasping the side rails, competently dismounted – no easy trick when wearing a long skirt, and was then handed her bag by Pedro.

"Madam your presence here raises a good many questions, if you would be good enough to accompany me to a carriage."

"Certainly Chief Superintendant, there seem to be several matters to be dealt with about your handling of this case." She said, in the sort of tone one might use to a butler who had just served the fish course before the soup. Then turning to me she continued. "And you Mr. Fowler, if you would allow the Chief Superintendant and I a few moments to leave the immediate area, had better continue with your coaling."

"Aye aye ma'am." I almost touched my forelock, but that would have been seriously out of character, so I settled for a serious stare into the middle distance. With that she turned and began to walk back along the side of the train, addressing Parkinson as she went.

"I was somewhat surprised that neither you, nor any of your officers, saw fit to approach me at King's Cross when I boarded the locomotive. I would have thought that the control of those boarding the train to have been a higher priority."

"You mean you've been on the engine, with the driver, since we left London?"

"Well someone had to be, and your own approach to the driver seemed to be a part of the problem."

Parkinson, aware of his loss of control, but unsure how it had happened, tried to find some way of regaining the high ground. His diminishing voice could just be heard saying, "I'm still a long way from satisfied with . . ." before the rest of their conversation was submerged by the surrounding hubbub. I positively leapt up the steps to the footplate.

"Pedro lean out and watch which carriage she gets into, and Stan you'd better tell me what's going on."

"Ruth saw them working their way along the train with the dogs, she knew that if they weren't stopped they were sure to discover both her and Charlie. She said that she had some hope of explaining her own presence, but could imagine no explanation that would cover Charlie. That was even before the business of having one of Rumanians on the engine. So she quickly tidied her hair and changed her clothes. Then she stepped out like a visiting Duchess to introduce herself, as you saw." He beamed with pride at her performance. "She said to tell you not to worry and that she'll travel in one of the carriages and keep her eyes open."

"Mr. Fowler," said Pedro gravely, "I must assure you that Stan and I both looked away while Ruth changed her clothes." Stan, one of nature's true gentlemen, gazed hopelessly heavenwards at this unnecessary declaration.

"I would certainly hope that you did," I said, whilst privately thinking him none too bright, "But more to the point, which carriage did she get into?"

"The third."

As we talked, Charlie had been peering out of his hiding place, watching the strange behaviour of the grown-ups; like most small children he accepted the complete irrationality of adults as normal. For myself, not knowing what else to do, I kept Charlie hidden and complied with Ruth's parting instruction about completing the coaling and watering. As we did so Antonescu's man finally turned up and was told to 'Stand there and keep quiet', which he did. I then announced our departure with the whistle and slowly moved off.

If not an outright pacifist, Stan was a very peaceable man, and would never normally countenance doing harm to another human being - unless to prevent some greater wrong from happening. In this case he had decided that the problems inherent with the extra man were sufficiently serious to merit drastic action. Hence his reference to Selby, when both of us could remember getting rid of a drunken but powerfully built lout, who had jumped into the cab as we were pulling out of the station.

Our reaction had been unplanned and unsophisticated, but successful. Stan had wedged a sweeping brush shaft into one of the grab handles at the cab entrance, so that it stretched across the opening at knee height. Then, having manoeuvred ourselves round him, we had simply pushed the man backwards in a concerted rush, precipitating a headlong departure through the cab doorway. Although we had accomplished this before picking up sufficient speed to guarantee lethality, there had still been a real chance of him breaking his neck. A better men than me might have been concerned about this danger to his welfare, and one day I hoped to become such a person.

This man was a tougher proposition than the drunk, but there were three of us - so it shouldn't have been a problem. Stan wedged the brush handle across the doorway and we moved round to position ourselves for the big push. We must have been dangerously obvious in our intentions, because the man frowned at us, understanding that any three people looking as determinedly nonchalant as us had to be up to something.

Having looked at us in puzzlement, he then glanced behind him and saw the brush handle, realisation spread across his face. Far from us catching him unawares, he knew exactly what we planned and in one swift and well practised movement he produced a small pistol from somewhere. That stopped us in our tracks, or perhaps in deference to the railway I should say *on* our tracks.

We could have stood there all night, staring at each other in our frozen tableau, unsure which of us had the advantage over the other. At close quarters, are three men with shovels a better prospect than one man with a pistol? Yes, they probably are - but who moves first and risks getting shot?

Fortunately, at that moment the situation was resolved when a medium sized lump of coal hit him quite sharply in the chest, this arrival of the coal, 'deus ex machina', astonished all four of us. Unhappily for the man, Stan and I recovered first and carried on with our pre planned rush. Before he could line up a shot he found himself taking two involuntary paces backwards, the brush handle caught him behind the knees and the inevitable cartwheel ensued.

Charlie looked crestfallen as he stood there, a picture of guilt, with coal dust all over his hands.

"I'm sorry Uncle, honestly, I didn't mean to make him fall off, but I was frightened he was going to hurt you." He was quite surprised when we took it in turns to pick him up and kiss him.

According to Pedro, who had looked back to watch, the ejectee had staggered to his feet and managed to swing himself onto the last carriage as it trundled past. Parkinson and Antonescu, not to mention the man himself, were going to be livid; but no matter what anyone might say, my direct instructions from the Prince of Wales had been to deliver the Crown Prince safely to our destination. That was exactly what I planned to do.

The next leg was 83 miles to York, would it be in this sector that the promised death threat came to pass? We were now playing a very different game to anything I had ever imagined.

Since marrying Ruth, I had become accustomed to the presence in my life of an intelligent second opinion, someone who brought a fresh perspective to any problem. It was only now, when that alternative view of life had vanished, just when I needed it most, that I realised the extent of my dependence on it.

I made Stan and Pedro repeat what she had said, before making her rather theatrical appearance to confound both Parkinson and his sniffer dogs. The logic of her behaviour was undeniable: far better to announce your presence, bold as brass and on your own terms, than be dragged from hiding as a guilty party. It wasn't her impeccable logic that concerned me, but the frightening consequences that flowed from it.

When it came to guile and natural cunning I suspected she could run rings around Parkinson, and his improbable assistant, but she was still just one unarmed woman against twenty armed and trained agents, of unknown allegiance. These were not odds that I cared for, but could think of no immediate way to move things in her favour. Then there was still that comment about 'equalising the numbers', which suggested there were enemy reinforcements waiting to join us at some point. Well they could pull the communication cord all day long, but it wasn't going to do them much good.

Now we were clear of the station I brought Charlie onto the footplate, and held his hand. It was a lot warmer near the firebox, and without someone to hold him he could freeze in this weather.

"Where's Aunty Ruth gone?"

"She wanted to talk to some of the people on the train, and she thought that you and I could drive the engine together – will you help me to do that?" He nodded eagerly, but silently, clutching my hand a little tighter.

Turning to Pedro I voiced a thought about his supposed defenders. "Did you hear that comment of Parkinson's about controlling Antonescu and his men by having enrolled them as Special Constables? As if having them pledge their loyalty to our sovereign lady the Queen is going to make any difference."

"I'm afraid the Chief Superintendant doesn't seem to appreciate the nature of the people we're dealing with."

"And I'll tell you another thing." I said to no one in particular. "If Sherlock Holmes really does exist, then it's obvious who he is."

"Scroop." Said Stan. I raised my eyebrows, unhappy to have my deduction stolen.

"Stands to reason." He said. "Tall thin man, wearing a wig, with a completely unbelievable name

– it has to be him. Now if you look in *his* pocket you won't find a picture of the Virgin, you'll find a magnifying glass."

I swallowed my pride and nodded. "I think you're right."

"There is one other thing." Said Pedro, "When I handed Ruth her bag, it felt heavy, too heavy. Could she have had a gun?"

I went over to my knapsack and felt inside, the Webley was still there. "No, we only had the one gun in the house, and I've got it. I can't imagine what she had in the bag."

"Aunty Ruth had a toy gun." Said Charlie. "I saw her put it in her bag." Still holding his hand I knelt down by him.

"What sort of toy gun was it Charlie?"

"One of the toy ones from the theatre."

"Was it one of the toy ones that goes bang when you pull the trigger?"

"Yes, she let Sydney shoot it once, she said that I was too small, it made a very loud noise."

"Bloody Hell." I said wearily. Stan looked disapproving and Pedro looked bewildered.

"She's carrying a stage prop, it's an old .22 pistol they use at Sadler's Wells, you load it with blank cartridges and it makes a flash and a bang. I'd forgotten all about it – but I suggested she should carry it when walking home from the theatre at night, to deter any unsavoury characters. The trouble is that if she pulls it on someone like Antonescu he'll assume it's real and pull his own gun. The stupid woman's going to get herself killed."

At this, Charlie's eyes widened and glistened with tears. Me and my mouth. I picked him up again and hugged him tight. "Take no notice of me Charlie,

106

I'm just being silly, Aunty Ruth is going to be fine and we'll all have tea together later. Now you come and help your Uncle Puff Puff sound the whistle again."

As we did so, I could hear Stan repeating to himself, in a wondering tone, "Uncle Puff Puff?" I was going to hear more of that.

It was coming up for one o'clock in the morning, and the snow which had been toying with us earlier was now coming down in earnest, what we could see of the landscape was a uniform white, the ground gleaming softly even in the darkness. I made up a rudimentary bed for Charlie in the storage locker, with folded tarpaulins and some clean engine rags. Pedro crouched down with him and told him about killing dragons in the Black Forest, it didn't take long for him to nod off. This was a journey of new experiences for all of us.

Meanwhile,
the newspapers reported . . .

GENTLEMEN !
Has there been a lessening in your youthful
vigour? Are you holding your own?
GENTLEMEN'S ELIXIR
Contains only the purest ingredients and
is guaranteed to rejuvenate failing powers.
As will be readily understood, our numerous
testimonials must remain confidential –
but you may be assured –
They Are Legion!
YOU WILL BE DELIGHTED
To receive so a longstandig a benefit
At all good chemists 5s.4d. a large bottle

TEETH : COMPLETE SET: ONE GUINEA
Single tooth 2s.6d. Five years warranty

Dr. Andrew Wilson, late R.N., recommends Mr.
Goodman as a very skilful and humane dentist.
Mr. Labouchere in 'Truth' writes: 'Mr. Goodman
has one of the largest practices in the world,
which enables him to employ capital and labour
in the most economical and effective way.'

Mr. GOODMAN Surgeon Dentist
2 Ludgate Hill, facing St. Paul's

SEVEN

I'm reasonably good at pursuing an aim, at achieving some sort of goal, but to do that you need to identify what it is that you're aiming at. Did I want Ruth back on the engine with me? Plainly not. My motive in bringing them aboard and hiding them was to keep them safe from possible kidnap. But that was only a valid concern now, if those she was with knew who she was, and thus recognised that she would make an extremely powerful lever to induce my cooperation.

Difficult though it was for me to accept the fact, the safest immediate option was for me to pretend to an unconcern about Ruth, I could scarcely go chasing her down the train and demanding that she return to the engine.

Parkinson seemed to be permanently angry, which is not the best frame of mind for rational deductions. But then he had that Scroop character with him, and if Scroop was actually Sherlock Holmes, and if Sherlock Holmes was as smart as everyone said – then what? Did those two people even share the same agenda? There were too many different and competing interests on this train, it was like a gathering storm, we needed some thunder and lightning to clear the air.

I suspected that my real objection was to a loss of control, and to the fact that, whether Ruth was identified or not, she was now in a situation where the possibility of random gunfire or other acts of violence was an immediate danger.

I even vaguely considered the lunatic option of simply stopping the train in the next town, telling Stan and Pedro to make a run for it with Charlie, whilst I took my revolver to rescue Ruth. But desperate though I was, it was still apparent that any such scheme would simply increase the chances of the sort of gunfight I wanted to avoid. I just hoped that she didn't try pulling her little blank firing pistol on a real murderer.

The one thing which seemed certain was, that without my cooperation, the only place they could hope to get their reinforcements aboard was at York, where we were scheduled to make another coaling stop. The plotters could have no idea that their remarks had been overheard, which meant that if I steamed straight through York it could seriously derail their plans.

I wrote a note saying what I wanted done, and put it into a hessian bag with a lump of coal as ballast. A fact that our passengers would have no way of knowing was that we didn't actually need the second coaling stop on this trip. The normal train makeup was 26 carriages and a standard tender, but we were pulling just eight carriages with the larger than normal Mark Five tender. This meant that, having coaled at Grantham, we had more than enough fuel and water to reach Newcastle - quite easily.

My note was a request to the next Station Master to telegraph ahead to York for them to keep us on the mainline, and not divert us to the coal siding. They might assume that we would stop at a platform, and perhaps I would, that could be decided later – as long

112

as the train stayed on the main line I would still have all my options open.

As we passed through Newark North at a steady thirty miles an hour, I waved to a porter and threw the bag onto the platform near him. It was a well understood routine that was sometimes used to pass operational messages. Although York was still 60 miles away they would have received my message in the next five minutes. I had been raised, and spent my naval service, in a time of communication by signal flags and heliograph mirrors, but now the ability to send immediate electrical messages the length of the country was a modern miracle.

Signal boxes had been equipped with the electrical 'talking telegraph' for some time now. These had a needle, giving a left or right indication, and the sequence of movements was the code for a signal: so that, for example, three clicks left meant 'Express train on your line'. However, in the larger signal boxes even this had now been replaced by telephone instruments, by means of which direct speech was possible between all parts of the network. The speed of technical change seemed to increase every year.

We had travelled little more than another ten miles before we came to the Dukeries signal box, where the Lincoln to Mansfield line crossed our track. Surprisingly the summersault semaphore signal on its tall tower was in the horizontal position, with the red light showing beneath it, we had a stop signal against us. Stop signals are a rarity for a Royal Train, I leaned out of the cab to look down the track. The signalman was waiting by the track side waving a lantern, to indicate he was coming aboard. He swung himself up onto the steps as we were still braking.

He looked at the three of us, settling on me. "Driver Fowler?"

I nodded, and he handed me a folded piece of paper. "Diversion message for you from London, you're going to Whitby, you'll be switched at York. The snow ploughs are out from Doncaster, watch for their lights and keep your speed down to a maximum of thirty, as visibility permits."

He didn't wait for a response, the railway was no more a democracy than the Royal Navy – you didn't discuss your orders, you carried them out. The signalman dropped back onto the track; he had no intention of being carried any further from his signal box than he had to in this weather. As he did so his colleague in the box switched the signal, the barely visible semaphore arm dropped to the down position and the coloured glass 'spectacle' covering the light moved from red to green, we were Clear to Proceed.

We had never actually come to a halt and were already picking up speed again. To see the railway system working efficiently was like watching a well oiled machine, this was a world I understood and felt at home with, it was a pity that not all our passengers agreed with me.

Standing next to the cab lantern I unfolded the paper, it was a handwritten transcription of the message. The words were in a careful copperplate, one of the benefits of universal education. Despite the message having been received on a telephone it was still written as though it were a telegram, the old habits lingered on. *'Destination now changed to Whitby Yorks stop Other instructions remain in force*

114

stop Further message on arrival stop HKSAJ' I showed it to the other two. Pedro seemed worried.

"Where is Whitby Yorks?"

"Whitby in Yorkshire, it's a fishing port north of Scarborough."

"Why would we be going there?"

"I don't know, but it's a long way from Newcastle."

"And the other instructions?"

"That must mean the instructions I was given to keep you in one piece, which was why Antonescu's man had to leave us so suddenly. For what it's worth the message seems to be genuine, those initials at the end stand for H.K. St. Aubyn-Jollie who's an Equerry to the Prince of Wales. I met him at King's Cross."

While I'd been explaining the message, Stan had got out the Line Book, which showed details of each line and junction, and was examining it in the lamp light. There was no official publication covering the network layout. Normally a driver new to any stretch of track would have a pilot driver with him on the first couple of trips, until he had, as they say, learned the road. However, since becoming a Royal Train driver I had compiled my own hand written booklet, containing notes both about the east coast main lines and most of the principal branch lines. This was what we were now consulting.

"We'll be switched as we're leaving York." He said, holding the booklet in both hands to keep it steady against the motion of the engine. "We'll turn east to join the coast line, but it's not clear which way we'll go past Malton, the line splits in two and both tracks join up again at Whitby." He handed me the book and I saw what he meant.

"In this weather they'll be bound to route us through Scarborough, to keep us clear of the worst of the snow. There won't be enough traffic to justify running snow ploughs across the moors from Pickering tonight." I made a rough calculation of the mileages on the likely route.

"Going along the coast will be about sixty miles from York, if we can maintain this speed that'll be two hours." And that seemed to settle matters, we were going to Whitby. I just wondered if this would upset the plotters, or did they already know about it? There wasn't a lot I could do about it either way, events would just have to unfold at their own pace.

*****

The Stirling eight footer is an excellent engine and an uncomplaining workhorse, but the design was more than twenty years old. One of the immediately noticeable signs of this is that the cab is not as fully covered as on the more modern engines, and heavy rain, or in this case snow, can be a dispiriting experience. However, my time in the navy had taught me a wide variety of different lessons, not just how to kill the Queen's enemies.

When operating in the tropics we would regularly rig awnings over the quarterdeck and other exposed work places, to shelter from the sun - well the same system worked just as well for rain and snow. The main difference was that engine drivers called it a storm sheet. At our reduced speed it was possible for me to tie the canvas sheet from the cab roof back to a couple of struts and a crossbar which fitted onto the front of the tender. This helped to keep us dry and made life more comfortable, at least for a while.

Now we were turning the place into a home from home, Stan even took the time to show Pedro how we made our tea, by hanging a Billy Can directly over the fire box door, it didn't quite get it to boiling point but was only one or two degrees short and made perfectly decent char. I had been wrong about him not coping with the hard work, from the look on his face he was thriving on it, even the weather hadn't dampened his enthusiasm. If he carried on like this the Rumanians were as likely to lose their Crown Prince to the railways as assassination.

I had the two firemen alternating between shovelling and acting as lookout, even if there wasn't much around here to look at, it was still important for everyone to have a job.

Whilst we were on the run, the fireman's job was essentially a balancing act between the temperature of the fire, the boiler water level and the boiler pressure. Each one of these constituents affected the other, if the water level was getting low he switched on the second injector, if the pressure was dropping he stoked faster and opened the damper wider. As I said, a balancing act.

I perched on the driver's seat on the right of the cab, the steel leg shield guarding me from the fierce blast of heat whenever the fire door was opened. I had my right foot wedged against the bulkhead and Charlie, having temporarily given up on his nap, balanced on that knee, I had one of my arms around him and he clung to me with one of his. It was a novel arrangement but comfortable enough, and he was still fascinated with it all, watching everything that happened. He seemed determined to fend off

117

sleep for as long as possible, this was too good to miss.

There were another twenty five miles to run to Doncaster, and like most of this stretch of countryside it was wide open and flat. The snow wasn't likely to cause any problems with drifting around here, there wasn't much for it to drift into – the snow plough was more by way of a precaution, in case conditions deteriorated even further.

The signals we encountered stayed on 'Go' and I kept us to a steady thirty, if the plough had still been in this section with us, the signals would have held us until it had left the track. Eventually, ten miles south of Doncaster, we passed it on a siding, its lights haloed in the snow, and exchanged whistles with its crew.

Until that point there had been three of four inches of snow on the line, but now on the cleared section of track the rails were once more visible in our running lights, standing out black against the whiteness. The only reason for our continued slow speed being the reduced braking effect on the icy rails. As long as I could maintain a steady thirty without stoppages, we would still have a reasonable trip. The conditions were less than ideal, but both the train and its footplate crew could cope – whatever our problem was, it wasn't a railway problem.

Doncaster is well known as the site of one of the biggest locomotive works in the country, in fact the Stirling single that I was driving had been built there. Unfortunately, as far as through trains are concerned, it is also well known as an uncomfortable, twisting, rattling section of line. It snakes around the south and west of the town, and all the while the multiple points and junctions are endlessly banging you this way and that. Even having dropped the speed for a while, I had had to put Charlie down to control the engine through this area and Pedro had taken his turn to hold him.

Our priority routing ensured that we had a succession of green lights, which meant that at every junction where there was conflicting traffic, we kept moving whilst they had to wait. Once through town, I eased the speed back up, and even tried taking it to 35 mph, but couldn't safely maintain it. It was now 2.30 in the morning and it was going to be a long night.

Stan had warmed a metal ballast block by the fire and put that into the storage locker under Charlie's makeshift bedding, he promised Charlie a story if he'd snuggle up in there, just as Aunty Ruth would have wanted. Eventually it worked, the child must have been exhausted.

Having settled our youngest passenger, Stan swung himself round the outside of the cab to edge carefully along the narrow walk way that ran down the side of the boiler, holding tight onto the chest level brass hand rail as he went. We had trimmed and checked the running lights at Grantham, but he obviously felt that in bad weather you can't be too careful, and if nothing else the lenses might need to be cleared of snow. At this sort of reduced speed it was possible, even if not altogether sensible, to make you way around the side of the engine whilst still on the move.

As we were nominally a Royal Train, albeit at a fairly low level, it meant that we carried a full set of four forward running lights to mark our status. They provided some illumination of the track ahead, and in these conditions they were, slightly, better than nothing. What we could have done with is an electrically operated naval searchlight; but it turned out that if we'd had one, and pointed it forwards, we would have been looking in the wrong direction.

As he clambered back into the engine cab, having checked the lights, Stan seemed to be suddenly galvanised into action and pushed me to one side; he was scrabbling for something without even the time to speak. He reached up to the forward bulkhead and pulled down the rabbit gun, swinging it immediately round to point backwards.

"Stop right there." He shouted, and raised the gun to his shoulder, ready to fire. Standing behind us in the gloom, on the heaped pile of coal and partially hidden by the storm sheet, was a figure in a black overcoat; he was almost invisible, almost but not quite. He had been using one hand to hold onto the guard rail around the top of the tender, no doubt wishing to avoid a coal slippage that would give him away, with the other arm held out to one side, like a tightrope walker balancing himself.

But now, having been challenged by Stan, he managed to hold himself upright on the rocking and shaking pile of coal and, completely ignoring the gun pointed at him, pulled a pistol from his pocket. That took a quite some level of arrogance, to assume that you could pull your own gun before the other man could even pull the trigger. His confidence was impressive but unjustified.

Before he could bring his pistol to the aim, Stan fired, a single round that hit him in the shoulder. The pistol flew from his hand, clanging against the top rail of the tender before disappearing overboard. If the other members of Stan's congregation could see him in action I wasn't sure if they'd give him a medal, or throw him out. The presence of Stan's gun, and the loss of his own, didn't noticeably inhibit the intruder, he seemed to be a man with a mission to fulfil - and he hadn't done it yet. He started once more to lurch unsteadily down the slope of coal towards us, as he did so a small figure stepped out in front of him.

The shot must have woken Charlie, the poor thing was having a singularly disturbed night, and he appeared at the door of the tool locker, looking still half asleep and confused. He stared at the man and then turned to look at me, wondering who this newcomer could be. The newcomer experienced no such hesitation, he could have had no foreknowledge of Charlie's presence, but could recognise a hostage when he saw one.

He reached forward to grab Charlie with his good arm, Stan moved the gun barrel, but did it hesitantly, not sure what to do. Had I been holding the gun I might have managed to squeeze off another shot before the two figures merged, but Stan didn't have the benefit of my past experience to guide him. I was standing behind Pedro, too far back to do anything useful.

Fortunately Pedro displayed the faster reactions of a younger man and swept the coaling shovel up from the floor. In his first wild slash he hit the side of the man's leg, which produced a gasp, but failed to stop him completing his grab for Charlie. As he gathered the unresisting small figure with one hand, his other hand was rapidly reaching for something in his coat pocket.

Pedro had full control of the shovel by now and brought it ferociously, two handedly, down on the man's head. The intruder's hat probably saved his life, but he still fell, taking Charlie with him. We separated them, I took Charlie back from him and moved forward to stand at the controls.

Stan took advantage of his comatose state to feel in the man's coat pocket and see what he'd been reaching for. It turned out to be a large folding knife, it looked like a flick knife, with a set of brass knuckles down one side. This wasn't an item to open your morning post with, it was purpose built to maim and kill. Stan held it up between his thumb and forefinger, shaking his head in despair at the depravity of someone who would handle such a thing - and then handed it to me.

Working together, the two of them sat the man on the floor, in the entrance to the tender, with his back to the bulkhead. Pedro slapped his face and shouted at him, the man shook his head to clear it and then focussed. Awareness showed on his face, not only of the fact that he had been addressed in his native tongue, but also the implication of who that could mean Pedro was.

He smiled as he completed the deduction and said something in Rumanian, it must have been offensive because Pedro hit him, an angry unconsidered slap around the face. The blow knocked his head sideways, but failed to wipe the smile from his face. I gave Charlie to Stan, taking the revolver from my knapsack and went back to join Pedro and the man. I squatted down beside him, to make it easier for him to hear what I was saying.

"He wants to kill you." I said, nodding to Pedro. "But I'm just an English engine driver, so I don't really care whether you live or die. If you answer my questions you can live, but if not then I swear to God

I'll put you in the fire box – slowly, legs first. Now tell me, who is Number One?"

His eyes widened in surprise, and he looked unwillingly at the glowing, red hot, fire box door, but the man had guts and although he had initially been taken aback by the threat, he controlled the reaction. He then calmly hawked and spat at me. The spit missed my face and when I looked down I saw that it had landed on my shoulder. I leaned forward, took his hat off and used it to wipe the spit away. Then I carefully placed the hat back on his head.

"That was a serious mistake." I said. "Now we'll try once more; who is Number One?" He tried to spit at me again, it didn't even reach me this time. His mouth must be getting a little dry from all the coal dust there was around.

"It seems that I was wrong about you, you're a lot more determined than I thought and I respect that. You can go, go back the way you came – over the tender." I indicated the way with my eyes and then stood back to give him room.

Pedro took a pace forward and grasped my arm. "No, he can't, he can't go back there to tell them what he knows."

I looked at him, a hard look, straight in the eye. "You will do as you're told on this footplate." And then, in an undertone. "Leave this to me."

Then I turned back to the man. "Go now, it's your only chance."

He stood up, uncertainly, looking for the trick, and then began to climb back up the coal.

"Stan," I called over my shoulder, still watching the man climb, "show Charlie the train in front of us, and then blow the whistle."

The man reached the top of the heap, at the back of the tender, readying himself to try and perform the difficult feat of clambering back across the coupling to the first carriage. It would have been an extremely dangerous manoeuvre for him, in a place where there were no steps or handrails and in pitch darkness, but not, I felt, quite dangerous enough. So although I know it's bad form, I shot him in the back, just as the whistle sounded and Stan was still encouraging Charlie to peer forwards through one of the portholes.

The man collapsed into the gap, a helplessly tumbling, flailing thing, to be run over by the rest of the train, carriage by carriage.

"What did he say to you?" I asked Pedro.

"He said - *You cannot stop us* – that was all. It was always going to be a waste of time questioning such a man. Although they are killers they would rather die than betray their cause."

I had a slightly different view. "On the contrary, I think he gave us the most important piece of information he possessed."

"Which was?"

"His behaviour when he discovered that you were Rumanian told us that whoever he was working for still has no idea of who you really are. That's far more important than whoever Number One is."

Stan had stepped back to join us, still holding Charlie, and looking at neither of us in particular, asked. "I don't think he was a Freemason was he? More likely one of Pedro's lot, I'm almost sure I saw him crossing himself." For a Welsh Methodist he had a lively sense of humour.

"Where's the man gone?" Asked Charlie, going straight to the heart of the matter.

"He had to go back to the carriage, before someone took his seat."

I wondered what was happening to Ruth, or to put it more accurately I worried about what was happening to her, and what I could do about it. The only consolation seemed to be that by controlling where, or if, we stopped I could prevent reinforcements from joining the plotters. That way, whenever the showdown came, and it surely would, the good guys should continue to outnumber the bad guys.

*****

We continued to push our relentless way through the darkness, all we could see were those swirling snowflakes close enough to be picked out by our lights, as they tumbled their way past us in the displaced air along each side of the cab. Beyond that was only darkness. Then the tiny halt of Escrick flashed briefly through our restricted field of vision, which meant that we were less than five miles from York.

The signals were supposed to be set for us, and I intended to steam through York like an ocean liner. If reinforcements were waiting anywhere, they had to be waiting at York, it was our last scheduled stop. Well they could wave as we passed. Disconnecting the communication cord braking system had been one of my better ideas, they could only equalise the numbers if I agreed to stop where they wanted me to. Perhaps that gentleman clambering over the tender had been planning to ask me nicely.

York crept up on us before we knew it. With our visibility limited by the blizzard, the first sign of the city was when the track split into several parallel lines, followed by the York South signal box. Then suddenly in front of us there was a blaze of light strong enough to penetrate the snow filled sky, the station itself. We steamed out of the gloom and into clear air under the station canopy, with lights all around us, it was like another world. York station has two parallel train halls, and the whole structure has a majestic sweep to it, swinging round in a long gentle curve. When it's not dark and snowing there's a splendid view of the Minster towering above the mediaeval streets, as you emerge from the northern end of the station.

There would be trouble about this later, if only we lived that long, but with no more than a preliminary whistle we sailed serenely along the main line platform at a steady thirty miles an hour. What few overnight travellers there were, stepped smartly back from the edge, our abrupt arrival didn't feature on any of their timetables. Scarcely had we emerged into the light than we left it again. With any luck, this surprise cancellation of a scheduled stop should have enraged someone in the carriages behind me.

As the lights of York North signal box slid past us, a signalman in the end window raised a hand in greeting, and moments later came the hollow echo from the steel girders beneath us, as we crossed the invisible River Ouse. We were already on the east bound track. York has an ancient and fascinating city centre but its suburbs, through which we were passing, are no more attractive than any other city, even when you can see them. That night we saw very little, beyond a few dim lights in the houses

126

immediately next to the track, our sightseeing would have to wait for another day.

We had cleared the city and were now heading into relatively unknown territory. I knew every mile of the Newcastle trip, daytime or night-time. I knew what was round each corner, how to gauge my speed on the banks and the curves, even what noise to expect from each of the bridges, I'd driven it a hundred times. But the run from York to the coast was one that I'd only driven on rare occasions, it was outside my home territory. Once we'd crossed the river we were into bandit country, if the rails didn't get me then the passengers probably would.

Meanwhile,
the newspapers reported . . .

SAD DEATH OF THE W.M. WHILE OPENING
MASONIC LODGE

Mr. Arthur Smith aged 43 years of Bridge Road,
St. Pancras, went on Saturday to the York &
Albany Tavern, Regent's Park, to preside at a
Masonic Lodge of which he was the Worshipful
Master. Everything was ready to open the Lodge
when there was noticed a sudden change from a
smiling happy face to one of pale insensibility.
Some supported him, others fetched brandy,
while messengers were sent for Doctor
Henderson, who upon arrival pronounced life
extinct. The suddenness of the unexpected death
cast a gloom over the assembled brethren.

A hastily convened conclave of those present
then resolved that, undeniably sad though the
circumstances were, it was not thought sensible
to forego the dining fee, which had already been
paid in advance, and that their meal should,
therefore, continue as planned. Many said it was
what their departed brother would have wanted.

EIGHT

The countryside remained flat, but the fleetingly glimpsed station names became less familiar; Haxby, Strenshall, Flaxton and Kirkham Abbey. Then suddenly the name of Castle Howard rolled past us on a dark and deserted platform, an imposing stone balcony on the first floor of the station building jutted out over the platform. This looked to be altogether too grand for the York and North Midlands Railway Company to have erected, no doubt the Earl of Carlisle took the view that his station should make some attempt to match his house.

From my notes our next station should be somewhere called Huttons Ambo, the fact that I could remember nothing about it suggested that it was probably no more than a country halt. After that there was Malton, the last serious station before making our way out towards Scarborough and the final run up the coast to Whitby.

I was still not sure how to play things when we reached Whitby, we would be arriving in the very early hours of the morning, and the chances of finding a fit and active constabulary on hand were remote. Unlike passing through Newark, where I had thrown a message onto the platform for the station staff to telephone ahead for me, there was no such possibility here, all the stations were closed for the night. It looked as though it was going to be another solo effort.

The line curved gently along the contour lines of the rolling landscape, with occasional low cuttings and small bridges; it was easy railway country and in daylight would have made a nice run. Malton came and went, more dark buildings and deserted platforms, I was maintaining a steady thirty miles an hour, the snow was ever present but not quite deep enough to slow us.

After Malton came Rillington Junction, even the signal box looked empty. Then it seemed that disaster struck. The three of us on the footplate were thrown violently to our right, only just managing to hang on.

Fortunately, Charlie was in his hidey hole in a state of exhaustion if not sleep. For a moment the left side wheels must have lifted from the track as the engine swung sharply in that direction, I held my breath waiting for the bucking and plunging that would accompany a derailment, but after hanging suspended in space for long enough to cause heart failure, the engine rocked back onto an even keel. I could only imagine that each of the following coaches must have had the same experience.

Even as my pulse rate was still settling itself I realised what had happened, we had been switched onto the Pickering line leading over Fylingdales Moor. It would still take us to Whitby, but in these conditions it was an insane decision. Furthermore, we had just taken what was probably a fifteen mile an hour turn at twice the correct speed, we were lucky to be upright.

There was every prospect that, even in this weather, the coast line would be driveable, less snow and a flatter run, but all bets were off on this route. The higher ground would mean a lower temperature and the more broken nature of the surroundings would vastly increase the risk of drifts. I reached for the Line Book to confirm my memory.

Yes, I had it right, just a couple of small halts and then Pickering, after which I had noted; 'A long climb to Goathland summit'. This was a line I had never travelled in my life, the sum total of my knowledge was that one depressing note. Should I stop here and fight it out, risking Ruth's life in the crossfire? Even rehearsing the words in my head made it clear that I wouldn't do that, I would procrastinate in the hope that something, anything, might turn up to lessen the odds against us. There had to be some hope of reinforcements in Whitby, even if the police were all in bed they could be woken up – but out here there was nothing.

I'm normally a decisive man, someone who weighs up the available choices, takes a decision and then does something about it. But now I was aware of myself vacillating, not knowing what to do for the best, like a rabbit frozen in the light. Pickering station passed us in darkness as I continued to dither.

Already I could feel, and the speed dial showed, that we were beginning to climb as the land rose up before us. From the dimly visible trees overshadowing us on each side I felt that we were running up some kind of gorge. If I were to retain any sort of initiative I would have to take the lead, I would have to be the one to act – leaving them to react. The available choices for such action didn't seem attractive.

Stan and Pedro were now taking it in turns to shovel the coal, this would need every last smidgen of horse power we could produce. The detail of the fire had disappeared, there was now just a gleaming white light which blinded you when the door was open, accompanied by a constant roaring as the air was hungrily sucked in. Conversation was impossible with that level of noise, but Stan and I knew what was needed and Pedro followed suit. Stan opened the second injector to top up the water level, and I set the exhaust blower to half open to help drag the air through the fire box.

The speed had dropped another two miles an hour, this was too slow, I moved the reverser a couple of notches to increase the torque and pulled the regulator another two inches further out to maintain our speed, and considered the situation.

There was a loud crack from somewhere behind us, like a distant gunshot, more solid than that but muffled by the snow. It might not even have been on the train, but of course it was. We all turned to look back, but there was no new intruder and nothing visibly different to be seen. The train had given a slight jerk following the noise, and I began to realise what it could have been. Looking at the speed dial confirmed my guess, we had suddenly regained that lost two miles an hour and were still accelerating.

Swinging out of the cab doorway I looked back along the train, where there had been a string of lights from eight carriages, now there were the lights of just four. The noise had been someone using an explosive charge to blow a coupling apart, the detached carriages had already disappeared into the gloom. The uphill gradient, would by now have reversed their direction and they would now be accelerating backwards towards the junction. Runaway carriages were a serious hazard, particularly in such awful visibility, but they were beyond our control. Attempting to chase them would be a fool's errand. Press on.

Counting the carriages off, working from the back; eight and seven were the baggage cars; six was occupied by a mixture of the Crown Prince's entourage and some train servants, for obvious reasons they had been located as far from the replacement Prince as possible. It was carriage five that caused the problem, that was Scotland Yard's accommodation, all our police officers were likely to have been in that one.

I was gripped by a depressing awareness of the limits of my imagination. I had completely misunderstood the reference, any talk of equalising the numbers wasn't about them getting reinforcements, it was about disposing of the police we already had. I could have safely stopped at York and resolved the whole situation. The knowledge of a missed opportunity made me feel sick. But as I've said before, no matter how bad the cards in your hand, you have to play the ones you're dealt.

A novelty on this train was the fact that we were using the new gangway connection coaches, these had connecting doors at front and back permitting free movement from one end of the train to the other; and all this whilst on the move. The Great Northern Railway had pioneered this system two or three years earlier, and some of the other companies were beginning to copy us, but so far its use was confined to experimental or special trains.

The only restriction on this freedom of movement was in getting to or from the engine. To do that we would have to climb over the back of the tender and drop down onto the buffers, before trying to open the leading gangway door. On a moving train this was not only difficult, but extremely dangerous. From our point of view this was made even harder by the fact that the gangway door would normally be kept locked from the inside.

This meant that, despite seeing Ruth and Parkinson get into the third carriage, we could no longer be sure they were still there. I had now lost any interest in identifying the assassins, as far as I was concerned a successful outcome would involve me leaving the train with Ruth, Charlie and Stan. It would be invidious of me to list them in order of priority, but I rather think that I just have done.

It would be nice if the Crown Prince made it as well, but there were limits to what I'd do to achieve that. As for Antonescu, Parkinson and Scroop, whichever of them was doing whatever to whoever, as far as I was concerned they could all hold hands and jump off the nearest cliff. And at the rate we were climbing we should be encountering some of those quite soon.

To compensate for our reduced weight and the fact that we had now picked up too much speed, Stan had stopped coaling and closed the fire box door louvers, this had once more made conversation possible. Pedro took the opportunity to voice what we were all thinking.

"What do we do now?" He asked.

"Do you know," Stan said to him in a thoughtful tone of voice, "if I were a gambling man, which thank the Lord I'm not sir, I might be tempted to put some money on the Captain here taking his revolver and going to look for some trouble." Had he read my thoughts, or was I simply a very predictable sort of man? They both looked at me, expectantly.

"Well, has either of you got a better idea?" Needless to say, Pedro, being young and eager, was keen to join in whatever might occur. I put a stop to that by pointing out that stoking and driving the engine, whilst taking care of Charlie and looking out for bandits was at least a two man job.

I wasn't sure how things were going to play out, but there was at least one preliminary thing I could arrange.

"Take control," I said to Stan, "I'm going to change the forward lights around."

"I'll do it." He offered, but I shook my head.

"Just keep her at about thirty and watch out for visitors from behind."

Following Stan's earlier actions, I leaned round the outside of the cab to grip the hand rail, and swung myself onto the outside walkway. At first there was a flat narrow ledge for your feet, but then came the massive drive wheel housing, rising nearly to the top of the boiler. The walkway ledge skirted around the outside of this wheel cover, merely needing to curve high enough to clear the connecting rod attachment, just offset from the centre of the wheel. This was what the engine was all about, it was where the engine power was finally delivered to the drive wheel, the noise and endless cycling motion made the whole thing seem alive.

Despite the slipstream of our progress and the all enveloping snow, as I edged along the side of the locomotive, the heat of the boiler was like an open fire on my face, and the temperature of the hand rail could be felt even through my gloves. Stepping over the external cylinder, I could feel the repeated sliding to and fro of the piston within it, through the soles of my shoes. How could anyone fail to be impressed by such a magnificent piece of engineering?

There's a broad steel platform at the front of the engine, we call it the running plate, and it supports the forward bogie wheels, once there it could provide a reasonably secure and defensible position, or so I hoped. It just needed a little help to make it more so.

The four running lights of the Royal Train were laid out as a row of three along the forward platform, below the boiler, and then one on its own on top, just ahead of the funnel. The platform itself was in constant motion, seeming to sway and jump about much more than the cab. The wind tugged at my coat and endangered my hat, and for most of the time I had to use one hand to grasp the safety rail.

Leaving the two outer bottom lamps on their original brackets I simply swung them round, pointing out to the side of the train. I then took the remaining two and arranged them to shine directly backwards, towards the cab. Satisfied that they were firmly in place, I made my way slowly back along the side of the engine. Another of my cunning schemes, it was to be hoped that it was more successful than some of its predecessors.

During my gymnastics with the running lights we had passed another two small stations, but the slope still continued, we weren't at the top yet. Even through temporary breaks in the snow, there hadn't been a light to be seen in any direction for a long time. This place was desolate, even in good weather it would be a typical upland heath: more sheep than people. If we ever met them, what few inhabitants there were would probably be hostile, more likely to stone us than help. I shivered slightly.

Stan had been obliged to open the regulator almost fully by the time I regained the cab, it seemed as if the slope had finally levelled off, but we were now having to plough our way through increasingly deep snow. This had to be it, the ideal position. If I could send everybody else on the train flying, that might give me enough time to get our little group into what I hoped was a safe position without being observed. I had Stan and Pedro wrap themselves in hats, coats, mufflers and gloves; while I took care of Charlie's outfit.

"Will you be a good boy for Uncle Stan?" I asked.

"I promise." He said solemnly.

Pedro hooked the rifle's sling over his shoulder and we were ready.

"Hold on tight." I shut down the regulator and applied the brakes with maximum force. The combined effects of the braking and the deep snow, brought us to a very rapid standstill, even managing to slide all the coal in the tender forward. That should have taken then by surprise in the train, I just hoped that Ruth wasn't hurt in the process.

"Go quickly, as fast as you can."

Stan stepped out onto the outside walkway once again, this time clasping Charlie to his chest with one hand, and reaching for the hand rail with the other, Pedro followed. This was the manoeuvre that I had considered too dangerous to attempt with Charlie whilst we were still moving.

As they edged along the side of the locomotive, I jumped down and moved as quickly as possible away from the train, dragging a piece of tarpaulin behind me to cover my tracks. The snow was far too deep to consider running, so I just plodded along, but did so very determinedly. Turning to look back, I saw my three fellow travellers reach the platform at the front of the engine. Then, miraculously, they disappeared, which was precisely what they were supposed to do.

They were now behind the carefully arranged, outward pointing lights and should be able to see anyone approaching – tucked in there, where they could see but not be seen. It should be very difficult to take them by surprise. There would even be enough residual heat from the boiler and the smoke box to keep them from freezing for most of the next hour.

I had moved about fifty yards out from the engine, when I turned and began to walk back parallel with the carriages, checking if anything useful could be seen. The first carriage behind the engine was the travelling kitchen and dining room, but the fact that the replacement Crown Prince had taken to his bed had left it unused. The catering arrangements seemed to be that everyone else ate sandwiches. The blinds were drawn, and from what little light emerged there can't have been more than a couple of lamps lit.

The second carriage was the Crown Prince's sleeping car and bathroom, with a similar appearance. Was the replacement still hiding in his bedroom to continue the charade, or were they interrogating him to discover Pedro's whereabouts? Or perhaps he'd been shot out of hand, without his killers even noticing the substitution. Frankly that last option would have suited me best.

Carriage three had originally been the drawing room, and four had been for Major Antonescu's men, and although they also had their blinds drawn, the amount of light visible suggested they were in current use. As I watched, considering what my next move might be, a door on the third carriage opened and someone jumped down; he was carrying a lantern, and once safely on the ground took out a pistol. Looking around the dull white scene he shouted a single word in a questioning tone, it sounded like 'Stefan'. That would be the man I dropped under the train, he was going to need to shout a lot louder than that to catch his attention.

Realising there was no answer, he began to trudge along beside the train, towards the engine. He swung the lantern nervously around as he went, but it was nowhere near strong enough to reach me, and simply served to make his own actions and state of mind all the clearer.

He climbed up onto the footplate and found the birds had flown. He looked in the tender and found the same. He then leaned out from each side of the cab in turn, shining his lantern at the immediately adjacent snow, but my tracks had been covered, and Pedro and Stan hadn't left any. The walkway along the side of the boiler was too hot for snow to settle. The only clue he might have picked up was the strange angle that our running lights were set at; but that would take a railwayman to spot – or someone smarter than this man.

He leaned out of the cab again and called something down the train. It sounded like more Rumanian, which is not a Slavic language like Russian or Bulgarian, but a Latin language, not completely dissimilar to Italian. It didn't need a trained linguist to deduce the likely meaning: 'There's nobody here and I can't see Stefan'. A second man leaned out of the doorway he had left and called back. Again, from the tone he used, an

141

intelligent guess would be: 'Alright you can come back in'. At any rate that's what he did, slamming the door behind him.

Beyond the pleasure at seeing how well my concealment of Stan, Pedro and Charlie had been, I was cold and clueless. My hope had been to see something that would suggest a course of action, but I hadn't, which left me very literally out in the cold. Rushed and intemperate action is almost always worse than no action at all, but doing nothing wasn't an option either. I had to retrieve Ruth before anything else made sense, and if I stood here much longer I would freeze.

I began to trudge towards the back of the train, but as I did so one of the doors on the dining car was flung open and Antonescu climbed carefully down, he clearly left the jumping to underlings, and made his way to the engine. Presumably he didn't believe the first man's report and was going to look for himself. He repeated the exploration of the engine and tender, but then stood there, planted solidly in the opening, looking like a bull about to paw the ground.

"Meestah Fowlah." He bellowed in his excruciating accent. "Meestah Fowlah – I know you are near, I know you hear me good. I have the woman Castlemaine, or maybe she your woman Fowlah – heh?" There was a pause, as he looked around and gave me a chance to beg him not to hurt her. I didn't take it.

"I don't want this woman, you take her. I must have Crown Prince, my job to take care of Crown Prince. We change over lady and Crown Prince – heh – what you say to me?"

While still unwilling to stand up and make a target, I couldn't see any benefit in pretending that I wasn't here, he knew the train hadn't been driving itself. So I replied.

"The Crown Prince is already safe, a lot safer than he would have been on the train. But if you don't want the lady, then you can show that you are an honest man – you can let her ride on the engine with me."

"Don't give me stupid Fowlah, I change over, one for one."

"You have already shown that I cannot trust you, getting rid of the carriage with the policemen in it shows that."

"I don't know nothing for carriages. English policemen no good – nobody get rid Antonescu so easy. You tell me where Crown Prince is then maybe you get woman. You keep giving me stupid talk then peoples get hurt."

"The Crown Prince has left the train, if you were watching what was happening you will remember that I slowed down as we passed the last station. The Crown Prince jumped off into the snow, there were security men waiting for him."

"You stupid boogah Fowlah, I know who you are. You are navy man with medal, special medal for killing Rumanian peoples, and you think I don't know this. Fat man Bertie he likes you, is him who give you medal, he think only you take care of Crown Prince. You wait and see - I show you how to take care of him proper when I get him. I take care of him real good, for ever. Where you put him?"

Quite apart from some surprise at his familiarity with the double meaning of the English phrase '*take care of*', and him calling me stupid, this presented

143

something of a problem. I thought about it for a moment.

"I don't believe you've even got Mrs. Castlemaine, if you had her you would prove it by showing her to me. I think you're a murdering swine and you've probably already killed her."

"You don't trick me no how, I got Castlemaine and you know it."

"Alright," I answered, "You keep the Castlemaine woman, she's a bit too aristocratic for me, and I'll keep the Crown Prince. I understand the Bulgarian Brotherhood are offering a big reward for him – then I'll have enough money to buy Castlemaine's daughter, and her sister and probably her mother too."

"No more funny talk, I kill you for funny talk, you give me Crown Prince or you never see woman again. You decide."

"I already told you the truth, you're just too stupid to realise it. I said that he left the train at Newton Dale station, that's the last little place we passed. That's what I said, and that's what he did. It's too far to walk but it will only take me a few minutes to get back there on the train. With this amount of snow they might not even have left the station yet. Give me the woman and I'll take you, otherwise we'll all freeze to death."

"You get woman when I get Crown Prince." With that he climbed down from the engine and returned to the carriage, slamming the door behind him.

The man was a fool, if he'd actually produced Ruth to prove that she was alive, I might not have been able to resist swapping Pedro for her. The only small objection to that course of action being the fact that once he'd got his hands on Pedro; then Stan, Ruth, Charlie and I were all dead meat. This man was so untroubled by killing people that he hadn't even bothered to ask about his missing man Stefan.

It was slightly surprising to discover that he knew exactly who I was, and so much about me, but all that proved was that whoever his employers were, they took their work seriously. So what? He might think that I was a stupid boogah, but I thought he was a cocky boogah, the sort who needed bringing down a peg or two.

And while we were on the subject, where had Parkinson got to? Probably in one of the detached carriages having a glass of sherry and a game of chess with Sherlock Holmes, while Major Anton-bloody-escu prepared to kill my wife. Well they could do what they liked, I intended to carry the fight to the enemy.

Secure in the knowledge that this train wasn't going anywhere without me, I cautiously made my way to the back of the last carriage. Holding the Webley, I walked slowly up to the closed communicating door, the one that had joined onto the recently detached carriages. I stood there and listened, but could hear nothing. So I made my way round to the far side of the carriage, walking along the track, below the windows. Every two or three paces I paused and listened again, but still nothing.

I was more than half way along when, just audible above the wind, I heard the side door of the carriage, by now behind me, being opened. I twisted round towards it, my gun hand leading the way. A figure was hidden behind the lower half of the door, swinging out from the carriage and holding onto the outer edge with his left hand. Part of his face and his right hand were visible in the open window space.

The hand was pointing at me, there was a sharp report and a flash - the hand was holding a pistol. But he'd wasted his first shot by allowing speed to take priority over accuracy, and the bullet did no more than tug at the side of my coat.

He must have realised he'd been hasty because now he was squinting, trying to overcome the transition from the lit interior to the darker exterior. The white background would help him, but his eyes had yet to acclimatise. The barrel of his pistol moved slowly from side to side as he tried to make sure he was pointing at me and not some passing shadow.

From his point of view, the trouble with this situation was that I knew something that he didn't. The Webley revolver fires a .455 calibre bullet, that's a big heavy thing nearly half an inch in diameter, and there's six of them. They leave the barrel travelling at 620 feet per second, which by my reckoning is pretty fast. Now this is undeniably interesting in itself, but you really have to consider it in conjunction with the fact that the walls and doors of GNR carriages are only two inches thick, and constructed mostly of wooden battens and planks. Then it becomes clear that to shoot at someone hiding behind the door you don't need to bother doing it through the window. So I didn't.

Whilst the crouching figure in the doorway was wasting his time narrowing his eyes to get a better shot, I gave him two in the chest, straight through the lower half of the door. He recoiled backwards, dragging the door with him and colliding with the frame. The door began to swing open again, I fired another shot, towards where it joined the carriage, my bullet hit the lower hinge and ricocheted away. But it had only been the door swinging free, it seemed there was no living hand behind it. The gunman had been thrown backwards into the carriage, presumably dying on his way to the floor – the place where most failed gunmen seem to go.

And then. . . . nothing. I looked along the row of windows, but nobody else was showing themselves, had he been a lone operator?

As the gunman and I had been shooting at each other there had been a particularly strong gust of wind, it had howled across the moor, and whistled insanely round the train. The gun he'd fired at me had only just been audible, even ten feet in front of me. There was a real possibility, or even probability, that the exchange of shots had been unheard by anyone. I should capitalise on that slim advantage.

The damaged door was too high for easy access from the ground, and there was nothing for me to climb on. I hastened, I positively snow ploughed my way, to the back of the carriage - to the jagged remains of the communicating door, where it had been torn free as the train came apart. I struggled awkwardly, using the ice cold broken coupling as a toe hold to reach the door. As expected it was locked, but equally as expected a hefty impact from my shoulder sprang it open. No time for subtlety. Not bothering with any sort of preliminary look I charged into the carriage, waving the pistol in front of me.

It was an open carriage, rather than being split into compartments, and three figures could be seen lying sprawled across the floor. The first, right in front of me, was the man I had shot at the side door, he was dressed in a black overcoat and though I didn't know all their faces I assumed him to be one

147

of Antonescu's. But whoever he had been, he was dead now. The other two were Parkinson and Scroop, bound and gagged but clearly alive.

Using the combined flick knife and knuckle duster that I'd confiscated from the man in the tender, I cut them free.

"Oh thank God you've come." Said Scroop apparently overcome with emotion. "It was terrible, they were going murder the pair of us." He scrabbled to his feet, rubbing at his wrists where the rope had been. Parkinson managed to restrain his natural warmth and good will, confining himself to a muttered: 'At last'. Then, strangely, he held his hand out, as if to shake my own. If vocal politeness was beyond the man, perhaps a graceful physical gesture would suffice.

But no, he wasn't expressing gratitude, he wished to exchange information. Looking me directly in the eye he used his handshake to form the identifying grip of a Master Mason. Unthinkingly I responded by returning the sign. On my part this was more of an automatic response to a fraternal greeting, than a willingness to explore the subject. But Parkinson had a different view and held my grip, continuing to fix me with his direct and meaningful stare. Unfortunately, any hidden meaning in his expression was lost on me and I probably looked a little blank in return.

Moving his face even closer to mine, he pronounced a word that I didn't understand the relevance of, and wasn't sure that I'd heard properly, it sounded like *Atlantis*. I showed my incomprehension with a puzzled look and raised eyebrows but he didn't repeat the word.

In view of the Masonic recognition we had just exchanged he was probably telling me which lodge he was in, which I thought to be more information than the situation demanded. I'm a little more choosy about my friends, and the simple knowledge that he was a Brother was nowhere near enough to overcome my dislike and contempt for the man. This whole damned train seemed to be packed with people I didn't care for.

"Masonic matters can wait for a more suitable moment." Was my brusque reply, a comment which caused him to look slightly surprised, I shrugged inwardly and pressed on with more urgent matters.

"What happened?"

"They simply outnumbered us, six of them came in with drawn pistols and tied us up. We didn't stand a chance. The one thing my superiors don't seem to have considered was the possibility that all the Rumanians might be involved in the plot."

He sighed theatrically, and shook his head. "But I'm afraid that's all too late now because the tragedy has already occurred, the Crown Prince and his secretary have both been killed. They were shot by Antonescu, or his men, I've seen the bodies myself. Which means that our duty now is clear, we must make our way as quickly as possible to the nearest place where there is access to a telegraph or telephone and alert the authorities. Proper steps can then be taken to round these people up."

This man still wasn't seeing straight. "We won't be going anywhere until Mrs. Castlemaine has been released, when last seen she was with you – where is she now?"

"The Rumanians who captured us took her with them." He gestured forwards to Antonescu's carriage directly ahead, not showing any great signs of interest in her whereabouts. I stared at him for a long moment before trusting myself to speak.

"She had better be unharmed when I find her." I said slowly, not bothering to waste my breath in overt threats, a blind man would have seen the signals I was exhibiting. But apparently not Parkinson.

"Fowler, you will return to the engine and take us to the nearest station – that is a direct order. I will take your gun and Scroop will take the dead man's. We shall then hold off the Rumanians until we arrive at Whitby, or wherever. At that point, and not before, we shall be in a position to pay attention to the missing Mrs. Castlemaine – if that's even the woman's real name."

He held out his hand for the Webley, I stared at him in astonishment.

"You mentioned that your superiors failed to consider adequately who might be involved, but the truth of the matter is that they gave that job to you. Our problems arise from the fact that you completely failed in that task, whether from cowardice or incompetence I neither know nor care. You allowed your charges to be butchered and now propose the same fate for Mrs. Castlemaine, a personal friend of the Prince of Wales, in order to save your own wretched skin."

"Fowler for failing to carry out the lawful instructions of a police officer you can and will go to jail."

"Which is a considerably better fate than awaits you, should any harm have befallen that lady through your ineptitude."

Every single thing this man said reinforced my original view of him. However, although the invective was satisfying, it was wasting valuable time. At any moment we could be joined by thugs from the next coach. No matter how foolish my next actions might be, they would not be improved by standing here - Parkinson was going to have to wait his turn in the lengthening queue for retribution.

Desirous of overcoming his inability to pick up hints, I pointed a finger at him. "I'm now going forward to try and release her, as I have already released you. If you interfere with me in any way, I will kill you."

I then turned and went to the communicating door leading up the train. There was a blind drawn down but it didn't completely cover the glass panel, by crouching down it was possible to see around the edge. The carriage ahead of me was fitted out as a travelling drawing room, with plush easy chairs and sofas, some small tables and a writing desk. Ruth was clearly visible sat on a chair, and surprisingly she seemed to be alone, though from her posture it looked as if her hands were tied together in front of her.

Why was she sat there alone, where were the rest of them? Could they be outside looking for me – that seemed to be the most likely answer.

There was no key on my side of the door and, not knowing if it was locked, I twisted the handle slowly and quietly, and then carefully pushed against it. The door moved, I pushed it fully open and stepped forward, my eyes completely fixed on Ruth.

As I took my second step she looked up, for the first time aware of my presence. I had just enough time to register her look of pleased surprise turning immediately to horror, before an arm clamped itself round my throat, and a gun barrel was rammed against the side of my head.

"Drop the gun, or I shoot - you first, then her second."

The door was kicked shut behind me and I dropped my gun. Resistance, as they say, was futile. He had been waiting for me behind the door, such an obvious and simple trick, and one which I should have thought of. There's no sicker feeling than the knowledge that you've just been trapped by your own carelessness. He pushed me along the carriage until we were near Ruth.

"Stand up – we go forward." He said to her. As she did so, she picked up her bag with her two tied hands: a woman picking up her bag, it's the natural thing to do. Well I certainly thought so, and so did the man with the gun for he said nothing. She moved obediently out to walk in front of me. The three of us were walking in line when I saw her bag fall to the floor, without realising why she should have dropped it. Then she came to a sudden halt, and so, of necessity, did I.

She swung round, raising her two hands in front of her until they were pointing over my shoulder. She did it in one swift movement. She was holding the completely useless blank firing pistol, and as it lined up with my captor's face she pulled the trigger. The muzzle was only inches from the side of my own face and the blast rocked me backwards.

But not half as much as the man behind me. With a clatter from his dropped pistol he fell to the floor, not bothering to say goodbye as he went. The floor in this train was getting to be quite untidy. I twisted round to see the cause of his collapse, and saw that one of his eyes had been quite neatly shot out. A mixture of blood and the viscous contents of one eyeball leaked slowly down his unmoving cheek.

"A blank firer is only a blank firer," she said, "as long as you don't put anything in the barrel in front of the cartridge, because that would be dangerous."

"What did you put in?"

"The last inch that I snapped off the sharpened end of a pencil."

"That would certainly do it." I nodded, and looked down at the fallen man. Had he been able to, I'm sure he would have nodded too.

FLEEING FINANCIER

The Antofagasta Mining Co. prospectus had offered fully secured loan stock at 10¼% interest redeemable at 12 months. The prospectus had stated that the loan stock was fully indemnified by the company's own reserves, and fully supported by the Bank of England. However, Mr. Harold Dowson, for the plaintiff, described the prospectus as 'fanciful nonsense' with no commercial validity. He said that upon enquiry the Bank of England had never heard of the company. Tho' he conceded that the picture of a gold mine on the company's heading might look well if framed.

Unfortunately, having received almost £15,000. of client's money in the first month of advertising, the gentleman describing himself as Senor Ernesto Gonzales of Santiago in Chile, disappeared from his lodgings, and was not to be found at his place of business. All was thought to be lost. However, by the greatest good

155

fortune, the plaintiff. Mr. Samuel Bedford of Tolliver Mansions, Islington, had business in Dublin. Having travelled to Liverpool to take the Irish ferry
he was staying at the Sefton Hotel in that city, when he saw in the dining room the person he knew as Senor Gonzales of Santiago.

When challenged the gentleman stated that he could not be from Chile, as his name was Jones and he came from Aberystwyth. He then began to wave his arms about and speak nonsense in a high pitched voice, pausing only to claim that he was speaking in Welsh.

A constable was summoned.

NINE

I cut her hands free and retrieved the dropped Webley, giving her the dead man's pistol. Parkinson and Scroop were now an irrelevance, an encumbrance, they had failed once too often and now would have to make their own arrangements. I had Ruth back, and we were leaving.

Turning down the lamps near the outside door, I pushed it open and then stepped quickly back, ready for trouble. But no shots rang out and nobody leapt at me. If there was another trap waiting to be sprung, then it would probably be successful, because I just didn't have the time to look too closely.

I jumped down, still alert for any other figures in a landscape, but everything remained as resolutely white as Ku Klux Klan convention. I helped Ruth down and together we moved away from the train before turning towards the engine. Visibility was between 50 and 100 yards, varying unpredictably as the wind curled this way and that across the hillside. As the night progressed the temperature was dropping, the snow which had been soft now seemed harder, sharper, and it hurt as it hit your face.

As we struggled on there was a slight clearing, between the whirling snow clouds, and the whole train was briefly visible. It stood out as an intrusion in this arctic panorama, the carriage lights looking insignificant against this display of nature, white in tooth and claw.

Even the engine running lights seemed to be flickering and weak against this natural majesty. But as I focussed on them I came to see that the flickering was no trick of the light, and it wasn't my imagination. The engine lights had appeared to be flickering because someone was walking in front of one of them; walking or fighting in front of one of them.

"Hurry, there's trouble." I said, though the best we could manage was an exaggerated sort of high stepped wading. Now that we were paying attention we began to hear faint voices from that direction, they sounded angry. Our defensive position on the front running plate, that I'd hoped to be secure behind the lights, had been discovered and was now being overrun.

We closed on the scene with agonising slowness. There was an ongoing scuffle, a disorganised scrum, with audible grunts and gasps of pain. The struggling figures were concealed, not only by the darkness but also by the fact that they were in almost waist deep snow. If someone fell over they disappeared from view.

However, as we came closer the conflict seemed to peter out, and they became just one group of figures. The only explanation could be that Stan and Pedro had been captured or killed. The group began to make its way around the far side of the engine, visible dimly as they passed through the lantern beams. As they did so there was a cry, no words, literally just a brief frightened cry. They'd got Charlie, and next to Ruth he was their ultimate prize, their free ticket out of any hole.

I fired the Webley into the air, and Ruth did the same with the dead man's revolver. Not because it would do the slightest good, but simply because we had to do something – anything. The figures halted, startled by our arrival. Anonymous white shapes of faces could be seen turning our way in the darkness. We had thought that we were already moving as fast as the conditions would allow, but now we moved faster. The bastards.

We caught them as they struggled away from us along the far side of the engine. Ruth and I fired half a dozen more shots above their heads as we closed on them, and then, frightened to fire any more for fear of who we might hit, we launched ourselves wildly at them, using the guns to batter any head in reach. Ruth didn't have the physical bulk to keep this up for long, and I no longer had the vigour of my youth; but for that first minute our bloodlust, fuelled by outrage, caused chaos.

Then the men ahead began to take carefully aimed shots at us, we were identifiable targets being at one end of the group. Ricochets banged and whined of the engine steelwork, if we continued standing here we were going to die.

We both dived down beside the locomotive wheels. We had put down two of their men in our mad rush, two men who had been carrying a third unconscious figure between them. One of these had pulled himself back up against an engine wheel, but would be no threat for a while.

The other one staggered after his comrades with blood running blackly down the side of his head where one of us had clubbed him. His presence between us and them discouraged further gunfire in our direction. But lying abandoned in the snow beside us was the unconscious body they had been carrying between them, one of theirs or ours?

We rolled the inert figure onto its back, and found Pedro. The departing group was now no more than an indistinct black shape, as the next bank of tumbling airborne snow swept around us. Pedro groaned and began to struggle blindly against whoever he'd last been fighting with. We held him down for a moment until consciousness returned more fully, and he blinked his way to recognising us. Then a gunshot sounded, just a single shot, followed immediately by a soft and almost inaudible smack as it hit the ground beneath the snow out to one side of us.

"That was rifle fire, they've got someone firing along the side of the train, and he's out of range of our hand guns. He doesn't even need to see us, if he just fires enough bullets along the side of the train one of them's going to hit us."

Together we pulled Pedro round to the front of the engine. He caught hold of me, looking desperate.

"Where are Stan and Charlie?"

"We know they've got Charlie, we heard him crying, and it makes sense to assume they have Stan as well."

He slumped back against the front of the engine, only the buffer next to him prevented him from falling to the ground. "This is all my fault, bringing my country's problems into your lives. Out of the three people you could have saved, you got the wrong one, you should have left me there."

Another man might have used soothing words and told him not to think like that. I preferred to do him the courtesy of telling the truth.

"You're quite right, out of the three people involved you would always have been at the bottom of my list. And for the avoidance of any further doubt, when Antonescu was shouting out to me earlier about swapping you for Ruth, the only thing that stopped me was the certainty that he wouldn't have kept his word. If I'd thought I could have trusted him – you'd have gone."

"I wanted to give myself up then, but Stan held the gun to my head and said he would shoot me if I moved." I'd have to have a word with Stan about that later, if there was ever going to be a later. "And was Antonescu right when he said that you were a hero in the navy for killing those Rumanian sailors?"

I sighed, it was all coming out tonight. "Yes that's right, but it was an entirely justifiable reaction to their illegal behaviour, and the medal wasn't my idea. I didn't have much choice in any of it."

"You must hate my people and think we are nothing but trouble."

"Not at all, it's true that I'm not keen on foreigners generally – most people aren't, but I'm not a complete bigot, one of my best friends is Welsh. I have nothing against Rumanians in particular, some of them might be very pleasant people, it's just that none of the ones that are seem to be on the train tonight. And Antonescu would still be an utter shit in any language."

"For God's sake, will you just forget about Rumania – what about Charlie and Stan, and what about the fact that we're going to freeze to death unless we can find shelter?" Ruth brought us down to earth, an extremely frozen earth. Then to reinforce the point, what sounded like a second rifle, began firing random shots along the other side of the train,

161

we were outnumbered and outgunned. If we were ever going to have a realistic chance of rescuing the two captives we would have to find somewhere safer than this to shelter, while we sorted ourselves out.

"Staying on the engine's out of the question, and trying to take the carriages by storm would be suicide now that they've got all their remaining men back on board." I said to Ruth.

"Your gun's empty and I'm on my last reload for the Webley. They can out shoot us in any situation, especially now we know they've got rifles."

"Could we make our way back to that last station?" asked Ruth, "even if it's closed we could break in and use the telegraph to get help from the police or the army."

"I think it's too far away to reach on foot." I said. "But even if we did make it, a small country station like that wouldn't have a telephone, at best they might have a telegraph for sending pre arranged coded signals. And frankly I doubt there'll be a code for 'We are under attack by Bulgarian assassins'."

As we spoke more bullets winged off the side of the engine, reinforcing the point that our position here was strictly temporary.

"We could try to reach the house, and see if we can get in there." Pedro suggested.

"What house?"

"There's a big house up on the hillside over there, there were no lights so it might be no more than a deserted ruin, but at least it would be shelter." Said Pedro gesturing vaguely over to the left of the line. "There was a gap in the snow while we were hiding at the front of the engine, and we could see the outline of it then."

I looked at Ruth. "What d'you reckon?"

She shook her head wearily. "I can't imagine leaving Charlie with them for the rest of the night, but I don't know what else to do that doesn't risk making matters worse."

"For what it's worth," I said, "they must realise that harming Charlie would simply guarantee they would be hunted down, he's too valuable to them just as he is." While I was saying it, I almost believed it.

*****

As my last job before leaving the locomotive, I took a chance with the random rifle bullets to go round to the rapidly chilling cab and took some detonators out of their box. I then set about fixing them to the rails beneath the engine and tender. It was dangerous work, if any exposed skin, around the edge of my gloves touched the bare rail then I would freeze to it.

The detonators are designed to be clipped to the line to warn oncoming traffic of some unsignalled blockage ahead. Each of them is a small explosive charge, set off by the pressure of the train wheel rolling over it; they do no damage but produce a very loud bang. Even being as far away as Pedro's dimly seen house, it would mean that no one could move the engine without me being aware of it. To be honest I seriously doubted that the train could be moved at all, without extensive to and fro shunting to break through the drifts which had already piled against the carriages. It was going to be some time before that particular problem reached the top of my list.

We headed off up the slight slope leading away from the railway track, in the general direction that

Pedro remembered. It was a painstaking business trying to keep our line of progress straight, and avoid wandering off into the wilderness. Once we'd lost sight of the engine we had to keep stopping to check how straight the tracks behind us were, to try and ensure that we weren't just going round in a circle.

It was an energy sapping trudge, quite apart from the uncertainty over our direction, the smooth surface of the snow concealed a tortured ground level of bumps, dips, gorse bushes and occasional ditches. After about quarter of an hour of this torment we spotted the dark bulk of a structure to our left, and turned gratefully towards it. It seemed a strange place to build a house, but I wasn't going to get into an argument about that tonight.

There were no visible lights, perhaps it was deserted, if it was I would break up the floorboards to start a fire, we had to find warmth and shelter somewhere. I couldn't imagine what sort of mad forbidding creature would choose to live in this God forsaken place, when with a little planning they could have had themselves sent to jail instead. But I kept such thoughts to myself.

There might once have been a garden around the house, and in their season marigolds and hollyhocks could have grown in sweet profusion. But this wasn't their season and all we had was more damn snow. Endless damn snow in every direction, surely the most useless substance known to man. Perhaps I was losing my grip, but the thought crossed my mind that had I wished to explore the Arctic or seek the Northwest Passage I should have stayed in the navy rather than becoming a railwayman.

The house, which had looked bleak from a distance, got no better as we came closer. A large two story building with a steeply pitched roof - whatever colour it was in daylight, it was black now. There seemed to be no obvious reason for its presence here, what on earth would the occupants do with themselves all day? The upstairs windows were in darkness, the downstairs windows heavily shuttered and the front door solid and unlit. Surely the place was deserted. The three of us stood in a row looking at it, the fog of our breath being whipped away by the wind.

"I don't think there's anybody here, it's probably been empty for years." I offered, Pedro had no comment, but Ruth tapped my arm and pointed up to the small semicircular glass window above the door.

"That window should have ice on it."

I saw what she meant, if the house were deserted then that exposed piece of glass would have been covered in ice, but it wasn't. Somewhere in this house was a source of heat, a lit fire.

I went to the door and pulled sharply down on the cold steel bar of the bell pull. Distantly we heard it ring, I pulled again, and again. At length the wavering shadows given off by a moving lamp showed in the glass panel above the door. Then the wandering light steadied, presumably as the lamp was set down on a table.

"Who is it?" asked a sharp female voice. Definitely not young, from the sound of it, but direct and unafraid.

"I'm sorry to trouble you." I said, addressing the locked door. "I and my two companions are from a train which is stopped on the line near your house, I'm the driver. The snow has blocked our way and we can go no further. Can we please come in?"

"If you are in fact the engine driver then your first duty should be with the train, seeing to the welfare of the rest of your passengers. I would suggest you would be better employed doing that, rather than talking to me."

"Normally madam I would agree with you, but I promise you there are very special circumstances which apply here. Please let us come in and I can explain everything."

"The track ahead may well be blocked, it was foolish of you to attempt to cross the moor in these conditions. But it can't be blocked behind you, as you've just come up that way. You should take your engine backwards all the way down the hill to Pickering, from where you may summon whatever help you need."

"Madam." There was a slight note of asperity creeping into my voice but, to paraphrase Oliver Cromwell, I was amazed at my own moderation. "I am a stranded railwayman, with two passengers, standing in a blizzard in the middle of a frozen wasteland. Whether or not you have a legal duty to assist us I am unsure, but you most certainly have a moral duty."

"Young man, if you'd care to leave your name and address, then the next time I feel in need of a lecture about my morals you may be confident of hearing from me."

This woman should be a barrister, she could reduce strong judges to tears and bring the Old Bailey to a standstill. I took a deep breath in the better to respond at length to this nonsense, but Ruth motioned me to silence and stepped nearer the door.

"We really are very sorry to disturb you in the middle of the night, but I promise on my honour that we mean you no harm. We have had to flee from a gang of armed criminals on the train, amongst other hostages they are holding my three year old nephew, Charlie, we're desperate. Please, please let us in, before we freeze to death, or they catch up with us."

"Well if that's the case, why didn't you say so in the first place, instead of this silly business about the line being blocked?"

"Because it sounds so far fetched, we feared you wouldn't believe us."

"I'm still not sure that I do, wait there for a moment."

Once again the patterns of light and shadow moved about in the window above the door. I stamped my feet and the others did likewise, once you stopped moving, your feet began to ache from the cold. Then she, and the lamp, were back. Her voice closer, from right behind the door.

"I'm going to open the door now." A key turned, two bolts shot back, and the door swung open to reveal a large gloomy entrance hall. The lady who had opened the door had moved back with it, to leave an empty space, and facing us from the far side of the hall was a second lady, also of a certain age. What lent the scene a particular novelty was that the second lady was holding a double barrelled shotgun, and holding it in such a comfortable and easy way that she was clearly familiar with its use. Needless to say, like every other gun we'd seen recently, it was pointing directly at us.

Pedro muttered, hopelessly, and half to himself; "This country is so different from the way I'd imagined it."

As we walked into the hall, I stopped in surprise, there were two things I hadn't expected. The first was a decorated Christmas tree, although the Royal family had popularised these some years ago, they were still very much a metropolitan affectation. The Germanic overtones made it unlikely they would ever achieve a wider popularity. But next to the tree was an even more surprising sight, and this one owed nothing to Prince Albert.

I was so overcome with relief that I could feel a lump in my throat. I was unable to stop myself walking over and placing a hand on it, to confirm that this was no illusion brought on by wishful thinking. But it was undeniably solid and real, and it would provide our first hope for doing something constructive to help Charlie.

It was in polished mahogany, two feet in height, and was fastened to the wall about four feet off the floor. On the front was a brass plaque saying: David Moseley & Sons, Manchester. There were two bells on the top, a trumpet style mouth piece was set in the middle at the front, an ear piece hung from a hook on the left and a cranked generator handle emerged from the right. Of all the improbable things I had never dared to hope for, these two ladies had their very own telephone instrument. Pausing in my admiration of it I turned to the owners.

"We must speak to the police immediately, will you work this for me please?"

"I'm afraid your too late." Said one.

"Has the exchange closed for the night?"

"Quite possibly, but more to the point the line's down in the snow."

"Are they sending someone to fix it? When will they be here?"

"Last year they came at the end of February, there's no point in coming sooner, it wouldn't last a week up here."

I slumped, emotionally and physically, my excited hopes dashed. They led us through to an inner room, a large kitchen cum morning room, where we were asked to place our revolvers on the table. It wasn't so much the guns they seemed to object to, as the bad manners of having them concealed about our persons. There is apparently a whole etiquette of gun handling when a guest in someone else's house.

A wood burning range was glowing and crackling and there was a vague smell of food, the whole scene was reassuringly normal, it seemed like another world. Ruth was escorted away to be given dry clothes while, in the absence of immediately available male clothing, Pedro and I were given two large blankets to drape ourselves in and left to hang our wet clothes by the side of the stove.

When a strangely dressed Ruth and her two minders reappeared we made our introductions, and then sat around the long pine table to recount the events that had led us to this place. The two ladies, who turned out to be called Gretchen and Magda, said they preferred to hear it from Ruth, so she did most of the talking. Pedro and I sat there wrapped in our blankets, like two Red Indians, adding comments to her account when asked.

On discovering Pedro's identity, Gretchen, the one with the shotgun, spoke to him in German, with Magda adding the odd comment. For two or three minutes they had an intense conversation, with Pedro appearing to answer a series of questions. At the end of which Gretchen turned to Ruth and I with the

169

simple comment: "We accept that this gentleman is who he claims to be."

"That was very fluent German." Said Ruth, in what was as much a question as a statement.

"We were born in Prussia and spent our early years there. After mother died, our father, Otto, brought us to England to make a new start. That was in 1848, what they called the Year of Revolutions in Europe; there was political unrest throughout Germany and Austro Hungary, and father believed we would have a more secure future in England. So Magda and I had our education split between the two countries."

Whilst the conversation continued Magda had produced two large frying pans and was cooking bacon and eggs on top of the range. The kettle was boiling and Gretchen slicing thick pieces of bread. The kitchens of Mr. D'Oyly Carte's new Savoy Hotel couldn't have produced a more mouth watering aroma.

Having decided that one of us was genuine it was only a short step to accepting the rest of our story, and from then on relationships improved dramatically. But behind everything was the spectre of Charlie in the hands of murderous strangers, it was impossible not to think about it. Stan being captured was awful, but he could analyze the situation and think it through rationally. Charlie would just be terrified.

Regardless of how exhausted or cold we felt, I suggested that our attempt to free them should be made without delay. Working on the principal that the human body is at its lowest ebb around three a.m. and it was now nearer to six a.m. than three, the sooner we made our move the better. Magda shook her head dismissively.

"It's presently fourteen degrees Fahrenheit outside, or in German, minus ten degrees Celsius. This means that out there on the open moor, away from the house, the surface of the snow will have frozen, but still won't be strong enough to walk on. You haven't a chance of creeping up on them, every footstep will sound like a window breaking. Not only that, but they will be able to shoot at you, outlined against the snow, while you will be unable to shoot back because of Stan and Charlie."

They were right about the surface of the snow, we had encountered that effect on our way here. Yet despite that, if left to myself I might still have argued, but Ruth reluctantly agreed with her. And so, eventually, did I. Whatever we did, committing suicide would be the least helpful option. I was at a loss, there was nothing useful I could do, but doing nothing was impossible. Ruth looked drawn and desperate, and I felt completely impotent, none of the available options were acceptable.

Having come to a baffled standstill, and unable to imagine any action that wouldn't create more problems than it solved, we talked about Magda and Gretchen, just to give us a different topic of conversation. We needed to take a break, even if only briefly from the scale of our problems.

It turned out they were horse breeders, but not just any horse breeders, they bred specifically for show business. They supplied circuses, and any other sort of stage show that required animals; not only horses – but that was their mainstay, and they travelled all over the country to do it. As Gretchen was explaining this, a look of surprise came over Ruth, and in the end she interrupted the story.

"You're the Schindlers aren't you? Of course, I should have realised, Magda and Gretchen Schindler – Schindler's Menagerie."

Gretchen came to a surprised stop, but wasn't displeased with the recognition.

"How did you hear of us? Most members of the public don't know anything about our work."

Ruth explained that not only did she work at Sadler's Wells, but that both she and I had been to see Buffalo Bill's Wild West Show in London that summer, and she knew that the Schindlers had supplied most of the horses for their British tour.

"Did you actually meet Buffalo Bill and the cowboys and Indians?" Ruth asked.

"In the cast everyone calls him by his real name, which is Colonel Cody, and yes, we met everyone. We were with them full time for the first two weeks, getting the animals sorted out, and after that there was always one of us going backwards and forwards every other week. In fact it was Magda who taught Phoebe that trick with the playing card."

"Who's Phoebe?"

"Phoebe Mosey, as was, she appears on stage as Annie Oakley. You must have seen her do that business, shooting a playing card in half, edge on, from about fifty feet away."

"We both saw that, it was astonishing." I said. "She did it right in front of us – and then she shot holes in the part of the card that was falling to the floor. How can that be a trick – we sat there and watched her do it?"

"Easy, you saw what you were supposed to see. The man holding it already has a card in two parts before they start, and she shoots at it with a blank. The man holding it is a professional card sharp who's been chased off every river boat on the Mississippi, so pulling a stunt like that is no trouble at all."

"But that doesn't explain how she shot holes in the half that was falling, we saw it recoil through the air every time it was hit."

"That's the bit that Magda taught her, it's simple once you know how. She uses a .22 rifle with a modified magazine and after that first blank shot the next three cartridges are loaded with 5 mm. round shot, with four or five balls in each cartridge, one behind the other. Being slightly narrower than the rifle bore, they begin to move around in the barrel and then spread out when they leave. All she has to do is be within the general area of the card and out of three shots she's almost sure to hit it with something."

"Is it all trickery?"

"Oh by no means, she's an amazing young woman and a real sharp shooter; it's just that particular trick, night after night, would be almost impossible without some help."

While Gretchen was talking to us, Magda had served the bacon and eggs and the mugs of tea. For five minutes nobody spoke, it was hours since we'd eaten. I should have been tired as well as hungry, but I was still brim full with energy, it just wasn't obvious what to do with it.

Having been born German, the Schindler sisters thought Hohenzollern royalty more important than we did, which led to some reluctance to treat Pedro as anything other than a Crown Prince. But having been thoroughly democratised by Stan and I, he said he would prefer to remain a commoner for the time

173

being, so Pedro he stayed. Magda asked him if he was looking forward to the wedding in January.

Ruth and I exchanged surprised looks. "Wedding - January?"

"He looked embarrassed. "I'm sorry that I didn't say anything, it was simply that it didn't seem important on the footplate, not with all that was going on."

"Is it anyone we know?" I wondered.

"Princess Marie, yet another grandchild of your Queen. Perhaps you can understand a little better now how desperate I was to enjoy this last chance for unsupervised freedom. In four weeks time my every move will be controlled and watched. Your own Prince of Wales is fortunate to live in such a modern country."

"Him and his wandering hands." Said Ruth. Gretchen laughed.

"You should have seen him trying to interest Phoebe into going for supper, in the end Frank, her husband, said that she would love to go – but only if he came too. Fortunately, it turned out that the Prince of Wales and Colonel Cody were both Freemasons, so Bertie took him off to a Lodge meeting one night. They got on famously."

"Both Freemasons?" Murmured Pedro in surprise, more to himself than any of the rest of us, but Magda answered him anyway.

"Yes, both of them, and so is father - are you?" All he could manage was an astonished shake of the head at such an outrageous suggestion.

"Is your father still living?" I asked, as she'd referred to him in the present tense.

"Oh yes, he's in his mid eighties now, and while he tires easily his mind is still as sharp as it ever was."

Prompted by this news, a vague possibility had begun to form at the back of my mind. A possibility that could tie a few previously random strands of this puzzle together.

"Does he live here, with you?"A minor frisson of shock flickered across her face, that I could ever have imagined otherwise.

"Naturally, this has been our family home since shortly after we arrived in this country."

"You said that he was a Freemason, was he a Mason before leaving Prussia?"

The sisters looked at each other, brows furrowed, needing a moment to consider the matter, then Gretchen answered. "Yes, he must have been because I can remember him introducing a fellow Mason from Prussia, an immigrant like ourselves, into the local Lodge."

"Would it be possible for me to speak to your father?"

It was agreed that, as our arrival had probably already disturbed him, one of them would take a hot drink upstairs and see if he was sufficiently awake to feel like talking to me. Ten minutes later found me sat at the bedside of the bright eyed elderly gentleman in question. Unlike his daughters, Otto had retained a strong German accent and was, as promised, in full possession of his faculties.

Having been given a brief outline of the reasons for our sudden arrival, he insisted on hearing more details from the horse's mouth and I was pleased to oblige. He listened with interest and was delighted to find that I was also a Lodge member, saying that the

175

English version was a lot more accommodating than the Prussian Lodge he had first joined.

According to him, there had been a sad but steady decline from the days when Frederick the Great had been the Prussian Grand Master; by the time he emigrated the movement had become political and strongly authoritarian, which hadn't suited his personal views.

When it was time for my own questions he was every bit as knowledgeable as I'd hoped. His information provided no complete answers, but certainly filled in several pieces of the jigsaw. The Masonic involvement remained a puzzle, and the more information I could gather the sooner I might crack it. I mentally filed his information away, thanked him and returned to the others.

It was time to bring some order to this talking shop, we needed to get down to cases.

"Let's concentrate on what's happening on the train. For a start, can we decide exactly how many men are we facing?" Nobody offered a comment so I continued.

"Well Antonescu started off with eight men, out of them one was killed in the tender, then there was the one I shot through the carriage window, and then there was the one Ruth shot inside the carriage. So that leaves Antonescu plus five, a total of six men holding Charlie and Stan."

"Don't forget Scroop and Parkinson." Ruth reminded me.

"We're going to have to ignore them. They already believe that one of the two dead bodies they saw in the sleeping car was the Crown Prince, as far as they're concerned their only interest now will be in getting out of here in one piece. When I spoke to them they made it clear they wouldn't even help you in the next carriage. If we ever get out of here in one piece - I'll break the pair of them."

"But if they aren't involved in the plot against me, then all you could accuse them of is incompetence, or cowardice." Said Pedro.

"As far as I'm concerned cowardice in the face of the enemy is a capital offence, and if the state won't take action, then perhaps I will. Anyone who isn't with us is against us, and don't you forget it." I turned back to the sisters.

"How long is it going to take us to summon help from whichever is the nearest town with a police station and a working telephone?"

"I think there's a police house at Sleights, that's about four miles from here, though I don't know about him having a telephone." said Gretchen. "And you can forget about the roads until the weather clears, they're no more than dirt tracks at the best of times. I'm afraid we're cut off until someone comes up the railway line trying to find out where their train is. Even after a severe snowfall like this we would normally expect to see them sending a snow plough along the line within a day or two."

"It was still snowing just as thickly the last time I looked." Said Magda. "I don't think they'll reach us tomorrow."

"Well that settles it, we don't have a day or two, we shall have to deal with this ourselves."

I looked at Ruth for inspiration, but her furrowed brow and chewed lip simply showed how intractable she found our predicament.

"I think that when we make our move, we'll only get one chance, we have to be as well prepared as possible." She said. "I don't want any unnecessary delay, but we're warm and secure locked up in here, while they're out in the cold with just a small stove to huddle round. We've got dry clothes and hot food, they probably don't have either."

"If it's true," Said Pedro, "that there are no actions we can take without jeopardising the hostages, then at some point we shall have to negotiate with them."

I knew that both they and Magda were right about not rushing into premature action, I just hadn't liked to say so. Somebody had to take a firm decision and it looked like my name on the dance card.

"I agree, there's nothing we can do now, by way of a direct assault, but at the very least we should be making a reconnaissance. Only then, when we have some idea of their dispositions can we decide what we're going to do." All that greeted this statement of the obvious was an assortment of concerned looks, which seemed to indicate a lack of any better ideas.

"If we can work out an approach that doesn't endanger Charlie, then we only need to remove another two or three of his men to even the numbers; then unless he's suicidal there will have to come a point at which abandoning this attempt on Pedro's life makes more sense than pursuing it." I paused to arrange my thoughts and think it through.

"It's obvious that sometime later today someone in authority is going to realise that we haven't turned up in either Whitby or Newcastle, and when that happens the search parties will be out looking for us. But all these things take time, hours or days, and I'm not sure how long a three and a half year old can survive in those conditions."

Ruth joined in. "I agree about the numbers, even now there are three of us to six of them, the odds aren't completely ridiculous, we have to be careful but we needn't be frightened."

Gretchen couldn't stop herself from querying the arithmetic, despite having been transplanted to England, the Hohenzollerns, the Hapsburgs and the Saxe-Coburg Gothas, still loomed large in her Germanic sense of hierarchy.

"Surely you're not suggesting that the Crown Prince should accompany you on such an expedition?" She sounded horrified, but Pedro replied for himself, even more horrified at her proposal that he should stay behind.

"There can be no question of where my duty lies." He said with great formality. I took this clipped remark to mean that he was signed up to an early start and some game shooting. With his background he should have accumulated several years experience of massacring central European wildlife, and be handy enough with a gun. The only difference today might bring would be the likelihood of the targets shooting back, which might lessen his enjoyment.

Between them our hosts had produced spare ammunition for both our hand guns and the loan of a third. We had considered every angle we could and done more than enough talking, it was time for some more detailed intelligence. The prospect of telling Aggie that we had calmly abandoned her husband Stan to his fate was not one I relished. Even if I was only taking a look, it was time we started this particular ball rolling.

I had already been given an assortment of jumble sale quality old clothes, only some of which fitted, but all of which were pleasingly dry. Our hosts said that they would use the time whilst I was out of the house to try and outfit Pedro in the same way.

179

They went upstairs on their quest leaving me alone in the kitchen.

In order to accustom my eyes to the darkness I extinguished all the lamps, except for one small one, which gave just enough light to move around. I then put on my original boots, as none of theirs fitted, after an hour by the range they were now only damp, and wrapped one of their mufflers around my face. The reloaded Webley went into my coat pocket, then I stood for a moment, reviewing my arrangements – that was fine, I'd done everything.

Suitably dressed for my Arctic reconnaissance I went to the back door, but as my fingers closed round the handle there was a noise. A soft scuffling sound, I froze, then slowly looked over my shoulder to check the kitchen behind me. I was alone, and anyway, now that I thought about it the noise had definitely been from outside. It could have been a fox or a badger, seeking what little warmth there was to be had from the back door. It could have been that, but it was more likely to have been a human being. Doing what precisely?

I slid the safety off the Webley and gripped it more firmly. There was a small un-shuttered window at the side of the inglenook beside the stove. In two paces I was there, trying not to steam it up with my breath. As we had approached the house and entered from the front, this was an aspect of the building we had not yet seen.

The dark shape of a man was stood with his back to the door, his coat collar high enough to meet his tweed hat. He was looking around behind him, he looked furtive. It was undoubtedly the shape and size of a man, and it wasn't Pedro. Whilst I wondered whether or not to shout for help, he turned to face the door, reaching out to the handle. He'd been very careful to look behind him – but his trouble was all in front of him - me.

In another two paces I was back at the door, I flattened myself against the wall next to it. It was unlocked and swung smoothly inwards, admitting a rolling wave of freezing air to sweep into the room. As the figure stepped into the kitchen I sprang out behind him, clamping my left arm round his neck and pressing the muzzle of my revolver against his right temple. Exactly the same move that had been applied to me on the train as I went for Ruth.

Kicking the door shut behind me, I pushed the man across the room, to pin him face forwards against the nearest wall. He said something, it could have been in Rumanian, or Chinese for all the sense it made. I took my arm from round his neck and warned him to keep his mouth shut and stay very still. I took a backward pace away from him, my gun still levelled at the middle of his body.

He stayed against the wall, as instructed, but turned his head to look at me, and despite my very clear instructions looked as though he were about to say something else. I gestured threateningly, pointing a gun at someone's face usually gets past the language barrier. Now that I could see his face he must have been at least seventy, but he still looked angry, and uncertain about keeping quiet. Eventually the gun persuaded him and his jaw relaxed into sullen silence. I stepped over to open the hall door and shouted:

"Can anyone hear me? We have an intruder in the kitchen."

In less than a minute I had a roomful of people, led by Magda still carrying what I assumed to be an

181

armful of her father's clothes. She opened the batting in a state of astonishment.

"What's happening? What are you doing with Seth?"

That last question revealed 'Seth' to be a known individual, and possible resident. "He came through the back door as I was getting ready to leave, I didn't know there was supposed to be anyone else on the premises, so I pulled a gun on him before he pulled one on me."

"I'm sorry, that's my fault, I hadn't realised the time. Seth has just arrived to give the animals their early morning feed. He comes in the kitchen for breakfast at this time every day." Having detached himself from the wall where I'd left him, Seth joined in.

"There's men out there, two of 'em as I saw. Creeping round in the snow. They thought I 'adn't seen 'em." His accent was indeed thick, but more Bradford than Bucharest. More to the point Antonescu wasn't waiting for me to set the ball rolling, he had taken the initiative. I hadn't imagined him to be this persistent.

When I said, "Bugger," it wasn't so much in surprise, but more an acknowledgement of my own inadequacy, this man was catching me unprepared every time. I needed to improve my game, and rapidly.

"This is a Christian household Mr. Fowler, we are all members of the local Methodist congregation, in fact I'll have you know that John Wesley himself preached regularly in Pickering. So we shall have a little less of your loose language if you please - you're not in the navy now."

"How did you know I was in the navy?"

182

"This might be North Yorkshire, and a long way from your idea of civilisation, nonetheless we still have newspapers, even here. Does the Crown Prince know of your background?"

Pedro, standing there half dressed in his new clothes, answered for himself.

"Thank you Miss Schindler, but Mr. Fowler has been admirably frank, almost brutally so. In fact ever since I started working for him, he and I seem to have had very few secrets from each other."

A TERRIBLE WOMAN

On Saturday at the North London Police-court, Mary Ann Turrell, aged 48, a strong looking woman, who stood in a defiant attitude with arms folded, was charged with being drunk and wilfully exposing her children in a manner likely to cause unnecessary suffering. Police-constable 94 N said that at 11.30 the previous night he saw the prisoner in Seven Sisters Road, leading her two little boys by the hand, neither wearing any other clothing than a shirt. It was raining at the time and the night was cold. Witness took off his cape and wrapped it about one child. The woman said she was escaping from her husband's violence, but enquiries showed this to be one of her drunken freaks.

The husband, a weak looking little man, said he lived with the prisoner at his own home at Osman Road. She was constantly drunk.

The prisoner – What about you? You drink brandy from a bottle, bottles at a time.

The witness continued that he had led a terrible life with his wife for many years. She beat him terribly if he would not give her money for drink. The previous evening she went out and he went to bed with the two children. She came home at 11 o'clock and asked for money. He told her he had none, she then took the children out of bed and into the street. The prisoner was allowed to give her version, and alleged she took the children away from him because her husband beat her, and was choking the children.

The witness (smiling meekly) – I could not beat her, she could double me up.

Mr. Holmes (a missionary) Said he knew the case very well, and added that the poor old man had led a terrible life with the prisoner.

TEN

I didn't hear the gun shot, but I did hear the clanging noise of what I assumed to be a bullet, hitting a cast iron drain pipe on the outside wall. It shocked us into silence, that is until I recovered my wits. I recognised the impact of a bullet, but that wasn't the point. The point was: this shouldn't be happening. Seth had been right, the people I had assumed to be cowering and freezing in the train, were now assaulting a solidly built house

"Move into the hall, all of you." I hustled them through the door, and as we went there came the solid smack of a second bullet, this time hitting the wall of the house.

"If that was supposed to hit a window, it was a long way off." Said Magda in a puzzled tone.

"I don't think it was supposed to hit anything in particular, it's more likely to be covering fire, designed to keep us in the house and stop us from seeing what they're doing."

"Which can only mean they're planning to move the train." Said Ruth. "Antonescu did say he had another engine driver."

I'd had enough of this, I had no intention of hiding under a bed until help arrived. Antonescu wasn't the only person who could be aggressive. "Pedro and Ruth, while I'm outside I want you to stay on guard in the house, look through the windows

187

if you want – but be very careful. Listen for any sound of someone trying to break in. Magda, Gretchen, talk me through the layout of the house please."

As we stood in the hall we could still hear occasional rounds hitting the brickwork. It turned out that despite the presence of shutters on most of the major windows downstairs. There were still some that remained uncovered. Added to which there were three outside doors and one external hatch leading to the cellar. The plain truth was that, despite the appearance of solidity, given our limited firepower and the determination of our attackers, this was not an easily defended house.

At some stage the mad Major was going to rush us, and when he did he could very well succeed. The two Schindler ladies, although willing and able to defend their property by wielding a shotgun or a pistol, weren't trained soldiers; and I strongly suspected that was exactly what Antonescu's men were. Ruth would kill to defend me or Charlie, in fact she had already done so, but she was another one who hadn't been trained to it. It was down to one well meaning amateur, Pedro, and one seriously out of practise professional, me.

Seth emerged from the ill-lit gloom, carrying two shotguns and a box of shells. That, together with our own two handguns and the pistol they'd lent us, was the extent of our armoury. This was going to be an interesting engagement, in all the wrong sorts of ways.

Ruth came downstairs, looking serious. "There are more than just the two that Seth spotted, there's at least three, possibly more. The trouble is all we can see are just vague shapes and shadows. They're not close enough, or clear enough, to take a worthwhile shot at."

Magda and Gretchen had loaded their shotguns and looked ready for a fight; dealing with large wild animals for a living meant they were tough, but would that be enough? A 12 gauge shotgun is an immensely powerful item, but even with a one and a half ounce load, very short range. It isn't much use against a man wearing a thick overcoat more than thirty five yards away. Hit him in the eyes at that distance, and you'd do some damage, but a body shot would do no more than aggravate him.

"Don't waste your ammunition, or give your position away, by shooting at anyone who isn't actually trying to break into the house." I told Ruth. "And tell Pedro the same."

"You're not planning anything stupid while you're out there on your own are you?"

"I promised there'd be no gung ho, didn't I?"

"Yes, but you have been known to tell lies."

I frowned, in what I hoped would pass for annoyance. "You just do your job and leave me to do mine – or I won't let you come on any more of my little trips."

Giving me the sort of warning look that suggested I'd be in serious trouble if I got myself killed, she left it at that. Her forthcoming annoyance was predictable and unfortunate, but unavoidable - the fact of the matter was that one of us needed to go out and disrupt things. Antonescu was having things far too much his own way for my liking.

Seth was unarmed, we didn't have enough guns for everyone, so I left him in the hall with Magda, whilst I took Gretchen into the kitchen. I explained what she had to do, and how much I would

189

appreciate not being shot when I came back in. Then putting on a pale grey stockman's coat of Seth's I turned down the light and stepped quietly out of the kitchen door.

The air was as sharp and biting as before, it was still fully dark and the snow continued to swirl blindly round in slowly descending clouds. The path from the kitchen door to the corner of the house was three feet deep in a soft drift, tucked into the lee of the house the surface here had remained unfrozen.

I moved with slow and silent steps, hoping there was nothing concealed on the ground beneath, that would cause me to stumble. I imagined myself creeping up on an unsuspecting rabbit, trying cautiously not to disturb it before I was ready to fire. At the corner I paused - more than paused - I became a part of the scene. I tried to relax into stillness rather than tensing myself into place. I made myself receptive, I stood, I watched and listened. There was nothing there, or rather nothing that was activating any of my senses.

There was no possible way of knowing what it was that would eventually alert me to the presence of another human being; something heard or something seen - just as long as it wasn't something unexpectedly felt. I waited.

After perhaps three or four minutes of icy immobility there was a gun-shot, the sound dulled by having to travel through snow filled air. It sounded as though it was on the far side of the house. Anyway it hadn't been aimed at me, it wasn't close enough. I swivelled my head slowly from side to side, letting my eyes do most of the moving, uncertain as to what range I should be trying to focus on. My feet ached from the cold, I should have brought something to stand on, I longed to stamp them to try and promote some circulation, but knew I couldn't.

Then at last, almost surprising me, it came: a few muttered words, directly in front of me, the language indiscernible. The sound alone wasn't enough, so I stared into the area it seemed to have come from. Then I saw one indistinct white shape separate itself into two. One of the shapes moved slightly but stayed in almost the same place, the other moved off to my right, towards the front of the house. The one who'd stayed must have been no more than twenty five or thirty feet away

But even at that short distance I was too far away to tackle him, I needed to get closer. The trouble was that getting closer would need cover, where to find cover out here? Then looking down at my coat I saw that, like my enemy, I was almost completely white, that would be my cover. As I wasn't planning to make any noise the thing that would give me away would be the movement. Not just any movement, but rather a movement that was apparent to my prey.

Unsure if this wasn't insanity, I began to walk directly towards him, although the term *walk* suggests a faster rate of travel than I employed. Keeping my head and upper body as still as possible, my arms to my side, the revolver now in my hand and pointing downwards, half concealed inside my coat sleeve.

I took slow and deliberate small steps; as we were still within the lee of the house the surface of the snow remained soft enough to step through silently. I moved in a straight line, aiming at the barely visible difference in the patterns of darkness in the snow. A difference which I now knew to be a man; a difference which he could have identified for himself by looking back in my direction and concentrating. That was something he hadn't yet done. His senses were swamped by the surrounding world of shifting whites and greys.

I breathed as shallowly as possible, through my nose, to avoid clouds of vapour and took small careful steps towards the dim outline, crouching lower the closer I came. Every step was a test, a test of how slowly I could put my feet down to avoid the squashed snow making crunching sounds. I was now close enough to make out the definite shape of a human being, he was, like me, completely covered in snow. Front, back, body, head, shoulders, the lot – all white. He was slouching, and occasionally shuffling his feet around, in his hands he held the shape of a rifle.

Did he have companions anywhere nearby? There was no chance of turning my head to look - the thought had only come into my head because I knew it couldn't be fulfilled. I wanted that gun, having a rifle would help to even the odds, it would be effective at several times the range of a handgun.

I stopped, at this distance surely any further movement was an unacceptable risk. How could he fail to see me at this range? I could almost count the buttons on his coat. Well if you want to put a naval gunnery term on the situation, it was the lack of relative lateral movement. Twelve inches sideways could be more dangerous than five feet forwards.

He was bored, you could tell from his stance. At length he looked to his right, and I took two more crouching paces towards him. He turned his head back, staring blankly straight above me, and then continued the turn until he was looking to his left.

I threw myself into the last few paces, leaning desperately forward to get at him sooner. He was aware of the movement and turned to face me, finally focussing on my presence. The sheer astonishment must have frozen his brain as effectively as the snow had frozen the rest of him. Instead of stepping back and levelling the rifle, he took half a pace forwards to identify the sudden flurry of movement, his rifle still held across his chest at the half port position.

Eventually, a full one and a half seconds too late, he began to move the gun, but too late to level it at me before my body collided with his – he still held the rifle, but now in only one of his hands, it was pointing straight up in the air. Perfectly positioned for killing birds, but useless for killing me.

My momentum and his lack of preparation ensured that we both went down, him falling onto his back in the snow, with me lying half across him. Whilst he struggled pointlessly to try and rearrange his grip on the rifle, I used my left hand to tear frantically at the front of his heavy coat, finally managing to rip it open. He started to say something, so I jammed my hand over his mouth, but he was twisting his head and squirming so much that he would soon free his mouth sufficiently to shout a warning. Come what may, he had to be silenced – now.

I rammed the Webley through the opening in his coat, and there snug and safe under the thick clothing, I pulled the trigger. You could say that he and I kept the shooting strictly between ourselves, no point in alarming the others.

The shot sent a spasm through his whole body, causing both arms to fly outwards, and the rifle to cartwheel away into the night. I'd really wanted that gun, but still, if I came back in spring it shouldn't be too difficult to find.

Another one down and only five to go. I came to my hands and knees, crouched like a lion over a freshly dead antelope, and scanned my surroundings. There were no hyenas in sight, and no voices called out in the jungle. I looked in the snow and saw the footprints of his partner, leading off around the house.

Keeping low and moving unhurriedly I began to follow, my every sense tingling with awareness – but now somehow oblivious to the cold. They had us penned in the house, an odd and assorted bunch of refugees. We were a group that had chosen to flee rather than confront them. Even knowing of their dead comrades on the train, including the one with half a pencil in his brain, they must be confident they had us on the run. That's a good attitude for your enemies to have.

Despite their probable complacency, that still wasn't enough - something here had me puzzled. Antonescu was pussy footing around when he should have been charging full speed ahead. Dead was how he wanted us, so why not just get on with it? In his place I would have been risking a hernia to get into the house, he only needed access to one room, or even the cellar. He had no need to hunt us down from room to room, killing us individually – that would be a dangerous and pointless waste of time.

Once he had any sort of entry point his safest bet would be to set fire to the place, and then stand back, ready to shoot anyone trying to escape. That's what I would have done, so why didn't he? Perhaps, despite appearances, he was a nicer person than me, some people are.

I was still considering the problem when there was a burst of Rumanian from up ahead. I was close enough to be confident of the identification, it was a language I'd been hearing a lot of recently. There was an answering voice from further away, also in Rumanian. This wasn't the discreet mutterings of the last two, this was a very public conversation, at high volume. More worrying was the fact that the response had been from Pedro. Pedro was talking to Antonescu, and I didn't know why.

I crept forward, in order to see as well as hear – but an easy kill must have made me overconfident. In the middle of the still softly billowing snowflakes I walked into my next target. Not carefully, or in a planned fashion, I simply walked into another snow covered figure that I had assumed to be part of the snow covered landscape. The same mistake that had killed the last man.

We were both startled and gasped, the impact had knocked the Webley from my cold and nerveless fingers, and this wasn't the time to look for it. He twisted towards me and we struggled and grappled with each other, like two schoolboys in the playground. Too close to throw a punch or deliver an effective head butt, we were reduced to a lethal but disorganised wrestling match. Each of us going for the other's eyes or throat, and all the while gasping for air from the shock and the sudden exertion.

But he was a hired man and I was my own man, my arrogance wouldn't allow me to be beaten by such a person. Slowly and brutally I overcame him, forcing him, first to his knees, and then onto the ground beneath me. Our bodies were invulnerable beneath the heavy clothing, the only exposed areas were our hands and faces.

By not wearing gloves my frozen fingers had dropped the gun, but now his own gloves stopped him from doing to me what I was doing to him. I pounded his face with my fists, I used the icicles that were my fingers to gouge his eyes, to tear at the side of his mouth and to try and wrench his nose off. If he hadn't been wearing such a thick muffler I would have bitten an ear off. There was no call for the Marquis of Queensbury round here, you do what you have to do, you're as dirty as you need to be.

I felt his body grow limp from exhaustion and the knowledge of defeat. Holding him down with one hand I reached into my pocket for the knife. I pushed the side switch, the blade flicked out and locked into place. Because of the clothing it would have to be his throat.

This was going to be messy, a splash of festive colour on the snow - but I hadn't started it and I hadn't kidnapped a three and a half year old child. He was one of the enemy, the same people who had tried to abduct Ruth from her own house – he couldn't be left here alive.

I repositioned the knife in my hand, the blade pointing forward from between my thumb and forefinger, a much more manoeuvrable position than the downward pointing dagger grip one sees in penny dreadful illustrations.

A cold round piece of steel nestled itself in below my right ear, pushing my head slightly to one side. It felt awfully like the end of a gun barrel – after a moment's consideration I thought it best to stop what I was doing.

"Meestah Fowlah, I tell you one time before you are stupid boogah. You think you catch Antonescu with your creep, creep, creep in the dark – you are very stupid. Get up on feet."

I did so, and took a step backwards, to allow his fallen henchman more room. As I did this Antonescu let loose a barrage of what was clearly abuse at the fallen man, ending it with a savage kick in his ribs. Another one of those and I wouldn't need to bother with the knife. Then he turned back to me.

"What you done with last man?" Using the hand that wasn't holding a gun he pointed back in the direction I had come from. This wasn't going to improve our personal relationship, but the facts would emerge soon enough, whatever I said.

"He pointed a rifle at me, so I killed him."

He grunted, a more neutral response than I'd expected, then turned and began to walk away. Almost as an afterthought he shouted to me over his shoulder. "You come, now." Then he turned away again and carried on walking.

He must have seen, but hadn't been bothered by the fact, that I was still holding the knife. So I folded the blade and dropped it back in my pocket, you never know when a nasty little thing like that might come in handy. This situation was inexplicable, but that was no reason not to take every chance offered.

The man he'd kicked was getting unsteadily back to his feet and I went over to look at the flattened snow where we had been rolling about. The man backed away warily, thinking that I wanted another go at killing him, but I was only looking for what I'd dropped. There it was, the blackness of the grip just visible, my revolver. There was snow in the barrel and snow packed in around the cylinder, it wouldn't fire like that but I stuck it in a pocket all the

197

same, and hurried after Antonescu's almost vanishing shape.

As I was now armed and undeniably hostile, and so was he, it wasn't anything like obvious who was in charge. That fact would probably reveal itself in the near future. Ignoring me, he called out and there was a reply, all in Rumanian – he was talking to Pedro again. Then suddenly in the darkness there were two figures standing together as I caught up. They both turned towards me.

"I'm sorry Mr. Fowler, but I have decided that this business must stop here and now. Too many people have been killed, and there are more lives in danger, I can't have this on my conscience. Major Antonescu has promised to release Stan and Charlie, and to leave you and Ruth alone if I give myself up."

"And you believed him? I warned you what would happen."

Pedro looked helpless, and held his hands out, palm up, as if to say; 'What else could I do?'

Antonescu pointed at me with his gun. "Who killed the peoples?" I stared at him, unsure of his meaning, so he asked again. "Who has killed the peoples? Is not Antonescu - is Fowlah killing the peoples."

"Like hell it is. I have only killed anyone who attacked or threatened me, everything I've done has been in self defence. If you don't want your men killed, then the answer's very simple – tell them not to attack me, hold my wife captive, or attempt to abduct a child. Is that simple enough for you?" I was beginning to get angry, which in view of his gun was less than sensible.

"My men is frightened, they in strange cold place. But I don't tell them to kill nobody – not yet.

198

Why you think I shoot at house walls and not windows, heh? Maybe I start the shooting with you, then we stop having the dead peoples." He prodded me with his gun to emphasise the words.

This was rubbish, we needed to get back to the fundamental issue that had started all this. "I couldn't care less if you like me or my methods, at least two of your men, and possibly more, are planning to assassinate the Crown Prince. Why don't you try explaining that? Preferably now."

Both Pedro and I stared at him expectantly.

"When I find these men, they dead men, but now I show you something." He transferred the pistol to his left hand, so that he was holding it by the barrel, and then he handed it to Pedro saying something in Rumanian as he did.

That left me with a snow filled gun in my pocket, Pedro holding the only pistol on display and Antonescu apparently unarmed. Looking at him, you could see that Pedro had no idea whether he should be pointing it at someone, or scratching his arse with it. He turned to me.

"The Major says that he has sworn an oath to the King that he would defend me with his life, and that all along his only interest in reaching me was to protect me from you. He apologises for his men and says that if I don't believe him I should shoot him dead, here and now."

"That's a meaningless offer – he only gave you the gun because he's sure that you won't shoot him with it."

Pedro handed the gun to me. "Then if you think he's lying, you shoot him."

A flicker of well justified apprehension crossed the Major's face. I weighed the gun in my hand, the barrel pointing vaguely in his direction. Bizarre though his actions were, I could think of no plausible explanation for his behaviour than differed greatly from the one he'd just offered. There was nothing out here, in the darkness and the snow, to have stopped him from shooting first me, and then Pedro, without a single independent witness.

Unless – unless - this a clever bluff to gain our acceptance for some Byzantine reason I had yet to fathom. Was the gun even loaded? I checked the safety was off, turned to one side, pointed the gun downwards and pulled the trigger. The kick felt like a live round and the immediate small hole in the packed snow of a footprint proved it. He hadn't been bluffing. I pushed the safety on and handed it back to Pedro.

"How does he feel about what I've done to his men, is he looking to get his own back?"

"He now accepts his judgement could have been mistaken, and that you and Ruth and Stan are my friends and have put yourselves into great danger to help me."

"Well if that's true we shouldn't have any more problems, we'll go down to the train, release Stan and Charlie, round up his remaining four men and get ourselves to Whitby as fast as possible."

Nobody rushed to argue with the suggestion, which I took for agreement. In a perfect world Antonescu and I might have shaken hands, as it was we settled for a slightly less aggressive mutual glare. His face didn't match his words.

The idea of deathbed conversion causes me no problems, only a fool wishes to die unshriven. And maybe Saint Paul really did see that light on the road to Damascus, but sudden divine revelation usually makes my nose twitch. What's the sub text – where's the ulterior motive? Cardinal Newman's conversion I could accept, but Antonescu's transformation into a pillar of the community and helper of dumb animals was a step too far. I didn't know in what way, or exactly why he was lying, but I'd bet my boots that he was.

I turned to Pedro. "Even if every single thing he says is the truth, even if he's whiter than this driven snow, I'm still telling you that he knows which of his men are the traitors. Because if he doesn't, then he should be shot for incompetence." Surprisingly it was Antonescu himself who answered.

"Maybe is two men I leave on train when we come here." He claimed that the two men Ruth and I had caught up with, carrying the comatose Pedro in the fight by the train, had been last minute additions to the security team. They had been included at the request of his boss on the Rumanian General Staff, and he claimed never to have seen them before.

Tonight, when setting off to try and force Pedro's hand, he had decided that those two, with significant head wounds courtesy of Ruth and I, should stay on the train to watch the captives.

I leaned towards him, for closer and more direct personal contact. "Stan and Charlie had better be in good condition when I see them. I'm an eye for an eye sort of person, and right now I've got my eye on you."

"I not harm old peoples and children. I put them in same car with Parkinson, so my men can watch them, all together." My only response was a guarded 'Mmmm.'

In theory, you could make out a case for Pedro, a real life Crown Prince, being the senior person present, but as he didn't have enough guile to steal the white stick from a blind man, that left me.

"Major, you will get your two remaining men together and disarm them. Then you and I with the Crown Prince will go back to the train. Is that clear?" He understood English a lot better than he spoke it, and his body language suggested he was bracing himself to tell me what I could do with my instructions. However, after a moment's silent fuming at my impertinence, and contemplating his options, he complied – turning his back on us to call for his men.

"Pedro, you stay with me, there's something definitely non kosher round here."

"You're Jewish?"

"Your English is good, very good, but you're too damn literal." He nodded as if he knew what I was talking about.

Having finished bellowing into the night Antonescu addressed me. "Is not good we leave man you kill to lie in snow like dead dog, we take him to barn, or some place, and cover him. Antonescu have respect for his peoples, if we not treat him proper then I have troubles from my men." He looked at Pedro for confirmation of this humanitarian concern.

"I think the Major's right, and I should go with them, it won't take us long and then we can go to the train together. Is that alright with you?"

I was uneasy at the delay but had to admit that it made sense to keep his few remaining men on side, besides after my latest bout of rolling in the snow I was now shivering uncontrollably again, and couldn't face an extended argument. So I said yes, and told them to come to the kitchen as soon as they were finished. It shouldn't delay us for more than a few minutes.

As I walked back to the house I realised that the early signs of dawn had begun to show themselves. There was no sunrise visible, there wasn't even a horizon, but behind the snow there was now a dirty grey background, rather than complete blackness. And unless it was wishful thinking the snow was slackening as the daylight crept in.

Back in the kitchen, in the light and the warmth, I cleaned the compacted snow out of the Webley's mechanism and barrel, giving Ruth and the Schindlers a hurried report on events to date as I did so. Magda handed round warm drinks, and Ruth put her coat on, ready to come with us to the train. Charlie was going to need some reassurance after a night with strangers. I glanced at my watch, they were taking a long time to collect the body – give them another few minutes.

Two minutes later, never very patient at the best of times, I'd had enough and went to the back door. I shouted out their names, and waited - nothing. I walked to the corner of the house and shouted again, louder, and waited again – more nothing. There was nobody there.

Where they'd gone or why, was less important than the fact that I'd been tricked. I wasn't sure if I ought to be angry or just weary. This wasn't even about Pedro's naivety and willingness to be duped – they were all as bad as each other. It was like trying to herd a flock of weasels, if weasels come in flocks.

I was surrounded by people with bizarre and unknown agendas. There wasn't a single one of our passengers who wasn't lying every time he opened his mouth. I should have known better; I should have dragged Pedro inside by the scruff of his neck and chloroformed him, that way I would know where he was.

Antonescu must have persuaded him into some course of action he knew I would disapprove of. It wasn't that I minded them getting themselves killed, but if their stupidity caused a problem for Stan and Charlie I might very well kill them myself. The idea that I had taken Antonescu's respect for the dead seriously was a blow to my self esteem. I rushed back in the house, I might not know exactly what they were doing, but whatever it was, I planned to stop it.

"They've gone." I said simply. "We need to get down to the train immediately."

Then leaving Seth and the two sisters to lock themselves in again, Ruth and I set off for the train. It was time we got things properly sorted out. As we came round the corner of the house we heard a slow sequence of bangs, from some distance away.

Ruth looked at me. "Who's doing the shooting, and what are they shooting at?"

"Nobody, those were the detonators I placed on the track underneath the engine. Somebody's got steam up and has managed to get it moving, They're stealing my train."

"With Charlie on it."

We exchanged shocked looks, though as my first thought had been for the train, perhaps we were shocked for different reasons. Even in the short time I'd been in the house the light had strengthened and the snow slackened even more. There in front of us we could see lights in some of the carriage windows, and the bright red glow from the engine fire box. Always a pleasing sight to a railwayman, except for the fact that it was moving slowly forwards, away from us.

There were two figures visible as outlines on the footplate, silhouetted against the fire light, a column of black smoke was pumping noisily up from the funnel, with a fast and regular whump, whump, whump. Every few second the big driving wheels would lose their grip and start to spin for a moment, steel wheels shrieking on the steel rails and the pistons racing. Then they would recover traction and press onwards

That's a drawback to the Stirling eight footer, the drive wheels were big, no doubt about it, but there were only two of them, it was never designed for a situation like this. I had no way of judging the expertise of the replacement driver, in slippery conditions like these anyone's performance might look substandard. Was it was one of Antonescu's men, or Stan at gun point? In practical terms it made no difference, once again we were obliged to try rushing through deep snow.

My legs were aching and I was panting hoarsely for breath, but Ruth was keeping up with me, if the engine hit a particularly icy patch we might have a chance. Come what may, we had to make the effort. It must have looked ridiculous, two figures struggling through the snow, trying to outrun a train. I hadn't thought about what we were going to do if we caught them – perhaps we could ask them nicely to stop, and perhaps they'd agree.

It never came to that, while we were still a hundred yards away the locomotive began to pick up a little extra speed, not a lot – but enough to make it clear that we would never catch it on foot. The snow was deep but not quite deep enough to stop them.

Seventy tons of hot steel with a powerful engine pushing it, will force its way through a great deal of snow, even without a plough blade on the front.

We came to an exhausted and gasping stop as we watched it disappear, leaving behind two black lines and a cloud of drifting smoke. Had I been the engine driver, watching our ineffectual pursuit, I would have waved two fingers at the stumbling figures and given them a derisive blast on the whistle. The actual driver never bothered, we weren't even worth taunting.

That bastard Antonescu hadn't just stolen Pedro – he'd stolen my train, the two injured men he'd left onboard must have been raising steam rather than guarding prisoners. As for Pedro himself he must be simple minded, if that's what having Royal blood does for your brain I'm glad to be a commoner.

Ruth put an arm round me. "Don't worry my love, we'll get them – I don't know how just yet, but we will." For a moment I believed her, which was better than nothing, and it was nice to have her arm round me.

I carried on down to the track, on the unlikely chance that Stan or Charlie might have been thrown out and be lying in the snow. I had no concern over the welfare of the wretched Parkinson, or his improbable friend, they hadn't helped me when I needed it and I was ready to reciprocate.

As we came closer we saw two black shapes in the snow, which turned out to be two bodies, carelessly thrown from the train like so much rubbish. Happily, if that's the right word, it was only the two men Ruth and I had killed, and not anyone we cared about. Even though we had been responsible for their deaths, the coarse brutality of their disposal shocked me. The bodies were rigid in their fallen positions, though whether from rigor or freezing I had no idea.

But the disrespectful treatment of the bodies seemed unimportant when compared with the scrawled message that had been left pinned to one of their coats. It was very simple and to the point, it said, 'Interfere with us again and next time we kill the boy'.

We looked at each other for a moment, we had no pre-arranged response to this sort of thing, eventually Ruth shook her head. "This makes no difference, they'll kill Charlie whenever it suits their book, no matter what we do. So we might as well keep after them." I agreed with her, but was glad that she'd said it first.

I thought that if there was ever the time to do it, somebody should at least put a tarpaulin over the bodies, to keep the foxes and crows away. But it would have to be someone other than me.

We turned disconsolately back to the house, it must have looked as if we were going to a funeral, it certainly felt like it. What we actually needed to do was to chase my train. An engine driver who's had his engine stolen is almost as sad as an uncle who's had his nephew nabbed. It just wasn't immediately obvious how such a pursuit could be organised. I asked the Schindlers.

"The snow's too deep to use a pony and trap, but is there a nearby road that some of your more substantial horses could reach?"

Gretchen looked doubtful. "There's a track from Beck Hole, just over the rise, that leads down to Grosmont, you'd need Seth to show you the way. But what are you planning to do?"

"It might not be very likely, but perhaps the engine might run into a drift and get stuck – or something. Whatever happens we can't allow Charlie and Stan just to disappear."

"But if they want to kill the Crown Prince, they've had ample opportunity, so why haven't they done so?"

"That's puzzled me, and I haven't worked out the answer. I'm not even sure that Pedro's the real target here - if he ever was. But what else could it be about? Somebody's going to an awful lot of trouble if all this is just to annoy me."

"If it's not Pedro that's important, then there has to be something, or someone else, on the train. Something or someone that you don't know about." Said Magda. Ruth and I looked at each other helplessly, Magda was probably right, it just didn't get us anywhere. Whatever the answer was, it lay on the train.

"Look we're only a midge's dick from complete disaster, so we don't need to agonise over the background any more – we just need to get out of here."

"A midge's dick?" Magda looked puzzled.

"It's a small unit of measurement."

"How small?"

"It depends on how excited the midge is." She suddenly worked out what we were talking about and shut up.

"D'you know, if you were going to try riding out of here, I think it would be faster following the railway line. Either one of them would do." Said Gretchen, half to herself. "It would be easier going than going along the lanes."

"They'd have to stick to the new line. Remember they're still moving the last of the Ironworks stuff out along the Beck Hole line, they wouldn't want to get run down." Said Magda.

I was confused. "Do you mean there's another railway line near here, a working line that I don't know about?"

They both looked at me for a long surprised moment, then Magda replied. "Well of course, your train came up the Deviation Line." She paused, looking at me expectantly as if this information would enlighten me. It didn't, so she continued. "They built the Deviation Line to avoid the steep incline below Beck Hole, where they used to haul the carriages up on a wire rope - so obviously that original line is still there, it's just over the hill."

"And are there trains still using that original line?"

"Oh no, not normally, but after the Grosmont Ironworks closed down two years ago the site was bought by a Mr. Gladstone from Hartlepool, so of course he's had his men taking it all down and moving the equipment up to Whitby Docks. They've almost finished with that site now, but before they leave they're using the men they have in the area to clear some of the remaining equipment from the old Beck Hole Ironworks. It must have been sat there for thirty years, I'm surprised it's not all rusted away."

"Ladies, as I don't know this area you're going to have to be more specific, what exactly does that involve?"

"Well it means that they're running trains along the Grosmont to Beck Hole section of the original line."

I felt as if I'd landed in a foreign country, a place where they spoke a language that sounded like English, but actually meant something completely different. I looked at Ruth, with the faintest stirrings of hope, she'd been trying to console me when she said there would be some way of catching them, it was beginning to look as though she could be right.

"Are you telling me that not only are there trains running along this disused line on the far side of that hill, but that those same trains go all the way into Whitby?"

"Yes, didn't we say so? The two lines join together at Grosmont."

"They're not likely to be using that stretch of line today are they?"

"I would imagine so, they just finished with the Grosmont site clearance on Saturday, and apparently they have about ten days work to clear whatever was left at Beck Hole. I heard that Mr. Gladstone doesn't believe in paying his men to sit around, so they'll be hard at it."

"No, that wasn't what I meant, will they still be working in this weather, the snow's closed this line – so why not that?"

"They don't have to worry about stranding passengers on the moor, and Gladstone couldn't care less about his men getting chilblains; they'll be working."

"How do we get there?"

"Down the stock trail from behind the barns. Whenever we have any shipments coming in or out, the railway company park the carriages on that line, so that we can load, or unload them without blocking the main line."

"Shipments? Shipments of what?"

"Horses, of course. Magda and I are the largest importers and exporters of horses in the country, and they all go by rail. So it makes sense for us to have our own loading area, and then when we're ready the railway company send an engine to take them to the quay. That's why we have the telephone, to organise everything. We don't usually keep our own locomotive – that would be wasteful."

"I can see that."

Ruth joined in. "None of that matters, we're just wasting time. Gretchen will you please just take us to the line, so that we can try and steal an engine."

"The sisters didn't look happy at being given so close an insight into our plans. Gretchen voiced their disquiet. "I'm not sure that would be a good idea . . "

But Ruth cut her off. "Charlie is three and a half years old and is being held by a gang of murderous cutthroats who will happily kill him just as soon as he becomes an inconvenience, or if he even cries too much. He's all alone, he's frightened, and he's in deadly danger. We don't need to know about your good ideas, we need to do something – now. Have you some alternative in mind?"

The sisters looked at each other, but not for long.

Magda stood up. "Gretchen, come with me." And then turning to us. "Get your things together and your coats on, we'll be leaving here in two minutes."

They returned wearing heavy coats and boots, Magda was carrying a carpet bag and Gretchen had a long canvas bag on a strap over her shoulder, it was almost as tall as her. I didn't bother enquiring into the contents of their respective luggage, we could make polite conversation later

The stables, which had been hidden in the overnight blizzard, and which I had barely noticed in

211

the grey dawn, could now be seen as a very substantial collection of wooden buildings. As far as could be seen under the snow they were all modern and well maintained. Although most of them were used for the winter housing of livestock, primarily horses, the term 'stables' wouldn't do them justice, they were too big for that. If they were all full, there could be hundreds of horses here, it was as they'd said, a large and serious business.

Gretchen let us in through a small side door. The snow had blocked all the roof skylights, but plenty of light came flooding through open double doors at the far end. Despite the open doors, the presence of several score horses made it pleasantly warm, even the smell wasn't too bad. Seth and two young men were shovelling muck into a cart, he came over when he heard us arrive.

"Those men last night were in here, one o' them doors 'adn't been fastened proper, there's four ponies got loose. The boys'll get after 'em shortly – they'll not 'ave got far in this."

Ruth and I were mounted on bareback ponies and told to 'Grip with your knees'. We did so and were led out, each of us on a leading rein from one of the sisters, who were themselves on considerably larger and more serious looking beasts. It was hardly the Charge of the Light Brigade, but as we'd discovered during the night, considerably faster than trying to make our own way through deep snow.

On any other occasion I would have enjoyed the journey, it was a fine crisp morning and the sun was shining but this wasn't a day in the country, it was the start of a chase, and the prize was two lives.

Meanwhile,

    the newspapers reported . . .

<u>*RED INDIAN CURE*</u>
It is an uncontested fact that no one
has ever seen a bald Red Indian
HOW CAN THIS BE ??
Eminent men have exercised their minds
on this knotty problem, to no avail.
BUT NOW AN ANSWER IS TO HAND:
A secret blend of North American plants
As used by –
<u>*Chiefs Geronimo and Sitting Bull*</u>
Guaranteed to ameliorate all hair loss
For the only genuine & original
000000
<u>*GOLDEN*</u> <u>*BEAVER*</u> <u>*LOTION*</u>
000000
DO NOT DELAY !!
<u>*Supplies are Limited*</u> *–* <u>*Order Now*</u>
Only 6s. 6d. per bottle

ELEVEN

The track led us between fields to cross over the brow of the hill and meandered down into the succeeding valley. On the sheltered side of the track the snow was only a couple of feet thick, but on the other side it had drifted almost to head height. As we made our way down the hillside we left the prevailing wind behind and the silence was unnatural, all that could be heard was the sound of the horse's breath, and the soft movement of their feet through the snow.

Then the track widened out and there suddenly, crossing in front of us, was the promised railway line. Equally as promised, it had been used this morning and the two glistening black rails curved away on each side of us. There was the white outline of what I imagined to be a wooden loading ramp alongside the line. They had a very well organised set up here, their own private branch line complete with a livestock loading facility. I looked around, but there was nothing to indicate any preferred direction of travel, so I looked at Gretchen who was holding my leading rein.

"Where will they be?"

"Beck Hole." She said, pointing along the track to our left. I set off in that direction.

Within minutes the sound of a train could be heard, and we dismounted to prepare ourselves. With

215

our feet on the ground the vibration was apparent, I could tell from its sound that the locomotive was labouring, clearly an engine under pressure. They must be hauling maximum loads, the sooner to finish clearing the site.

As it came into sight it wasn't travelling at high speed, perhaps twenty miles an hour, but too fast to try jumping on. I had gone furthest down the line and stood between the tracks, waving my arms like semaphores, and then periodically pointing back up the track behind me, as if warning of some problem ahead. The engine note changed as the driver pushed the regulator back in and the puffing subsided.

I stepped to the side of the track as the engine approached and the driver swung himself out to take a better look at me. I crossed my arms above my head to signal 'stop' and reinforced it by mouthing the word. Behind me he could see three agitated woman making similar gestures, there was clearly a problem so he stopped.

As he slowed to a halt I ran alongside him, the cab floor level with my head. Then I lunged out and grabbed at the hand rails on each side of the cab steps, and hauled myself up. The driver, still unaware, stretched out one of his hands to be grasped, whilst his other hand still pulled on the brake lever. His fireman was busy turning the handbrake wheel on the far side of the cab. The steel blocks squealed and screeched as we juddered to a standstill, making conversation impossible. Eventually halted, he turned to me.

"What's the problem?"

In brief, I told him, but it took a while for him to grasp what I was saying, and even then he was uncertain.

"I can give you a lift as far as Grosmont, and then you can try the telegraph or the telephone."

This was a waste of time, discussion wasn't the answer. "I'm sorry but you're not giving us a lift anywhere – you're getting off – right here."

They weren't happy, but when faced with a pistol the two men climbed down and obliged me by uncoupling the loaded flat car behind the engine, and thus the rest of the train with it.

The urgency of their braking could even have put flat spots on the wheels, there's only so much braking effort you can apply to a fully loaded train before you start to cause damage, but why should I care? I'd wanted an engine and now I'd got one. The two ejected crewmen began to trudge their way back along the line to report the theft of their train, and I gave Ruth a hand up into the cab. Gretchen and Magda were still walking along the line towards us.

"Are those two taking the horses back?" I asked, nodding my head in the direction of the advancing pair.

"I rather think that they intend to come with us." Said Ruth.

"This isn't a Temperance Society outing, do we actually want two middle aged ladies getting in the way, especially as one of them seems to be bringing her fishing rod with her?"

"Considering they saved our lives last night, and then produced a railway engine out of thin air this morning, you could be a little more appreciative of whatever help we can get."

"Saving Charlie and Stan is far too important to be concerned about reciprocal politeness. The engine being here was just a coincidence, and the fact they

217

gave us a bed for the night doesn't mean we should hinder ourselves with two useless passengers."

"You don't know they're useless, you're just prejudiced. Shut up and leave this to me."

"You'll need some help." Said Gretchen, by now standing alongside the engine. It sounded more like a statement than a suggestion. "Magda and I will come with you, the idea that your little nephew should be held as a hostage is completely unacceptable."

Then without waiting for an invitation, they climbed onto the footplate. I was uncomfortable with the idea of such free access to an engine that I was in charge of, but had to acknowledge that on this particular engine their proprietorial rights were at least as good as mine.

Both ladies were dressed in long gabardine coats, leather boots and men's flat caps, if nothing else their outfits were serious. Gretchen unhitched the long green canvas case and stood it up a corner of the cab, looping the strap round a convenient handle

"That's very good of you, and we're both grateful for all the help we can get." Said Ruth, the calm voice of reason. "But do you understand that there's likely to be some shooting, and this could be extremely dangerous?"

Magda sighed, "Yes we understand all that, but it remains the case that if Christian people are simply onlookers to evil being done - then there isn't much point in holding such beliefs. We're very busy with the horses at the moment, and this sort of thing is terribly inconvenient, but after hearing what you said about Charlie we've both agreed that there's no alternative."

"So you're prepared to join us in taking what might be desperate measures to rescue Charlie?" Asked Ruth.

"I would have thought your friend Stan would have explained to you, being a Methodist isn't the same as being a pacifist. If desperate measures are called for to save life, then the sooner and more effectively you take them, the better." She nodded meaningfully to the green canvas case. Having been told to shut up, I simply raised my eyebrows in query. Magda's own eyes followed the direction of my gaze.

"Oh that - well what did you think it was – my fishing rod?" They both smiled that anyone could be so stupid and Ruth silently pursed her lips, whilst avoiding eye contact.

"It's an MLM." She said, but as I showed no signs of recognition she explained.

"A magazine equipped Lee Metford, it's a type of rifle."

"But if you had a rifle, why didn't you say so last night?"

"It might have escaped your notice Mr. Fowler, but the visibility last night was, for the most part, less than thirty yards. That's shotgun distance, not rifle distance, which is why we produced two shotguns. Today, however," she said, looking out at the sunlit landscape, "Is a wholly different kettle of fish. And now, although it's pleasant to chat, if this thing's got enough steam pressure, or whatever it uses, wouldn't it be a good idea to start us moving?"

Ruth was still avoiding my eye, but showed her loyalty by not laughing, at least not openly. As the steam pressure was still at the same level as when I stopped it, I repositioned the reverser and opened the regulator and we slowly began to head north.

Our purloined engine was one of a fairly common type, especially in this part of the world, it was a class referred to as a Bogie Tank Passenger, or more simply a BTP. These machines were manufactured at various different sites around the north east, and although some of the details varied, they all shared the same layout of four driving wheels of about five and a half foot, followed by four bogies, with a small integral coal and water bunker forming the back part of the cab. A typical shunting engine design.

We were somewhat crowded on this particular footplate, but the bigger picture seemed more important than worrying about our personal space, so we happily rubbed shoulders and jogged elbows. I showed Ruth how to shovel the coal, and eased the regulator a little further out to build up some speed. Our departure with no load behind us was a very smooth affair, no wheel spinning histrionics and no need for forced air. I checked my T's and P's, and confirmed that all the needles were where they ought to be. That's pretty much what driving a steam engine is all about; Temperatures and Pressures, just watch those and keep shovelling the coal and everything else will fall magically into place.

When we left King's Cross I had been the respected driver of a high speed locomotive, drawing a Royal Train, with several dozen important people aboard. I now found myself, in borrowed clothes, the driver of a stolen shunting engine, accompanied only by my wife - the slightly homicidal theatre manager, and two deeply religious horse breeders.

It had somehow come to pass that in this condition we were seriously planning to apprehend a bunch of heavily armed desperadoes, whose motives I could only guess at. The asylums of this country are filled with people who would regard this as madness.

*****

Although there was packed snow between the rails, the lines themselves were clear and we began to make a reasonable speed. Having spent the first couple of minutes establishing our new routine Ruth raised our most pressing issue.

"What do we do about their threat to kill Charlie if we interfere with them?"

"Well if we do catch up with them they won't necessarily know that it's us driving this engine. And then what's the alternative? I don't believe Antonescu, or whoever wrote that note, has any intention of simply doing the 'right thing'. I think it's just like Pedro said, when the hostages are of no further use they'll be killed. Our only hope of stopping that happening is to be there."

"Be where?" Asked Gretchen.

"Whitby, I suppose."

"But ask yourself – why Whitby – why divert you there instead of Newcastle?"

"I don't know; I can't imagine any connection between a Yorkshire fishing village and the Rumanian Royal family."

"Well I can tell you one thing that it isn't." Said Ruth. "It isn't anything to do with Pedro. I agree with Magda about there being something, or someone else on the train that we don't know about. If anybody had wanted Pedro dead they could have already done it. All this business about him being under threat is just like watching a magician waving his right hand in the air, while all the time his left hand is doing the business. He's not involved in what's going on, he's just a smokescreen."

Magda was nodding agreement as Ruth spoke. "The only reason they could have for going to Whitby is to meet a ship - apart from the port there's nothing else it could be. Unless of course this is an international plan to steal a train load of kippers."

We silently pondered kippers for a moment or two, as the engine banged and rocked its way along the uneven rails of this old and rarely used track. Although Ruth had already had several hours to adapt herself to life on the footplate, Gretchen and Magda were surprised by the roaring heat of the firebox and what was, for them, the continual need to hold onto something, but they soon adapted. No doubt if you're used to breaking in horses, then the motion of a steam engine is pretty small potatoes.

Daylight began to dawn in my brain, I was finally joining the consensus, this wasn't about Pedro. Once you had established that then everything else might make some sort of sense.

"We were taking Pedro to Newcastle to visit the Armstrong Mitchell shipyard, the idea was that he would order a battleship for the Rumanian navy. But if you think about it Armstrong Mitchell is one of the biggest and busiest naval shipyards there is, they build warships for half the navies in the world. How impressed will they have been about the credit worthiness of the Rumanians, especially when it comes to paying for something like a battleship?"

"So somewhere on that train is enough cash to pay for a battleship." Said Gretchen, continuing my thought process.

"That would never work, enough cash to buy a battleship would occupy a huge amount of space. There would be packing cases full of the stuff." Said Ruth. "We would have surely spotted it."

"Perhaps so, but the basic idea's good. A more likely method would be to use those American money transfer documents, they're called Bearer Bonds. There was an article in the Gazette earlier this year, they guarantee payment of a stated sum to whoever has physical possession of the document itself, and apparently you can get them in this country now."

"In a sufficiently large value?"

"Yes, they're only issued by governments or very large companies, and the whole idea is that they can be for any sum; hundreds of thousands of pounds – or even millions. I agree with Ruth, I bet all the security has nothing to do with Pedro, but it's just to guard some bloke with a briefcase chained to his wrist. Whitby's a quiet little harbour, with no military garrison and only a limited police presence, perfect for a job like this. All they have to do is get their man to a waiting ship or steam launch and be over the horizon before anybody knows what's happening. I think they've got every chance of succeeding."

"But surely they could be tracked through the banking system." Said Magda.

"No, that's the whole point of a Bearer Bond, it's the legal property of the person holding it, no matter how it was acquired. It could be safely deposited with any major bank, no questions asked."

"For all I care they can take it, and welcome to it." Said Ruth. "But they're not going to get away with hurting Charlie, even if I have to swim after them."

Although we were already going as fast as was safe on this track, in these conditions, I had them shovel more coal, and opened the regulator to maximum. Driving blindly at full speed on an unknown track is more than foolish, it's also dangerous, but I was doing it anyway. Catching up with a faster train, travelling an hour in front of us, had been no more than a vague possibility, but now there was the glimmer of a realistic chance of doing it I thought that some risks were justified.

I started to show Ruth the basic engine controls, stop and go being about as basic as I could make it – if this came to fighting I might be otherwise engaged for a while.

In my time in the navy I had always tried to lighten the mood before going into action, the men usually appreciated even the weakest of jokes or light hearted remarks, we needed an excuse to diffuse the tension and hide the nerves. And not just their nerves, the three of them all assumed that I knew what I was doing, and that as a decorated naval hero I would somehow swashbuckle my way through whatever was to come. It was nice that they had such confidence in me, but the reality was that a large piece of luck would come in handy anytime round now.

I gestured to the holdall bag that Magda had brought.

"Let me guess, if you've got a rifle in the other bag I suppose you've got a couple of grenades in that one have you?"

224

"Bottled beer and ham sandwiches." She said. "Would you like some?"

Ruth, Gretchen and me all said yes at the same time, so she handed them round. Then she produced and lit a small cheroot for herself, holding and smoking it as casually as any man. It's entirely possible that my mouth dropped open at this stage, for despite having seen low foreign women, in low foreign dives smoking cheroots openly, I had never before seen it in this country.

Mistaking my surprise for disappointment, she took the tin back out of her pocket and offered it round. Ruth and I mutely shook our heads. This had to be the result of the ladies' Germanic parentage, the Black Forest was probably full of cheroot smoking women with rifles.

Now that Crown Prince Ferdinand, as the Schindlers politely still called him had vanished, together with what was left of his security detail, there was a subtle change in the atmosphere. Whilst Pedro, under any name, they respected as being German royalty and thus only one step below their Prussian hero Bismarck; they had remarkably little time for the niceties of East European politics.

As far as they were concerned anywhere east of Vienna was 'The Balkans' and heedless of geography they vaguely lumped Rumania and Bulgaria into the same category. When I had mentioned that the purpose of the planned Rumanian visit to Newcastle had been to order a battleship, Magda had shaken her head and tutted, saying that '*it shouldn't be allowed*'. Despite having spent most of their lives in England, the Schindlers still viewed the world through autocratic Prussian eyes, and it was only marginally less worrying to have them as allies

225

rather than enemies. A change of subject seemed to be called for, before we got on to Teutonic theories of racial purity and the operas of Richard Wagner, who had by all accounts been as mad as a box of frogs.

"How did you come by the Lee Metford, I thought they were only for army issue?"

"I think you're right but when we were supplying horses to the Wild West Show, Colonel Cody was so impressed by Gretchen's shooting skills that he insisted on presenting her with one. Goodness knows where he acquired it, but he's the sort of man who has friends everywhere."

"What range is it capable of?"

"Normally you would say 750 yards, but the Colonel had it fitted with diopter sights, which are more accurate than the usual leaf spring variety, and we're using smokeless cartridges instead of the army issue black powder. In good conditions I would expect about 850 to 900 yards."

Ruth was astonished. "But that's half a mile, is it accurate at that distance?"

"I'm a good shot, but not as good as Annie Oakley, my eyesight's not as sharp as hers. I can normally achieve a twelve inch group at 850 yards. The trouble is that in these circumstances we can't just open fire on anyone on your husband's train, we're going to need to be extremely careful - one of these .303 bullets can pass straight through one person and kill the person stood behind them. Quite apart from Stan, Charlie and the Crown Prince, there are the two Scotland Yard detectives to consider, we don't know exactly who the enemy is."

"And don't forget Sherlock Holmes and Doctor Watson." I added sarcastically.

"Are they onboard?" Asked Gretchen, her face bright with interest. I peered at her suspiciously, there were a very limited number of people who could safely take a rise out of me on this subject, and she wasn't one of them.

"My understanding was that they were entirely fictional, the Prince of Wales tried to assure me otherwise but I remain unconvinced. If they are onboard I have no idea who they're disguised as."

"Oh I think they're real alright," said Magda, "Colonel Cody told me that he'd been introduced to them, and he seemed perfectly serious."

I concentrated on the line ahead to avoid getting drawn any further down what I was sure was a dead end.

The gorge that we had been in had slowly flattened out on each side of the track, and white rolling countryside now surrounded us. I was looking out for the new line that should shortly be visible over to our right, when I saw the smoke. It was train smoke, there was no mistaking it. It was on the new line and it was not far ahead of us. I leaned out of the cab to see more clearly, and we seemed to be catching it.

"What have they been doing, that we've been able to catch them?" asked Magda.

"Pretending to be a snow plough. And anyway the Stirling engine is built for speed, which is why it has those huge eight foot diameter driving wheels, they work perfectly at 60 or 70 miles an hour or more. But at low speeds, particularly when trying to force a path through snow, that size of wheel won't exert anything like the traction that the much smaller wheels on this thing can produce. They've just been using the wrong engine for the job."

If my guess was right then the points, where the old line we were on joined the new line, would be the 'run through' variety that would only need changing for a train leaving the new line. If I was wrong we would derail, I wasn't planning to stop and look – if in doubt, charge in head first. I warned the girls to hang on.

The relative angle between us and the Stirling narrowed, and his column of smoke moved into a position where it seemed to be directly ahead of us. There was a sudden rattling and swaying as we ran through the points, and suddenly he actually was directly in front of us, about 250 yards away and closing. Then the back of his rearmost carriage disappeared into a circle of blackness.

Within seconds we followed him into the tunnel, with the usual rush of increased noise and smoke. This had to be the approach to Grosmont station, but he had no intention of stopping and neither did we. I still wasn't sure exactly what I wanted to do, beyond an unformed desire to interfere with them in some way. Nelson was famous for telling his captains to Engage the Enemy More Closely, it was time for me to do the same.

Grosmont station came and went, no one was visible, either on the platforms or on the train ahead. Did they know that I was behind them? Did any of them bother looking backwards? They had no reason to suppose they were being followed, so probably not, surely all their attention would be on where they were going.

I explained to Ruth exactly what I planned to do and how she was to cope with the controls, she's an intelligent practical woman and so although it was all new to her I felt sure she'd manage.

The back end of the rearmost carriage was slowly coming closer as we caught up with them. This was the carriage in which I'd shot one of the Rumanian security men, as he'd leaned out of the door to shoot at me. The same carriage in which I had last seen Parkinson and Scroop, were they still there? Gretchen's rifle was comforting to have, but as she said, not much help in this situation. Whatever happened here was going to be at a much shorter range than 850 yards. I turned back to Ruth.

"You're happy about using the regulator and the brake? You'll remember to take the one off before you use the other?" She looked apprehensive, it would have worried me if she hadn't, but nodded her understanding – before leaning forward to kiss me.

"Magda, watch that gauge, put more coal on as necessary and keep the pressure around the 140 mark, alright?" She also nodded her agreement, but didn't look tempted to kiss me.

"Gretchen, I want you on the right hand side of the cab, so that as and when opportunities present themselves, you can lean out and give me covering fire, alright?"

"I'll be there."

Then, with a revolver stuck in my belt, I grasped the coaming round the edge of the cab side with my left hand, and leaned out into the wind, reaching forward with my right to grab onto the forward edge of the cab wall. The slipstream hit me, pushing my clothing back against my body, and I could smell the Stirling's smoke as well as our own.

Unlike my own locomotive, where there was a clearly defined ledge around the side of the engine, making it possible to step carefully but safely, this engine offered no such luxury. The first five feet

229

provided no more than a narrow one inch lip on which to try and wedge the side of my shoe, I clung on with my hands clamped to the edges of the cab upperworks. In two long steps I was on top of the second row of driving wheels and able to take hold of the boiler hand rail.

I glanced ahead, we were only yards away, and still closing, but more slowly now as Ruth had moved the regulator arm slightly forwards to restrict the flow of steam to the cylinders. Slowly I made my way over both sets of wheel guards and round to the front of the smoke box to stand on the front running plate. Standing there at the front of the engine, I felt like a Viking standing on the prow of his longship.

There was now only 25 yards of empty space between me and the broken connecting door at the back of my own train's rear carriage. I leaned round the side of the boiler, looking back to wave at Ruth that she should continue to close the gap.

Once inside there would be no game plan, just improvisation, disposing as best I could of any hostile person I encountered, even Parkinson and Scroop. They'd had every opportunity to help, but so far had chosen not to, there could be no neutrality in this matter - if they got in my way they would pay the price. Where, or in what condition, I would encounter Charlie was a mystery.

The final two yards of space between us closed to nothing, and our front buffers nudged against his. My transfer wasn't elegant, I took one step across the running platform and then jumped, colliding with the connecting door and collapsing through it.

I landed on the same piece of floor that the dead security man had hit; my face was resting in the dried pool of his blood. The door banged violently shut behind me and my whole body flinched reflexively. At the same time Gretchen put three shots through the top half of the carriage, breaking a thousand unidentifiable tinkling things. If Ruth was following our plan she would now be easing off on the regulator to fall back, safely out of gunshot danger. I didn't bother looking, my concerns were in here.

As the pieces of roof level debris were still showering the area ahead of me I stood up, holding the back of a seat to steady myself. They must have felt the bump as we had pushed against their buffers, but there was nobody visible. Were they hiding, or in the next carriage - who knows? I ran forwards, allowing no time for thought, if you pause in this game, you're lost.

There could have been someone crouched behind any one of the seats that I rushed past, someone who could have easily shot me as I passed, the fact that I'm still here to tell you means they didn't. It doesn't always work, but the navy taught me that onward momentum usually beats careful consideration, go for the sound of guns and don't give them time to think.

A dark shape flickered across the glass of the communicating door through to the next carriage, I dived sideways between two rows of seats, as five or six rapid shots sprayed themselves down the middle of the carriage. That sounded to me like a revolver being emptied, let's hope I'm right and it's not a nine shot pistol. I charged the communicating door, concentrating solely on how hard I could hit it with my shoulder.

The door exploded open, hitting someone crouched just beyond and sending them flying. I swung down to one side, my gun pointing at the fallen figure. I didn't recognise him but saw that he was still holding his gun, it wasn't pointing at me, he was temporarily too dazed.

I don't like armed men standing behind me, so I shot him in the head before he recovered. As the gun fell from his hand I noticed it was a nine shot pistol. He'd still been loaded and ready to fire but hadn't been fast enough when I started my charge. That was my first piece of good luck, how many of those did I have?

This was the 'drawing room' car with scattered easy chairs and sofas, where I had found Ruth. In the very brief glance I'd had before hitting the floor I hadn't seen anyone else, but nothing in life is that easy. A shot banged into the wall above me, I ignored it for the six seconds it took me to reload the Webley, then risked a look. There were at least two of them, one of them was holding Charlie as a shield. Charlie looked dirty, dishevelled and terrified – his face was streaked with dried tears. The child was gasping in terror rather than breathing.

I didn't recognise the man with the gun, but it wasn't Antonescu. He stared at me, almost smirking in triumph, the face of a man with a Royal Flush.

The onset of blind rage came flooding in – but no you can't go down that road – swallow the rage - stick to what you do best. Now more than ever, do it the way you've always done it, keep pushing.

"Give me the boy, or I'll kill you both – you've got five seconds before I start shooting." And I meant it.

Coarse laughter, accompanied by two inaccurate shots was the answer. That particular sound of laughter was one I'd heard before, in brothels and bars, wherever sailors on shore leave congregate. It was drunken laughter.

That ruined everything, my whole rationale was to confuse and wrong foot the opposition, to make it clear that standing up to my headlong charge was suicide. The trouble was that in order to be successful it assumed a degree of rationality on the part of my opponents. If the headlong rush wouldn't work on a couple of drunks, without risking Charlie's life, what would?

"Alright, so you've got the boy - but you can't kill him without me killing you. Is that what you want - is it?" There were muttered comments as they spoke to each other, that was a step forward. From the sound of the wheels, even without looking outside, it was obvious that we were slowing down. Not braking, that would have caused the couplings to run together, just slowing down. They were planning something. But it opened up another possibility.

"So far I've killed four of your men, do you understand me, four of your men dead. And you seriously think I won't kill you? You're so drunk you can't even shoot straight – give me the boy and I'll leave the train."

"Heh – how you think you leave the train mister? Can't you see we going?"

"Same way I got here, I jumped on, and I'll jump off. Do you want to die for the sake of that boy?" I got to my feet and stood there, in full view, in the classic duellist stance - sideways on, my right arm pointing rigidly at the one who wasn't holding Charlie.

"Try shooting me, go on try shooting me – you lumps of shit. I'm bulletproof you can't touch me, I can kill you both before you finish squeezing the trigger. Try your luck boys and see where it gets you." Whichever way this turned out, it was going to be strictly one performance only.

Both of them fired, and so did I. Charlie screamed, they missed and I didn't. The one I'd been aiming for fell down, I swung the revolver to line up on his friend's face. It was a picture of shock, he hadn't expected that.

"Let the boy go and you can live, hold onto him and you die. Do you want to die? Do you really want to die?" I stood facing him, determined to keep my hand steady. I was right at the back of the carriage and didn't want to get any closer. At this range, even on a moving train, I could still hit a man down the length of a carriage, but if I got much closer, then even a drunk might get lucky and hit me with a wild shot.

He was holding Charlie in front of him with his left arm, and pointing his gun at me with his right. Charlie was starting to wriggle. The man looked panicky, he knew he couldn't maintain this stand off for long before his left arm gave up. He started to move the gun, it looked as though he was thinking of clubbing Charlie to keep him still.

"Touch the boy and die."

He was wavering, not knowing what to do. I pointed my gun at the ceiling, feeling horribly naked without the fire power.

"Put the boy down and let him walk to me – I give you my word as an English gentleman that you can live. Let him go and you live."

Slowly and unhappily he lowered Charlie to the floor. "You give word as gentleman that I live?"

"I promise, you will live."

Regrettably, like so many of my promises, this one was written on water, but just for once it wasn't my fault. The door behind him banged violently open, almost coming off its hinges, and a rush of men tumbled into the room. My recollection is that they were all armed to the teeth and shooting furiously.

It's like organising a firing squad, if you put a large enough group of people together, and tell them to start shooting, in this case at me, there is a tendency for each of them to assume that some of the others are bound to hit the target. The result being that none of them really bothers to aim as carefully as they ought - the man next to you will probably do it for you.

Well that's the best explanation I can advance for the fact that six or seven men blasting away with handguns failed to hit anything other than the scenery. I dived back through the door to the next carriage and ran for it. This was worse than being in the navy, at least they gave you a tot of rum when the pirates had been shooting at you.

I staggered and weaved my way back down the carriage, stray bullets whining around me and noisily breaking things, all the way bitterly aware of my humiliation. I had come to rescue Charlie; I had found Charlie, I had seen Charlie, and then I had run away. How utterly useless. So much for the daring hero, I would have done more good asking Gretchen and Magda to make the attempt.

As I reached the torn and broken connecting corridor at the far end of the last carriage, it had become obvious that the gunfire behind me was no longer an immediate danger. They had turned out to get rid of me and had succeeded, and now that I was running for my life it looked as if none of them thought it worth chasing me, I was no sort of threat. The only thing left for me was to make my wretched and undistinguished exit. I pulled the last door open and stepped out onto the swaying platform.

Despite my clear instructions for Ruth to drop back after I had made my leap onto the last carriage she was still there. The front of the stolen locomotive was still bumping against the buffers beneath me. My salvation was at hand, so I took it and jumped across the gap. No one was going to give me a medal for this performance. But now we needed to back off and re think our approach.

Grasping the hand rail I leaned around the front of the boiler, the funnel chugging away next to my head and looked back at Ruth. I had no idea what she thought was going on. I waved for her to slow down, we needed some distance between us and the gunmen.

Her reactions were faster than I'd anticipated and her application of the brake sharper. My feet slid forwards along the running plate and for a horrible moment I thought that I was going to be run over by my own engine. Luckily one of my feet caught against the broom holder, and my desperately scrabbling hands managed to grasp the clock handle levers on the front of the smoke box door.

As I gasped for air and tried to recover my wits a bullet hit the smoke box, inches from my face, small fragments of something sharp and hot hit my cheek. Some bastard was shooting at me. I swung around the side of the boiler, crouching down over the front wheel guard, and using the sand box as some slight protection.

I heard two more bullets in quick succession, but beyond them not hitting me had no idea where they went. I looked up around the edge of the sand box, despite Ruth's dab on the brakes we were still only about fifteen yards behind them, and seemed to be moving back towards them. This was a horribly exposed position.

There was a shout. "Heh – you – watch this."

Standing in the remains of the connecting corridor at the swaying rear end of the carriage was Stan. His shirt was torn, his hands were tied and his face covered in blood, he looked concussed and dazed. Standing behind him was another man with a gun, he held Stan's collar with his left hand and pressed a gun to Stan's temple with his right. From what I could see of the man's face, he was smiling.

"I get big laugh, I watch you kill your own man." With that he tried to push Stan out of the doorway and onto the track, where the engine I was standing on would immediately have run over him.

But Stan had come to life in a desperate last attempt to save himself. Unable to move his hands or arms he was writhing this way and that, trying to wedge himself in the doorway, his shoulders on one side, his feet on the other. There wasn't a chance that I could shoot what little I could see of his attacker, without an equal chance of hitting Stan.

I stood up and turned back to look at Ruth. "Stop! Stop now!" Nothing happened – in desperation I waved my arms in the air and repeated myself. Ruth did as she was told and applied the brakes, much harder than before.

Men standing on the outside of railway engines, especially ones that are braking hard, really shouldn't wave their arms, I know this because when you do that it means you're not holding onto anything. So having done what I shouldn't have done - in due accordance with the laws of physics, I was launched forwards into the void, still waving my arms and shouting as I went.

It hurt when I landed, but nowhere near as much as it would have done if it hadn't been for the three feet of snow that I landed in.

Hands were moving me about, competent hands, warm hands. A face was hovering low over mine, the lips were moving, it was saying something slowly and clearly, I could almost understand it. Beyond the face there was a bright blue sky, I was lying on my back. Then I remembered.

I was lying in the snow, I struggled to try and push myself up. The hands pushed me back down again.

"Just lie there, don't try to do anything for a minute, I want to make sure you haven't broken anything." Having established the lack of breakages I was allowed to stand up, which took somewhat longer than I would have expected. Ruth had to make a grab for me as I swayed dangerously, like a tree in a hurricane; I nearly went over. We clung together for a while as my head cleared and stability returned.

My belly was sore, it felt as though I'd been kicked. I put my hand on it and found the revolver, I was going to have a perfect gun shaped imprint there for the rest of the week, I'd been lucky not to have done more damage, either to me or the gun.

Then my brain worked out what had been happening. "They were trying to throw Stan out of the train, so that we'd run over him." I said, not knowing if they'd been successful.

Ruth was suddenly horrified, realising that she'd overlooked Stan in her rush to be with me, and leaving me still swaying and trying to stay upright, she set off back towards the train. As she did so, Magda came round from the front of the engine and shouted to us "He's still alive."

As I was still fairly useless for the next few minutes, the three women worked together to untie Stan and get him up into the engine cab. The gunman had finally managed to throw him from the train, but fortunately his struggling had given Ruth sufficient time to come to a halt before we actually ran over him. Our engine had stopped just three feet away from his body.

Meanwhile,
  the newspapers reported . . .

MAN FOUND IN DRESS

Before Mr. Rose at the North London Police-court on Monday was plasterer Mr. Norman Williams, aged 21. Following reports Police-constable 347 Y had attended the Moon in View public house, Clerkenwell, where he arrested the defendant after finding him dressed in women's clothing. Defendant objected saying that he was causing no trouble, however, witnesses stated that he had twice been into the Ladies Convenience to the obvious outrage of public decency.

Defendant responded that he had merely been obeying the calls of nature, and that he meant no harm. Mr. Groves replied that whether he meant any harm was not the issue, but rather the great offence to good taste, to which the affronted witnesses bore eloquent testimony.

When asked by the Magistrate why he was so dressed, defendant responded that all his own clothes were in the wash and he had simply borrowed some of his sisters. (Laughter)

When pressed still further, he admitted that he was being pursued for outstanding debts and had hoped to escape his creditors by use of a disguise. He added that the Police-constable's actions had not been helpful in this regard.

The Magistrate then added an additional £2. to his debts.

TWELVE

I told them what had happened and what a distressed condition Charlie had been in, three grave faces looked back at me. Stan was sitting on the floor, wedged up a corner of the cab, alive but heavily concussed and not yet properly conscious.

Ruth broke the silence, she looked me straight in the eye and said quietly; "Whoever harms that child, it would be better if a millstone was hanged around his neck and he was thrown into the sea."

Although both the product of church schools, Ruth and I were not normally given to quoting scripture at each other, the rarity of the event served to emphasise her intensity. It might have been a New Testament quote but she had a very Old Testament look in her eye, the two Schindlers were nodding their agreement and looked ready to join in.

I'm usually the one who has to be told not to overreact, but it was becoming clear that the people responsible for Charlie's condition would be lucky if they were already be dead when we found them. My travelling companions meant business.

For me it would represent a departure from my normal routine, I usually only killed someone when there was a sound operational reason. The concept of a vendetta or revenge killing had always struck me as being a somewhat European habit, rather like eating garlic; more the sort of thing that foreigners did.

243

Nonetheless, it would probably be diplomatic if I lent a hand, her motives were basically good and one has to help out.

The Schindlers, no doubt as a result of living so far from civilisation, were quite adept at dealing with the injured man. I suppose that if the nearest doctor or vet is a seven or eight hour round trip away one develops an ability to cope alone. Between them they had examined Stan and decided that, although it might be a while before we could expect any account of events during his captivity, he was likely to make a full recovery. To be honest, good friend though he was, Stan wasn't quite as high on my private worry list as Charlie; but it was still a major relief.

I started the girls on the stoking routine again and moved off. We'd been stopped for fifteen minutes and unlike before we could no longer rely on snow drifts to slow down the Stirling. Both engines were now running along tracks that this engine had cleared earlier, our speed advantage had vanished

*****

Gretchen wanted to know, "Were any of the men on the train the same two men you saw with Antonescu at the house?"

"In the heat of the moment it's difficult to be completely certain, but I'm almost sure they weren't"

"Then that means we're running into some difficulty with the numbers, initially there should only have been two of Antonescu's men left on the train, the two with head wounds from the fight by the locomotive. You do look at these people before you kill them – don't you. Did they have head wounds?"

"Of course I look at them you stupid woman, and no, there were no visible head wounds, well not before I shot them." I said, somewhat annoyed at this suggestion of a slap happy approach on my part.

Yet you've just killed another one and seen several more, none of whom you recognised, and none of whom had visible head wounds. Like some explorer in the Amazon jungle, you seem to have discovered a whole new tribe of people."

There was a lengthy silence as we all digested the certainty of her logic, everybody looked suitably grave, though nobody seemed sure what to do about it. Deciding that my immediate priorities lay more with engine driving than second guessing a bunch of gangsters, I concentrated on the running the locomotive smoothly; hopelessly following in the wheel tracks of my own train. This was now a clear line, curving its way easily along the flat land beside the river. All we could do was to follow them, presumably right into Whitby, and journey's end, whatever that might involve.

We thundered onwards, the speed dial was flicking nervously at sixty, this must be slightly down hill. The tank engine was really earning its money today – playing with the big boys. I turned to Gretchen.

"Will you make sure all the guns are reloaded please."

She looked me in the eye. "It's all in hand." I looked back at her for a moment longer than strictly necessary, the adrenalin was making her look younger. Or was it just the excitement making me less fussy – who cares? She must have been every day of fifteen years older than me; it's just as well that I'm so much in love with Ruth or I might have wondered if she'd ever had anything other than a horse between her legs. The thrill of the chase can do strange things to a man, and from the look in her eye, to a woman as well.

As the river lazily wandered its way to and fro down the valley, the railway line cut across it on a succession of small bridges, marked only by a change in the note of the wheels. With Stan still dazed, the three women and I talked our way around the various ramifications, who the unknown men might be, was Parkinson really a Scotland Yard officer?

Magda was still chewing through the basics of the problem. "If the person who organised your diversion to Whitby was trying to organise the delivery of the stolen documents, or whatever else, to a boat then surely that boat would have had to have been here yesterday."

"I would imagine so, whoever sent that diversion message would have no reason to think that I would precipitate a brawl in the snow by stopping to look for Ruth. Their intention was just what they said – that we should go to Whitby. That's where all this is going to end, and probably by boat, that's the only way they could hope to escape the inevitable hue and cry."

"But if they expected us there yesterday afternoon, will they have waited?"

"Well I'd wait 24 hours for a battleship's worth of easily negotiable Bearer Bonds, wouldn't you? But you're right there's likely to be a new degree of urgency in their movements. If we've guessed correctly they'll want to load and leave as quickly as they can, in order to be in international waters before the authorities work out what's happening."

"Do you think they'll just leave Charlie behind when they go?" Asked Ruth, her tone suggesting she'd already guessed the answer.

"If it's the Bulgarian Brotherhood, that Pedro was telling me about, then there's not a chance of them leaving a witness. They've got a long and established record of killing hostages, even at his age Charlie will have seen too much to be allowed to live."

Up ahead I could see the river moving gently back in from our left, it had broadened out here, less of a fast moving beck and more of a shallow meander with flat muddy islands visible. A steel lattice bridge crossed diagonally to a village on the far side, from my memory of the stations passed so far, this should be somewhere called Ruswarp. We couldn't be any further than two miles from the end of the line.

As we moved onto the bridge I saw it, but too late to avoid a collision. There was a low black object laid across the track near to the far end of the bridge. I couldn't see what it was, but knew immediately that the precise nature of the blockage was irrelevant, it wouldn't have been put there unless it was sufficiently heavy to derail or stop us.

With my left hand I pushed the regulator lever fully forwards to cut the steam supply, and with my right hand pulled the brake lever fully back. The resultant noisy deceleration was gratifying but wholly inadequate, we skidded on, the steel wheels sliding along the steel rails.

"Hold on." I shouted. "We're going to hit something." I checked Stan and saw him blearily pushing a foot against the base of the hand brake stanchion. There was the hard bang of a very solid

247

contact and a sideways lurch, followed by a juddering and bouncing. Gretchen had cannoned into me and was holding on tightly as I braced myself against the controls. We were off the rails but still moving, was our journey going to end in the river?

The front right hand corner of the engine caught in the steel side rails of the bridge, and with a cacophony of tearing metal slowed us down far faster than the brakes ever had. After an endless period of banging and hammering we came to a stop, derailed, but still upright and still on the bridge. A sudden silence surrounded us, broken only by the subdued hiss of escaping steam from a fractured pipe, - that and the gasp of someone in pain.

Gretchen unwound her arms from around me and stepped away, seeming awkward and embarrassed by the unusual proximity, her breasts having been pressed against my back. The awkwardness answered my unasked question about whether she ever had, or not – it would seem not.

Magda and Ruth were in a heap on the far side of the cab, with Stan crumpled up with them. Ruth was underneath, and it had been her gasp of pain. She had been turning as she fell, and her right ankle had twisted under the combined weight of two falling bodies. Feeling it, I couldn't tell if it was broken or not, but when she tried to move it she cried out in pain. Gretchen knelt down to take a more expert view. This was turning into a disaster, I wasn't getting a single thing right. If there was a naval recruitment office in Whitby perhaps I should see if they'd have me back.

With the help of some willing locals, who had come to see what all the noise was about, Ruth and Stan were carried off the bridge, while the rest of us followed slowly in their footsteps. Our dishevelled procession wound its way past the church and up the main street to a large and imposing stone house, the choice of venue being directed by Magda, who seemed to feel that having landed on top of her she was at least partly to blame for Ruth's misfortune. Luckily no one blamed me for not looking where we were going.

The elderly gentleman who owned the house was a friend of the Schindler's father, Otto, and seemed happy to open his door to us. While Magda organised one of our helpers to fetch a doctor and then began to tend to Stan, Gretchen explained to the owner that we needed to use his telephone to speak to the police, was it in working order?

"I don't see why ever not, I haven't used it recently but I would imagine it's still working."

He took us through a green baize covered door into the back hall and showed us the instrument, apparently it was the first, and so far the only, one of its type in the village. He was justifiably pleased with this opportunity of showing it off. He gave the generator handle several turns and then held the black ear piece to his ear. After a short wait, during which nothing happened, he repeated the procedure. It then burst into life, and the faint sound of a voice could be heard. He responded.

"Ah yes, good morning Ethel, it's Mr. Dorrington here, from Ruswarp . . . . . Yes, very well thank you, and you? . . . . . The thing is we need to speak to the police station in Whitby can you connect us please?"

After another pause he gestured me to come forward and passed the ear piece to me, pointing out that I should talk into the mouthpiece on the front of

249

the box. Fortunately, working on the railways, I had already had some experience with the device and was able to use it quite confidently. Ethel announced that she had succeeded in making the connection and a new voice echoed through down the wire.

"This is Sergeant Pickles speaking, to whom am I addressing?"

Having been a regular visitor to Yorkshire for some years I was aware that Pickles was a perfectly standard name in this part of the world, rather than an attempt at humour. I proceeded to give what I thought was a succinct outline of our position, and explained the presence of a child hostage on the stolen train.

"So you're saying that you were travelling on a train from London, which got stuck in the snow on Goathland Moor. But now the train has gone off without you, is that correct?"

"I wasn't just travelling on it, I was the driver, but otherwise yes, that's right."

"So what do you want me to do about it?"

"As I explained they have taken a small child as a hostage and we have good reason to believe they will do him harm, you must get all your men together and stop these people. The train will probably be arriving in Whitby as we speak."

"When you say; *all my people*, there's only me and young Harrowby here."

This was a complete waste of time, I looked helplessly at Mr. Dorrington, he smiled encouragingly back at me. Try a slightly different approach.

"Tell me Sergeant Pickles, has any unusual ship or boat arrived in your harbour in the last couple of days?"

"Well nothing as you could say, *unusual*, there's our regular fishing boats, but they're always here, and then there's two of the London colliers." He paused for a moment's thought. "Then there's that Russian navy ship, of course, that's down at Bog Hall."

"A Russian navy ship?"

"Yes, that's right, it's a two masted black steam ship, quite a fancy looking job; but still not exactly what you'd call *unusual*. We quite often have visiting navy ships."

"And it's at somewhere called Bog Hall you said – where exactly is that?"

"Bog Hall? Well it's by the dockyard." He sounded suspicious that I didn't already know this. I was gripping the ear piece of the instrument so tightly that my hand hurt, but I had to remain calm.

"Please humour me Sergeant, is this Bog Hall place part of the port of Whitby?"

"Well of course it is, it's on the north quay, where the railway line goes down to the docks."

That was it, the magic phrase: 'Where the railway line goes down to the docks'. Despite the importance of the information, my shoulders slumped as I gave an involuntary sigh. We'd found them, but whether there was enough time left for this information to be useful was unclear.

"Can you see this place from where you are Sergeant?"

"Please stay on the line." There was the sound of retreating footsteps, shortly followed by the same footsteps returning. "Yes, I can see it from the side window, there's smoke coming out of the funnel, it'll be high tide shortly so I imagine they're getting ready to sail."

"Did you see if there was a train anywhere near it?"

"Oh yes, that arrived half an hour or so ago, it's pulled up right next to the ship."

"Sergeant you have to stop that ship from leaving, a child's life depends on you. You and young Harrowby need to get down there now. You have to stop them – by any means possible, do you understand me?"

"Now you listen to me, I can understand that you're upset at missing your train, but Her Majesty's Constabulary do not exist to go haring about on wild goose chases. Why if we were to . . . ." His voice was continuing as I silently replaced the ear piece on its hook.

Ruth's face was a study in desperation, Gretchen put her arm on mine.

"You exhibited great self control Mr. Fowler, I rather think I might have shouted at him."

Mr. Dorrington seemed to take Sergeant Pickle's shortcomings as a black mark on the community. "I am sorry Mr. Fowler, but Wilfred's normally not so bad - for a policeman."

I looked at Ruth. "I'm afraid that with that twisted ankle you'll have to stay here, but I'm going after them, it's probably too late, but who knows?" I turned to the others.

"Mr. Dorrington I need a carriage, or at least a horse, immediately – and I mean immediately. Gretchen give me your rifle."

"Mr. Fowler, I shoot my own rifle. Mr. Dorrington, make that two horses, and as Mr. Fowler said – immediately if you please."

Dorrington left the room at a medium canter, his eyes agleam, nothing this exciting had happened in Ruswarp since the last Viking raid passed through.

"Gretchen your help has been invaluable, without you and your sister we would never have got this far, but that's got to end now. You can't carry on risking your life for strangers, you stay here with Magda, Ruth and Stan. I'll go on alone, it would be better that way."

The lies came easily, but it was all for the greater good. I wanted her along but she had to be an eager and determined volunteer, not simply going through the motions for the sake of politeness.

"Mr. Fowler, I'm pleased to note what a completely useless liar you are, your intentions and desires are written all over your face." My give away face probably sank at that, but she carried on.

"Taking up arms against another human being is a major step to take, but any presumption by these people that they can throw a Methodist lay reader to his death must be dealt with firmly, which is exactly what I intend to do."

One could see her point, allow this sort of behaviour to pass unchallenged today, and by tomorrow there'll be Methodists being thrown off trains all over the shop. Still, it was clearly better to be a Methodist than a Freemason, I'm not at all sure the members of my Lodge would have been as keen to avenge my own intended death.

"Not forgetting Charlie."

"No, Mr. Fowler I had not forgotten Charlie, he is the object of our forthcoming efforts, and is constantly in our prayers."

"Will your prayers be accompanied by the occasional use of gunfire?"

"As long as such use is on a scripturally sound footing, then yes."

"Is there a scripturally sound footing for the use of firearms?"

"Don't be sarcastic with me young man."

That was exactly the response I'd hoped for, but you could tell from her knees together attitude that she knew what I'd been thinking about her. That's always disturbing - to realise that the person I'm talking to has discerned just how low and disreputable my views of life are. Mind you if we we're going to include bullets in our repertoire then the odd carnal thought, in her case very odd, would scarcely be noticed.

I went to the door, and bellowed. "MR. DORRINGTON, THE HORSES PLEASE."

I knelt down by Ruth to hug and kiss her goodbye. She held me tight for a moment.

"Be careful darling." Was all she said, it was all she could say, as we both recognised that a little gung ho might shortly be called for.

It was turning out to be another busy day, I'd already wrecked a locomotive and a steel bridge. Now, with the assistance of a German horse breeder I was going to try and sink a Russian warship. I heard the snorting of horses and the jangling of their tack from outside the front door.

ISLINGTON GAZETTE
Editorial Comment:
The rampant socialism of the County Council is once more manifested in the absurd and extravagant proposal to make tramways and even railways, free to the working classes, at the expense of that unhappy section of the population who are ratepayers. We have already had a variety of instances of the way in which the Council is being used by professional agitators to promote anything and everything which will satisfy the cravings of democracy. The funds of the metropolis are now looked upon as the legitimate plunder of the trade unions, and the Council does nothing but consider fresh means of giving them access to them.

If there are free tramways for the working or any class, there is no earthly reason why, as has been properly said, there should not be free meals, free house rent, free clothing, free everything. If we come to this, we come to a dangerous sapping of the independence of the class benefited, and the nearest thing to universal pauperism of the wages class.

THIRTEEN

"Rutland it really is you, how wonderful. I'd recognise your voice   anywhere, even down a telephone. In fact with projection like yours you scarcely need the instrument. How are the audiences?"

"Ruth darling, what a treat to hear from you in this frozen wasteland. Though I don't know what you mean by: 'How are the audiences?' There isn't a seat to be had, as always - you know how it is when people see the name Rutland Barrington on a bill. And just don't ask about the theatre – we're on top of a cliff, it's even called the West Cliff Saloon for goodness sake, it sounds like the Wild West. The wind comes howling across the North Sea in a straight line from Siberia, if they have the front door and the back door open at the same time all the bloody scenery falls over – my dear you've never seen anything like it."

"Rutland you've always been troubled by wind, but as long as you're putting bums on seats, that's what it's all about."

"I suppose you're still going to bed with that saturnine railway man, you do know I could make you much happier, and I give matinees, there's nothing like an afternoon performance."

"That railway man is my husband and yes I'm still going to bed with him, and no, you couldn't do it better – nobody could."

"I don't know about that, I heard a whisper that you and our fat friend Bertie were making the beast with two backs."

"That's incredible it was only two nights ago when he came . . ."

"So it is true, you dirty little beast."

"No – not like that it's not, he was chasing Marie Lloyd and I just happened just to get in the way. But since you raised his name that saves me from doing so; Rutland you're going to love this, it's got everything. It starts with Bertie, then there's stolen Bearer Bonds, foreign desperadoes, Freemasons and an angelic little kidnapped child. And solely because I've gone and twisted my ankle at the last minute, I'm going to have to let you in on it with Fowler and me - and incidentally cover yourself in glory in the process."

"My dear girl if D'Oyly Carte hears about this he'll have Gilbert writing a libretto."

"The local paper I'm looking at says that you have a matinee due to start in less than fifteen minutes, is this with the full company?"

"Well George Grossmith's gone to America with that book of his, The Diary of a Nobody, it's been a huge success."

"Yes I know about that, but I mean the chorus, are your numbers up to full strength?"

"Absolutely, you know Rutland Barrington; a big man and a big performance – no half measures. But I do hope this isn't some charitable nonsense. Mmm no - you're too hard headed for charity, so why not spill the beans to your Uncle Rutty?"

"Cancel the matinee, give the audience their money back and tell them to go home, or if you like you can send on a juggler instead. When they read tomorrow morning's paper and find out what you've been doing they'll still love you for it. This is the publicity stunt of the century."

"I couldn't possibly cancel, they're already in their seats."

"Use the fire alarm, that'll get them on their feet."

"There could be mass panic, old ladies will be trampled to death in the aisles."

"Old ladies aren't in short supply and it'll be cheaper than refunding the tickets."

"Yes, there is that. But what about the cast, do they stand down? They're all kitted up and ready for Overture and Beginners."

"No, no, you keep the cast in full dress ready for the Act 1, we're having a slight change of venue - but just the men, you don't need any of the women."

"You speak for yourself dearie, I've got a long felt need."

"So I've heard, but we don't have time for your vulgarity now, this is going to have to be extremely fast, so just keep quiet and listen."

"Ah - the story of my life, one domineering woman after another riding rough shod over me. But God knows I could do with the entertainment, and you've always been a diamond in the theatrical rough. So go on darling – roll all over me, tell me the worst."

*****

Gretchen led the way, her horse seeming sure footed against mine, but that wasn't because of any difference in our mounts, it was the result of comparing her expert horsemanship with my own unfamiliarity. Wherever possible she broke into a trot, or was it a canter? I've never known the difference, and quite frankly I've probably eaten more horses than I've ridden on. My horse did what hers did and I hung on, that's always been a skill of mine; hanging on in unlikely circumstances. Nonetheless she had insisted on carrying the rifle strapped across her back, rather than mine, on the grounds that she didn't want it to be damaged if *anyone* fell off.

The track made its way along the flat land to the north of the river, in summer these would probably be water meadows, but for now it was just another thousand tons of snow that had fallen heavily to earth. The flatness and relative lack of trees allowed us a longer view of the line ahead than previously.

The newly revealed view showed a surprising addition to the landscape, four figures also on horseback, also making their way along the track to Whitby. They were too far away to see any detail, but something about their shape or clothing suggested they were men.

I had no real grounds to believe they had any connection with our ongoing saga, but it was quite a coincidence. If we'd had any spare capacity we would have gone faster to catch up, but we were already going as fast as we could. They stayed a group of distant black shapes travelling at the same urgent speed and in the same direction as us.

All the while I was consumed by a gripping fear of what we would find when we got there. I felt like the prisoner in the dock nervously waiting for the verdict, would I be freed, or would I be hanged?

Our track passed under a majestic viaduct, crossing the valley from north to south, I presumed it to be carrying the Scarborough to Whitby line. If railways had brought nothing else to this country they had certainly produced some outstanding feats of civil engineering. Nobody had been building anything like this since the mediaeval cathedral builders, and before them the Romans. I felt a slight surge of pride to be even marginally connected with such an undertaking.

Then, as the line swung round to follow a sharp left turn of the river, we could see up on a headland in front of us, the unmistakeable outline of what had to be Whitby Abbey. Ruined and roofless, but still imposing itself on the skyline. That showed just how close we were to our goal, the four figures ahead of us were still pressing on as fast as ourselves. It was now obvious they had to be connected, why else would any group of people be chasing this same train so urgently?

"Wait." Said Gretchen, reining her horse in sharply, and causing mine to follow suit. She pulled a small pair of binoculars from her pocket and stood up in her stirrups, training the glasses on the four mounted figures.

"I thought so," she said, turning to me, "those are Schindler horses."

"How can you tell?"

She shrugged. "Their shape, gait, footprints." She gestured to the lines of hoof prints we had been following, as if that would somehow clarify things for me.

"But who's on them?"

261

"No idea." She said shortly, as we urged the horses on again.

There were now small boats to be seen, moored in the widening estuary of the river to our right, with the tops of cranes and the masts of larger craft visible ahead of us, they had to be alongside Sergeant Pickle's Bog Hall quay, where all our questions would be answered. The track bed of the railway line had widened out and there were now four separate lines, and sure enough, one of them branched off to the right, towards the water. We followed it.

As we did so our missing train came into sight, the engine still giving off wisps of smoke and steam in the cold air, above it could be seen the two raked masts of the Russian ship. Without speaking Gretchen pointed off to one side, where four horses stood in a group, presumably hers. There were no riders to be seen.

While still a hundred yards away, we dismounted without speaking, the ground here had been largely cleared of snow by the routine traffic of a working dock. I pulled out my revolver and Gretchen uncased her rifle, it was a long, gleaming, and impressive piece of equipment. If she was as good as she claimed, it could make a significant difference.

I ran towards the train, it looked to be deserted, the window blinds were raised but no occupants were visible. Gretchen was running alongside me, she had thrown off her coat and was holding the rifle across her chest, she looked businesslike and ready for a fight. Perhaps my views on going into action alongside women might need to be reviewed. As we closed on the train there was a prolonged rattle of gunfire, machinegun fire, there was the sound of breaking glass and the solid impact of heavy rounds. Some workmen over by one of the sheds ran for cover, a sensible move.

We looked at each other, shocked. This wasn't the Khyber Pass or any other far flung Imperial outpost, this was Whitby Dock; home to fishing boats and colliers. We should have encountered potted shrimps and kippers, not a machine gun.

"And you queried the fact that I had a Lee Metford rifle." Said Gretchen with justifiable pique. "Perhaps I should have asked Colonel Cody to get me one of those."

From the rate of fire it had to be a Maxim gun, none of the other machine guns that I'd ever heard of could match the Maxim's output of 500 rounds per minute. That was going to make any assault on the ship an interesting business, but if that's where Charlie was, then that's where I was going.

As the machine gun fell silent, probably to load a new belt, we heard the sound of individual gun shots from near the locomotive. Then two figures ran round the front of the engine, and crouched behind the front bogies, peering guardedly back at the ship. It was Pedro and Antonescu.

Gretchen and I looked at each other again, even more surprised.

"Are they part of the disease or part of the cure?" She wondered aloud. I made no answer, as I had none.

Although offering no more than partial protection against .303 machine gun bullets, the train concealed us from the ship's view, but there was no cover between us and the two men. In the absence of an answer to her perfectly reasonable question, I pointed my revolver in their direction, the muzzle of her rifle followed my lead.

"Do you know, I had never realised that being an engine driver could be quite so – bracing." She whispered as we crept stealthily towards the crouching backs of my two former passengers. I do like a companion who keeps their head when all around are being shot at.

"This is where it gets dangerous." I said quietly. "Even if we can't control events, I intend at least to change them." With splendid verbal economy she restricted her own comment to four words.

"That's why I'm here."

"Then let's do it."

I moved away to one side, gesturing that we should stay apart, I didn't want us to make an easy single target. We continued our silent progress, until we were within 20 yards of them, at which point I announced our arrival.

"Don't make any sudden moves, because I don't trust either of you. Now turn round very carefully, with your guns pointing downwards."

It was probably the shock of hearing my voice so close behind them that initially caused them to freeze, rather than the words themselves. But having digested the meaning they slowly complied, their pistols pointing firmly at the ground. I might not have sounded pleased to see them and certainly wasn't in the mood to listen to any carefully prepared cock and bull story. I leapt straight into what I considered to be the heart of the matter.

"Where's Charlie?"

It was Pedro who answered. "Charlie? Isn't he with you?"

"Don't be funny with me, or it won't just be your moustache I cut down to size. Where is he?"

There came the sound of the Lee Metford's bolt being operated and a round sliding into the breech. From the corner of my eye I could see the gun barrel pointing at Antonescu. From his face he realised that he was very close to the end of the line, in more than one way. He started to say something to Pedro, but was interrupted.

"You can speak in English or German, but if you use any other language then I will assume you're planning hostile action, and if that happens I will do whatever is necessary to stop you." They might not have been surprised to hear threats from me, but coming from such an unexpected source as Gretchen, it carried more weight.

"Major Antonescu was just saying that you probably think we took your train."

"Well if you didn't, then who did?"

"We don't know, other than to suggest it could be those two injured men of Major Antonescu's that we left on board guarding the prisoners."

"Well if that's true, what are you doing here? And furthermore how did you travel?"

Pedro simply pointed to the group of horses we had just passed.

"That makes sense." I said to Gretchen. "They must have been the group of four we were following earlier."

Another rattle of machine gun fire hosed around the quay on the far side of the locomotive, there were even some stray bullets that made it between the wheels, and under the engine. I made sure that I was stood behind a wheel, to lessen the chances of being hit, and had the others do the same. The fact that this had nothing to do with either Pedro or Antonescu was now blindingly obvious, even to me.

Visible on the quay through the engine's wheels, and lying in ungainly tumbled poses were the clearly dead bodies of what I was sure were Antonescu's two remaining men. The Rumanian security services were having another bad day.

Lying alongside the quay was the Russian naval vessel, a steam corvette or gunboat from what I could see of it. There was smoke rising from the funnel, and the unmistakeable blue and white Andreevsky flag hung from one of the yardarms, a British courtesy flag from another. A line of gold Russian lettering on the bow gave her unreadable name. Half a dozen of the dark uniformed crew were on the edge of the wharf waiting the order to cast off the shore lines, this was sailing time. Although Whitby's inner harbour is tidal it was obvious there was enough water to float her, you only had to look at the trembling and slight movement of her to see that she wasn't aground. There was nothing to stop her departure, including our little group, three men with revolvers and one woman with a rifle, against a machine gun equipped warship – it wasn't even good enough to be a joke.

"Are you sure that Charlie's not still on the train?" I asked Antonescu, knowing he could understand me perfectly well.

"I have look - I am sure." He said, and so dogmatically that I believed him. All four of us knew what that implied: if he wasn't *on* the train then he was lying dead in a ditch where he'd been thrown *from* the train, either that, or he was on the ship. An abject sense of failure swept through me, they'd got the money, they'd got the child, and all I'd done was kill Pedro's security detail; one by one. My usual contribution to international good relations.

"How can the Russian government possibly hope to get away with such an act of piracy?" asked Gretchen. "The Royal Navy is the most powerful military force in the world, even if this ship escapes there will surely be a reckoning. Something that will make even this much money pale into insignificance."

"I honestly don't know." Was my weak and inadequate reply.

I stepped to the front of the engine and peered carefully round to get a better look. When I saw the whole ship, rather than just bits glimpsed through the engine wheels, I knew she had a point, and that there was something wrong. My professional sailor's eye swept over her raked masts and funnel, the angle of her stern, her sharply swept bow line. All the parts of the vessel that cannot be easily changed or disguised. Then I scrolled backwards, my mind running through the hundreds of different varieties of warship I'd seen in my life. It took some moments, but then I had it. I turned back to the others.

"The Russians aren't supposed to get away with it, the plan is that the Russians should pay, and pay heavily, for this act of piracy. That isn't a Russian ship, the Russian naval ensign, the Cyrillic lettering, they're all just a disguise. That's a steam gunboat built in Britain, thirty or more years ago for the Ottoman Navy – the Turks."

"So they're Turks?" Asked Pedro in astonishment.

"No, that's hardly likely - the entire Ottoman fleet has been tied up at Constantinople for the last twenty five years, they haven't got the cash to pay their crews. Their navy might be impressive on paper, but in reality it's no more than a collection of empty aging hulks. The chances are that whoever planned this operation stole that ship from its moorings, it wouldn't be difficult, most of them don't even have watchmen onboard. Moved her to some quiet backwater and spent a couple of thousand pounds getting her re-commissioned."

"But the sailors?" Queried Pedro.

"The sailors are the cheapest part, they could be the sweepings from the dockside bars in any major port, from Piraeus to Hamburg. All they need is a handful of half decent officers and an engineer. The main armament probably doesn't work either, they don't need it, all they needed was a cover to lay the blame on someone else. I would think that at the earliest opportunity the ship will be scuttled, and at that point the trail will disappear."

Six more of their sailors had appeared onshore, all with rifles held in front of them, they began to move away along the quay to our left.

"I looked at the others, baffled. "Don't ask me what that lot are doing."

"They're going to open the bridge." Said Gretchen. "There's a swivel bridge in the middle of the harbour, you can't see it from here, but it has to be opened before they can reach the sea. After all that gunfire they'll be going to make sure that nobody has raised the alarm and is trying to keep it closed."

One of the ships boats, a small steam cutter had a line attached to the vessel and was laboriously hauling her bow out, to point into the middle of the harbour. All the officer's eyes were on that, and I knew at once that I was going to do something deeply foolish.

"Give me the rifle." I demanded. She clutched it more tightly and took half a pace backwards.

"Certainly not, I'm probably the best shot here, tell me what you want to hit and I'll use it."

I stepped forwards, reaching my hands out to take it. "Don't argue, just give it to me – I'm going aboard the ship."

"So am I."

"You can't," said Pedro, "it's already moving, the bows must be twenty feet off the quay."

"Well if the bows are being swung off the quay, then what do you think the stern's doing?" I asked curtly, surprised that he needed to have something so simple explained.

Even as I was speaking Gretchen had already begun to run back along the landward side of the train. She had the right idea, that would be the best line of approach – I set off after her.

She stopped at the end of the last carriage and waved me past her, presumably not wanting too many of our faces visible at once, and trusting my assessment of the situation above her own. I looked cautiously round the end of the train and saw that we were only a short way behind the stern, which was, as it had to be, now pivoting against the quay. Just then there was the rapid hammering of smoke being pumped from the funnel, as the engine came under pressure, it sounded like a train leaving the station. Simultaneously there came the thrashing sound of the screw, churning the water under her counter, as she began to make way.

Ten years of civilian life fell away from me; I was back in the navy – leading another raiding party.

Only this time, instead of a boat load of heavily armed, hairy arsed matelots, I had me and the lady horse breeder. Nobody onboard was looking backwards, the action was all in front of them. I broke cover, sprinted across the open quay and jumped. I was aware of movement behind me but didn't look. The rumbling thunder of the ship's engine covered the sound of my pounding feet.

Landing on the planked deck, I stayed in a crouching position and reached for my revolver. Gretchen landed next to me, the rifle once more strapped across her back, I gestured her to stay down. Then out of the blue something unseen, but large and very solid, hit me in the back and knocked me over. It was Antonescu, I assumed the next heavy impact I heard to be Pedro landing. I had just doubled my available force.

I moved forward to a position behind the after deck house, where we were hidden from sight, even if somebody did turn round. Time for a quick word to enthuse the troops.

"I know we're outnumbered, but if I'm right about the quality of the crew, then as long as we can remove the officers, they should be like headless chickens."

"And if you're wrong, then we're all just chicken shit." Said Gretchen, with emphasis on the last word. The three of us turned to stare at her, our mouths open in astonishment. This woman had hidden reserves of vulgarity, a pleasantly attractive feature I thought. Pedro apparently disagreed, as he uttered a shocked, 'Gnädige Frau!'

"Don't look at me like that." She hissed at the three of us. "If I'm expected to behave like a

270

hooligan then you'd better expect me to speak like one."

"Both of you shut up. This isn't a democracy, you will stay hidden and keep quiet until I say otherwise." Reinforcing my words with an aggressive glare, I stood on a small access hatch and chanced a look above the deck house.

The navigating bridge on this ship was a raised open walk way, stretching from side to side just in front of the funnel. There was a ship's wheel, a binnacle and an engine telegraph in the middle, and stretched wire railings all the way round. It was occupied by three officers and a helmsman, with a rifle carrying sailor stood at each end. The Maxim gun, with its crew of four sailors was on top of the forward deck house, towards the bows – it was facing forwards, like everyone else round here. Together with the six men who had let go of the shore lines there were at least ten more armed sailors visible on deck.

The deck continued to thump and shudder beneath our feet as we moved slowly out into the middle of the harbour, it was a comfortingly familiar sensation but it did nothing to change the glaringly obvious fact that we were massively outnumbered. Their crew didn't need to be highly trained and motivated, they could swamp us by sheer weight of numbers any time they wanted.

I tried to ignore the pressure of expectation from my small band of cutthroats and concentrated on how to proceed. There had to be some trick or diversion, something that would help to reduce the overwhelming odds against us – but whichever way I approached it, there simply wasn't.

Even if we killed two men each with our surprise opening salvo, which was improbable, that would still leave at least twelve people and a machine gun shooting back at us. Plus the crew of the launch and any reinforcements coming up from below deck. That wasn't bravery it was damned stupidity and would do nothing to help Charlie. Would I have been more use staying ashore?

No I wouldn't – it's time to find your backbone Fowler, the odds aren't what I might have chosen – that's hardly surprising. No matter how many guns they've got they can only kill you once. There's always a time in any operation when rationality isn't enough, when the arithmetic breaks down, at that moment you just have grab the baton and run for it. It's worked so far. The trouble was, the navigating bridge was beyond accurate handgun range, we were going to need the rifle for that.

"Gretchen, you're going to stay here. If you stand on top of this hatch you can rest your rifle on top of the deck house. When the rest of us get into position near the funnel and I give the signal, I want you to shoot the man on the wheel and then all three officers, but remember start with the man on the wheel. Whoever tries to hold the wheel must be shot – alright?"

"If they are not immediately threatening anyone, then I can't shoot them in the back, that would be no better than murder."

"Do you doubt that their own intentions are evil and murderous?"

She mutely shook her head, unable to disagree, but a long way from happy. And she wasn't the only one feeling unhappy, this was exactly the reaction I'd feared, I pursued the point.

"That group of men represents the head of this particular mad dog, if we cut it off we could bring this nonsense to an end. There is no way to sidestep this issue - if you remove the helmsman the ship will go off course and probably run aground."

As I listened to my own words I was sharply aware that this particular ethical point had about another two or three seconds of talking time left, before I socked her on the jaw, snatched the gun and did the job myself. It would only take one of them to look backwards - and we were goners. This is what you get for going into battle with civilians, they want to discuss their orders.

Her jaw firmed and her eyes narrowed. "I'll shoot the ship's wheel to pieces and can promise that it will be unusable. Then if any of them shoot back at me I'll return their fire, that will give us the same result."

I breathed a sigh of relief, as soon as they were aware of our presence she was going to have lots of people trying to kill her. Although this particular depravity might have been new to her, she must have encountered many other forms of human malice. No matter how scenic her surroundings, there would be the usual percentage of the locals slandering their neighbours, abusing children and beating their wives. Bishop Heber was pretty much on the money when he talked of a place, 'Where every prospect pleases and only man is vile'.

I turned to Pedro. "I want you and the Major to make your way along the right hand side of the deck. Your job is to get close enough to kill the Maxim gun crew and then make sure that nobody replaces them."

"We'll take care of that, what will you be doing?"

273

"I'm feeling tired so I'll probably go for a lie down."

"Ah yes, the English humour, most droll."

I moved round to the left side of the deck house, signalled Pedro to start moving on his side, and set off myself. Once the three of us had moved past the shelter of the after deck house we were in the open, but no one was looking our way. The sailors on deck were lining both the side rails near the bows, their rifles held ready to deal with anyone who tried to stop us, the Maxim gun crew and the navigation bridge personnel were all focussed in the same direction.

Up ahead it was now possible to see the object of their interest, the swivel bridge. It was still closed, blocking our way, there were even carriages and people crossing it. But on the left side of the harbour the group of six armed sailors could be seen approaching it, their job would be to take over the bridge controls and let us out, to the open sea and freedom.

Pedro, the Major and myself were almost in position when there was an urgent shout from over the far side rail. The people on the bridge all turned to look at the source of the shouting, then they turned back to see us. We had been spotted by the crew of the steam launch, and for the avoidance of any confusion that was the steam launch that had been hauling us off the quay, the steam launch that I had forgotten about.

It took all of one or two seconds for the officers on the bridge to deal with their complete astonishment at our presence and then order their men to shoot us. Although the Maxim gun was unable to open fire, as the navigation bridge stood between us and them, no such difficulties hampered the individual sailors.

"Pedro – get back – now!" I shouted, whilst doing that exact thing myself. A ragged volley of shots blasted out, it sounded like the first day of the grouse season. More encouragingly, as I scuttled to safety, I also heard Gretchen's rifle firing, and doing so systematically and carefully. Pedro, Antonescu and I collided in heap back behind the deck house, the very shelter we had just left. Gretchen stepped down off her platform showing no visible sign of stress, and then calmly but quickly reloaded her rifle.

"They opened fire on me, and were also trying to shoot you, so I was obliged to shoot back." She said, explaining what I had known to be inevitable, before climbing back to her firing position. Talking things over with her had paid dividends.

I joined her to take a look. She had cleared the navigation bridge, all that was left were three crumpled bodies, the others presumably having fallen to the deck. She began firing again, this time at the Maxim gun. It was only going to be a short while before they realised that now the bridge party were already dead or missing there was nothing to stop them using their weapon on us. Blasting bits out of the now empty navigation bridge would be a cheap price to pay for our removal.

Her pin point performance with the rifle was crucial to our survival, the Maxim gun was beyond useful handgun range, and had we alerted them to our presence by a fusillade of largely inaccurate pistol shots they would have surely replied in kind. She was every bit as good as she'd claimed; cool, methodical and deadly accurate. If only we'd had two of her we might have stood a chance.

After the first two members of the Maxim gun's four man crew had gone down, the other two sensibly dived for cover. However, the individual sailors had all now taken their own firing positions, aiming their rifles at us from behind masts, the forward deck housing, and any other available protection. No matter what we did, we were stuck. As long as we kept them away from the Maxim gun, we could probably maintain a standoff, but there was no chance of breaking out from this position. Not against that many guns.

The ship was now in the mid stream and still pointing in the right direction, now that we were clear of the quay the engine note had slackened though as far as could be seen we were still under positive control.

Ahead of us the swivel bridge was now visible, it spanned an opening not much wider than the ship, between two stone piers. Nothing could leave the inner harbour without passing through that gap. As I looked, the group of sailors arrived at the swivel bridge and started clearing people off it. The ship swung slightly to one side, aligning itself more precisely with the opening. That confirmed it, they had manned their battle stations' wheel, which would be somewhere below decks. Clearing the navigation bridge had been worth a try but hadn't done the trick.

Rule number one in this sort of situation is: don't stand still while they're shooting at you. I gripped the long steel lever handle on the deck house door, lifted it and pulled backwards. Inside there was an empty mess room area with tables and chairs, which was of no interest at all, but over on one side was a companion-way leading below decks, which was of considerable interest.

Leaving the others on deck, I ran down the steel steps, the engine noise was much louder here – it was a standard below decks layout with a corridor running from side to side across the ship, and a fore and aft corridor off that, down each side. I raced back to the upper doorway and gathered them all inside, wedging the steel door closing lever to try and delay pursuit. If we couldn't stop them steering the ship, perhaps we could close their engine down.

It didn't matter which of the long corridors we went down, I chose the left. There were two lamps, fixed to the bulkhead on steel gimbals, they gave just enough light to show that on our left were a series of wooden doors, clearly leading to cabins. While on our right there was just one door, a steel door with two lever handles; it was an engine room door, all engine room doors look the same.

I never saw the shooter, but a shot sounded from the far end of the corridor, four of our own in return seemed to dampen his enthusiasm, for no more followed.

As I expected, once through the door we found ourselves on a small steel grille platform at the top of the two deck high enclosed space. The machinery was spread out beneath us, a steep steel ladder led down to the engine room floor. Surrounding and engulfing us was the smell of hot oil, the roar of the fire box draught and the frame shaking thump of the piston

It looked like a single cylinder engine, acting on a single shaft; there were a great many similarities between this and my day job. I understood much more about steam propulsion now than I ever had whilst actually in the navy. This should be the work of moments to close them down, then they could steer round in circles for all I cared – without an engine they wouldn't be going anywhere. The masts on a ship like this were more for ornament than use; it would take them hours even to begin to rig her for sail.

"Pedro, make sure you're fully loaded and come with me. You two stay here and kill anyone who looks like a threat" Then shoving the Webley into my trouser waistband I stepped, face outwards, onto the steel ladder, and slid down on the two slightly greasy handrails, my feet touching nothing until the deck at the bottom. It's like riding a bicycle, once you've got the knack . . . . Pedro followed me, face to the ladder, one step at a time.

It was much lighter in here because of the overhead skylights, light enough to see two engineers in oily boiler suits moving to hide behind the coal bunker, they looked to be unarmed and frightened, as long as they stayed that way we'd get along just fine.

I planned to shut down the steam supply from the boiler to the cylinder, that would halt everything within one or two revolutions. There was an oval metal plate on the front of the boiler, it said Money Wigram, Blackwall, London, 1860. That was the name of the shipyard on the Thames and the date it was built. Before I could begin to identify the relevant levers I was aware a shower of broken glass dropping around me.

Because of the all engulfing engine noise, this event was effectively silent and, foolishly, I stood there for a moment wondering why it would suddenly start raining glass. I looked up and saw faces peering down through the now open skylights, the faces were accompanied by gun barrels. This was beginning to be tedious.

Shots could be heard now, even above the engine noise, some were theirs and some were ours. Gretchen and Antonescu had seen the newcomers and were giving us covering fire, but the crew on deck didn't even need to look – they had only to point a gun over the edge and shoot downwards. Bullets were humming all around the place and ricocheting off everything in sight. We still had to find Charlie, and couldn't afford to get trapped in here, but there was more than one way to skin this particular rabbit. I hustled Pedro back up the ladder. It was only a small platform and too crowded to fit us all on.

"You two get back in the corridor. Gretchen, you see that metal contraption sitting on top of the boiler – yes that thing there. That's the boiler safety valve, shoot it off."

"Won't that be dangerous?"

"I sincerely hope so, that's rather the point."

So she did – without further hesitation – lift – aim – fire - whoomph. A ferocious jet of super heated steam blasted its way upwards, making a howling noise like the end of the world. Any faces that had been looking through the skylight when that went off would just have been scalded back to the bone.

She and I stared at each other, shocked at the violence of it. "Schiess." She breathed, in an astonished tone.

"We've now had shit in two different languages." I said rather primly. "What shall we have next, Merde perhaps?"

Realising that this was the second time she'd cursed in the last ten minutes, she had the grace to look embarrassed. I was going to have to assure

Magda that this regrettable coarsening of a previously good woman was none of my doing, my own language had been, almost, impeccable throughout.

Having accomplished all we could in the engine room, and having tired of the possibilities of the after deck, it seemed like a good idea to try our luck forwards. And so, shutting the engine room door behind us on the nightmare of escaping steam and random bullets, that was where I led us. We looked into the cabins we passed, even though it seemed unlikely that a significant hostage would have been abandoned back here. They were all dirty and untidy, and completely empty.

As the demented shriek of escaping steam began to lose its intensity it was possible to hear sledge hammers behind us, they were smashing the wedged handle on the door from the deck. Then the sledge hammers stopped and gun shots rang out – they were inside and coming in this direction. I hurried us forward.

Having come to the end of the engine room space on our right, the corridor opened out onto a large hallway, illuminated by another skylight. Unfortunately, it was here that nemesis and the end of our naval escapade awaited us.

INSULT TO A MARRIED WOMAN

At Clerkenwell County Court, on Wednesday, before Judge Eddis, Edwin Wittrick sued Ellen Gates, nurse of Trinity Asylum, Acre Lane, Brixton, for 15s. rent. Plaintiff said the defendant was a lodger on premises owned by him. She paid 2s.6d. a week, and when she gave up possession on June 15th. she was 15s. in arrears. Defendant said she left the premises on June 8th, and called a witness, who corroborated the fact. The Judge – I will give judgment for 12s.6d. with costs.

Defendant – I cannot pay it. I have been grossly insulted by that man. He surnamed me Ellen Gates, spinster, when he knew very well I was a married woman, and a mother of children (Laughter)

The Judge – Calm yourself Mrs. Gates, I will make an order for the amount to be paid in two monthly instalments.

Defendant (Quite overwrought) – I won't pay a farthing of the money, because of his insulting ways. I am sure the worry of this case will make me ill. (Laughter). May God forgive him for his wickedness to me – and I, a married woman. (Laughter)

FOURTEEN

The four of us emerged into the open space in a disorganised rush, unsure whether to worry about what was behind us or what was in front, and with no clear aim in view. Facing us from the far side of the hallway, was a tight group of sailors, who looked as if they knew exactly what they were supposed to be doing. There must have been at least twelve of them, arranged like an impromptu firing squad in two rows, the back row looking through the gaps in front of them. All of them held rifles, pointing straight at us, the only thing missing was an officer at one side holding up a sword and ready to shout 'Fire'.

Instead of the officer, there was Scroop, allegedly Inspector Carlton Scroop of Scotland Yard. Focussing on a completely irrelevant point, my first thought was how pleased I was that I hadn't believed a word he'd said in the first place. I was also pleased to note that none of my companions had been foolish enough to try shooting their way out of this obvious dead end.

To complete the scene he should have said something languidly sarcastic along the lines of: 'Ah – Mr. Fowler, how good of you to join us'. But not having read the same novels as myself he simply snapped something incomprehensible, and undoubtedly foreign, at the sailors. It sounded like a prelude to opening fire. I was damned if I was going to beg for mercy from someone with such a very silly name, but it did seem appropriate to say something.

"There's no need to be petty about this, just because we've buggered your engine. All you need do is give us the boy, and you're free to go."

Scroop, or whatever his real name was, Smashngrabski or some such, responded by looking puzzled. If nothing else that at least stopped him opening fire.

"Boy, what boy?"

"Young Charlie, my nephew."

"You mean the boy on the train?"

"Yes, where is he?"

"How the hell should I know where he is? This isn't some home for straying orphans, if he's your nephew – you tell me where he is."

There had been a marked change in his demeanour, no more diffident humility now, and also the clear hint of some Slavic accent creeping through the English vowels. However, his answer had temporarily left me with nothing to say, if Charlie wasn't here then where was he?

"When did you last see him?"

"Not since you snatched him back, when you were doing that thing with jumping on and off the different trains."

"But that's the whole point I didn't snatch him back. I tried, but failed. And then you left that note saying you would kill him if we interfered again."

"Why not? I wasn't sure if you and that woman were together or not, one of you might have thought that the other one had the child. If you don't have him then I have no idea where he's gone, and couldn't care less."

The sailors who had come along the corridor behind us had taken our guns, and from amongst them there now came an unpleasantly familiar voice. My old friend Chief Superintendant Parkinson, supposedly another of Scotland Yard's finest.

"Fowler, you were warned not to interfere, but you wouldn't be told. I see you no longer have Mrs, Castlemaine with you, where is she this time - hidden in the galley perhaps?"

"Far from it, she's summoning help, there's a militia garrison in town and by my reckoning they should be here at any minute."

He laughed, unpleasantly. "No there isn't, there's no militia garrison within miles of here, which is precisely why we chose it. You should have learned by now that you can't fool me, I ran rings round you on the train. The massed ranks of Scotland Yard and some blundering Rumanians, you never stood a chance." He was unstoppable, in full flow.

"Every single one of you swallowed the Chief Superintendant Parkinson nonsense, especially you, with your prickly little game playing. And all the time you and Antonescu were no more than puppets, I pulled the strings and the pair of you danced. You were both so utterly predictable. Neither one of you did a single thing that I hadn't planned." He laughed again.

"You want me to call you *Mister* do you? Very well then, *Mister* Fowler, I'll give you a useful tip. In your next life, which is coming sooner than you thought, you should stick to engine driving - because you're no bloody good at anything else."

At that moment a man in a dirty white boiler suit came from the direction of the engine room and whispered something in his ear, it was one of the engineers bringing the bad news. This was going to be nasty.

It was, he came to stand directly in front of me and hit me hard across the face with his pistol. Two sailors behind me held my arms, if they were trying to prevent retaliation they needn't have bothered, but they were useful in keeping me upright. He hit me again, this time in the stomach, it was right on the spot where I'd landed on the Webley. I threw up, but he was quick on his feet and I missed.

"I'm not even angry with you Fowler, I'm too professional for anger, that was just a display. You're a steam engineer, you have fifteen minutes to repair the thing you damaged. If it's not ready by then I will shoot your friends one by one at fifteen minute intervals, until it is."

"You can shoot who you like but it will take me at least thirty minutes to put a temporary plug in that hole, and after that another thirty minutes to get sufficient steam pressure back to move you. So if you shoot anyone I'll stop work, then you can kill the lot of us in one go. That's what you intend doing anyway."

From everything I could see about the man, he was telling the truth about not being angry, he was just extremely determined. An emotion I found more worrying than anger. He moved even closer to me, gave me an almost sad little smile and then grasped me violently by the throat. I was lifted up onto my toes, and forced back against the two sailors holding my arms. He was an extremely powerful man, and even though he was only using one hand he was effectively strangling me. Lights exploded in front of my eyes and then darkness swept in from all sides, I was dying. Then he relaxed his grip slightly, allowing me to start a hoarse and agonised struggle for breath.

"You still don't understand it do you? There is no room for negotiation or haggling. You've been outclassed and have nothing left to bargain with, except the speed at which your friends are going to die."

I could find no flaw in his reasoning. "I know that, and I'll do what you want. All I'm trying to say is that even if I'm a dead man, if you give me something to hope for on their behalf, I'll work faster and better. I know you've out manoeuvred me, the facts are all around me, but I can still give you something that you want."

He wouldn't lower himself to express interest by responding, but simply stared at me, silently. I took that as a sign to continue.

"Let the woman go and I'll plug that hole faster and more effectively than any engineer on this ship. Then when that's done and your own engineers can confirm that we're raising steam, you let the other two go."

"And do you seriously think that I'll ever let you go?"

"No I don't, and what's more I don't want you to. Because of the damage that I've already done to the boiler it will never work at full pressure until it's been in a shipyard. I'm willing to stake my life on the fact that I'm the only man aboard who could run that engine room without blowing the whole damn ship up." I paused, staring at him, but he made no comment – he was interested.

"My request is that I don't go ashore, I stay onboard. On a one to one basis, you might well be a better man than me, but think about what happened before you turned up. With no one to support me except some mad old woman and these two ineffectual nobodies, I managed to make mincemeat out of half your crew. Let me run the engine for you, I reckon it was probably good for about ten knots before I arrived, well I reckon I can probably give you enough steam for maybe five or six. And that's five or six knots more than anyone else could manage."

"And then?"

"Well if I'm onboard, then it would be in my interests for the ship to escape, because if the Royal Navy catch us they'll blow this thing out of the water. They'll be angry and they won't care about prisoners. I know because I was one of them, they'll kill everyone on board – me included. I've had enough of being an engine driver and I've had enough of being married to a nagging wife, it's time I went back to sea. After I get you out of here successfully you can pay me, and then I'll help you to organise your next job a bit better than this fiasco."

"I don't make deals with failures, get into the engine room and start work."

"As soon as I've seen the old woman ashore."

"Start work now or I shoot her to death slowly, in the knees, in the elbows, in the shoulder. I can make it last for hours."

He swung his gun in Gretchen's direction, and calmly pulled the trigger, the report was deafening in such a confined space. The bullet gouged a piece of timber from the decking very close to one of her feet, before ricocheting into the bulkhead behind her. The sailors around her flinched, but she didn't. Her sang froid immobility was all the more impressive in light of the fact that she must know that the next bullet was going to do her serious injury. I'd taken this about as far as it would go. I tried a change of tack.

I looked him straight in the eye, and spoke with all the earnestness I could muster. "I didn't want to say this in public, but tell the sailors to let go of me, I have something to show you."

He nodded to the men to release me. I took a step forward and held out my hand, as if to shake his. He looked wary, but nonetheless took my hand. I made the same Masonic recognition signal that he had given me on the train, but this time I accompanied it, in low and confidential tones, by what I now hoped was the correct form of words.

"On the train I was unsure of your position, and have been taught to be cautious. But I now give you greetings Atlantis, I am a friend of Adam's from Ingolstadt."

Otto Schindler, although old and frail, had been delighted to talk to me. His visitors in winter, at such an isolated house on the moors, being extremely few and far between; and on the subject of Freemasonry he had been an invaluable source. His own membership of the craft going back to his days in Prussia, and my mention of Parkinson having used the word 'Atlantis' as a Masonic password had stirred the relevant memories.

Apparently, Germany had been the heartland of a movement called the Illuminati, which Otto had described as a perversion of Freemasonry. Its tenets were supposedly visionary and mystical, but in reality it was strongly nationalistic and anti Semitic, and promoted notions of a centralised and autocratic government. They believed themselves to be above the law, and were thought to have been implicated in several plots involving assassination and blackmail

It had started in Bavaria over a hundred years ago and despite being banned in most European states it lingered on as an underground movement, usually trying to attach itself to any sympathetic strands it could find in the Masonic movement, from which it had at one time sprung. He had speculated, without any certainty, that the composer Wagner might be a fellow traveller.

According to Otto, the term Atlantis was the name of a Lodge in Bavaria, which he understood to be heavily infiltrated by Illuminati members. The mention that I had made to being 'A Friend of Adam', had been a reference to the name of the movement's founder. I hoped it would be enough to convince Parkinson of my bona fides, if only temporarily.

He seemed astonished and for an immensely long ten seconds stared hard at me, trying to read my mind through my eyes, and I truly began to wonder if my information had been correct.

Then he spoke to the two sailors who had been holding me, I didn't understand the words but I knew what he was saying. He was saying: I'm releasing him for now, but stay with him, watch him, and if he so much as coughs the wrong way – kill him.

To me he said, "I acknowledge your greeting and will do as you suggest, but be very careful about your actions – trust will flow from results." Then he beckoned me and Gretchen to follow him, and went quickly up the companion-way leading to the deck.

Less than five minutes later, the ship's longboat had left Gretchen ashore on the north quay, back where she'd started from. Before putting her in the boat I'd asked Parkinson, as one Illuminatus to another, that she be given the rifle back, saying that it was her father's gun that I had borrowed, and that a woman with a rifle clearly posed no risk to anyone but herself. She stood on the quay looking suitably forlorn and lost, apparently not knowing what to do next. No matter what happened now I had at least paid my debt to her. The steam launch was still towing us, at perhaps two knots towards the swivel bridge, the longboat was heading back to help them.

Ahead of us, under the control of the shore party, the two sides of the swivel bridge did what they were built to do. They each swivelled neatly to the side and left our way to the sea wide open.

I still had no idea where Charlie was, but must now assume him dead somewhere, thrown carelessly from the train. An unwanted thought of Ruth came to mind, and a lump to my throat. Would I ever see her again, and if not, then what would she think of my actions? She would probably remember me as no more than some sort of foolish glory hunter, desperate to win another medal, and more newspaper mentions. In truth it wasn't like that, I just sometimes seem to find myself in situations that require decisive action.

Perhaps I should never have jumped aboard in the first place, or allowed the others to follow me. But there was no reasoned argument on earth that could have persuaded me to leave Charlie a helpless captive. The fact that I turned out to have been mistaken on that point was no more than hindsight – and hindsight's never worth a damn.

In arranging freedom for three out of four of us, I had made a far better deal than the circumstances warranted, but this was still going to end badly.

Parkinson really was going to get away with this, and I was going to help him. Right up to the moment that I blew this rotten ship and all aboard to pieces – that first explosion had been only a mild introduction to the interesting things I could do with a steam engine.

DISPUTED STATURE

The Plaintiff, Mrs. Oliver, deposed that on the evening of August 8th last, she was returning home with her husband, carrying a bottle of ale. As they were passing the defendant's house she stepped on a coal cellar cover, which gave way, her leg went down the coal hole. The bottle she was carrying broke and her right hand was cut. Cross examined – George Johnson, who resided opposite , said that on August 8th last, he saw a lady fall about three yards from the coal plate in question. He saw the plate and found it fast, not out of position. A second witness, Mrs. Thornhill, said that she witnessed the fall and saw the plaintiff wrap her hand in a handkerchief. Mr. Reed – Did you say, It is good she is not stout, or she would have been worse hurt? Witness (A stout lady) – Some people get fat no matter how little they eat, and I want no insinuations (Laughter)

Mr. Reed – It is not an insinuation. I simply ask whether you made that remark.

Witness – I get fat on hard work, and I want no more of your

293

nonsense.(Laughter) I shall ask the Judge to protect me.

The Judge – Very well then. There was no reflection upon yourself.

Witness – Thank you sir.

Mr. Reed – Do you think –

Witness – I cannot say what I do not know.

Mr. Reed – Will you listen to the question?

Witness – As a lady being stout I will.

Mr. Reed – Is it possible that –

Witness – I cannot say.

Mr. Reed – Will you listen to me madam?

The Judge – Listen to what he has to say, and then answer.

Witness – Yes I will; but I don't like his insinuations about being stout (Laughter)

Mr. Reed – Do you think the plaintiff fell owing to the pavement being uneven?

Witness – I cannot say because I am stout. (Laughter)

FIFTEEN

It had been many years since Captain Corcoran had first donned naval uniform, and it was generally agreed that it suited him. There is a certain type of man that seems to be destined by nature for leadership, and he was one of them. Unlike some officers, his popularity with the men seemed to be the unsought result of him simply being himself. So there had been none of the lower deck grumbling that was occasionally heard with sudden changes from the established routine.

The circumstances were unusual, highly so, but their orders had been specific, time was of the essence - if they were to have any chance of success it would have to be done at the double. Fortunately, although it wasn't his company's normal base of operations, he had been to Whitby before, and was familiar with the town's layout. So he had no doubts about the fastest route to follow as he doubled his men down the hill towards the harbour.

Though the temperature was still not much above freezing, it was a crisp bright day, and sun was glinting off the snow covered headland and Abbey across the harbour. A good day for action he thought. In order to make clear the deadly serious nature of their mission Corcoran had drawn his sword. That, together with the sight of two columns of Royal Navy Jack Tars jogging behind him through the normally peaceful streets of this quiet seaside town, with rifles held at the port, quite literally stopped the traffic.

A few startled shoppers called out encouragement; 'Good Luck Boys', being the usual greeting. He courteously acknowledged each one with a nod of the head, but had no breath for unnecessary speech. They came along the Fish Quay, feet pounding rhythmically in step, and onto Marine Parade, it didn't matter if their target saw them coming. People emerged from shops at the sound of the booted feet, and carters pulled over at their approach to give them a clear run through. A growing group of interested bystanders followed nervously in their wake, to see exactly what sort of trouble this portended. It had been a long time since Whitby had seen the like.

The masts of the Russian naval vessel were visible even before the bridge itself. She was quite a lump of a ship, with a plume of smoke rising from her funnel, and two stylishly raked masts. She was closer to the bridge than he'd imagined, he increased his speed for the last hundred yards.

Then he spotted the cause of the trouble, there were six of them, all in dark uniforms. He didn't recognise the nationality of the uniform, it was sufficient to know that they weren't British uniforms and that they had, therefore, no right to be brandishing weapons on a British street. The presumption was that they were from the Russian warship, which was why they seemed to have taken over the bridge controls. His orders had been clear, this sort of nonsense needed to be dealt with very firmly indeed.

The men were in a defensive stance around a cast iron structure no more than four feet in height, from which protruded a large wheel on each side. He might not have realised the purpose of the machinery at first glance, had not the placing of the men made it obvious that this was the bridge control. They were pointing their rifles outwards as though expecting attack, although prior to the arrival of Corcoran and his squad, the most likely source of attack would have been from the massed flocks of seagulls wheeling noisily about the harbour and lower town.

As far as the inhabitants were concerned the bridge routinely opened from time to time to allow ship movements, and then closed again, it was a normal part of daily life. Only the presence of the armed shore party made today in any way unusual.

On almost any other day of the year they could simply have given the bridge man a half sovereign to ensure the bridge opened at their approach; there would have been little or no evidence of wrongdoing and their purpose would have been adequately served. Unfortunately, the presence of the Royal Navy meant that today was not going to be one of those days. The only thing achieved by the armed men was the confirmation that the Russian ship's movements were anything but routine, and looked more like an escape than a normal departure. All this was clear to Corcoran as he reached the bridge approach.

"Rackstraw take ten men and cover the approach from the inner harbour, be ready to fire on my command."

Then turning to the, by now quite sizeable, group of interested onlookers who had come to see the fun, Corcoran waved his sword in the air to get their attention and called out. "I'm afraid you people are going to have to stand well back, it looks as if there's going to be gunfire. That's right move well back there."

At the mention of gunfire the crowd began to edge backwards, to the very slight cover afforded by shop doorways and peering round street corners. The rest of the ratings deployed to cover the approach from Bridge Street, some lying prone, some behind lamp posts and some behind a commandeered fishmonger's cart.

The actual swivel bridge itself was only the central part of a handsome stone construction carrying a road across the harbour. The men around the bridge control were now isolated in the middle of this roadway, forty yards from the shore line, with the open section of the bridge behind them and no sort of cover in front of them. It was an extremely exposed position, a fact which Corcoran's deployment had now made clear.

Their instructions had been to clear civilians out of the way and take possession of the controls, no possibility of opposition had ever been mentioned, the men's apprehension was now clear in their every movement. It had been seen when they arrived in Whitby that the gap between the bridge piers was only a little wider than the ship itself, and the intention had been that, having ensured the way was clear for departure, they would jump down on to the ship's deck as it passed through.

Even the fact, they had already observed, that there was some sort of problem with the ship's engine hadn't seriously worried them. It was a delaying factor certainly, but now that there were two launches towing her she would still be through the gap in five or ten minutes. After which, assuming that the engine could be repaired or sails hoisted, there would be nothing to keep her from the open sea. Captain Corcoran's unscripted arrival had changed all that. Behind them, the steam launch hauling one line, and the longboat hauling another, had passed through the opening and the bow sprit of the ship was slowly moving into the gap.

Corcoran stepped forward onto the open stretch of roadway leading to the centre of the bridge, completely unprotected and without cover – regardless of personal safety and in the finest traditions of the service. He carried no gun, simply a drawn sword and immense force of character. "You are completely surrounded and outnumbered, you will surrender now or my men will open fire."

The six men had retreated to the edge of the chasm, through which their ship was now beginning to pass, and could be seen casting worried glances both at Corcoran's line of armed sailors and at the approaching ship. It seemed a close run thing, which of these two conflicting forces frightened them the most. The pressure was too much and their group coherence was breaking down, two of them had now lowered their rifles and were arguing with the others, accompanied by gestures to the impassive line of naval ratings. Some of the others responded angrily, with counter gestures back to the ship. As the bows moved steadily between the bridge piers behind them, the dispute between the men became even more heated.

One of the Russian sailor raised his rifle and pointed it directly at Corcoran, shouting something as he did so. Corcoran's response to the threat was brief and to the point. "Don't be such a bloody fool."

But the man was jittery, nervous and unresponsive to reason, he tensed himself to fire, then the harsh crack of a gunshot startled the seagulls. A brief red mist of blood spray could be seen around his head, the rifle dropped from his dead hands and half a second later he followed it to the ground. The world came to an amazed standstill and mouths dropped open in surprise. Corcoran turned, slowly and majestically, to look behind him, his eyes scanning both his own men and the assembled crowd beyond them.

"Who fired that shot?" He demanded. Puzzled heads were shaken, there was a complete and utter graveyard silence, only an imbecile would have confessed. He didn't bother asking a second time but turned back to the remaining five sailors.

"Put down your guns immediately." He called, in such commanding tones that disobedience was never a realistic option. Even if they didn't understand his words, they knew that continuing to hold their guns was a bad idea. The five remaining rifles were quietly laid on the ground.

Then the Maxim gun started firing again, and a lashing hail of bullets sent jagged flakes flying from the stone edge of the bridge pier. Then it climbed slightly to reach the small group of men standing close to the edge. Corcoran and two of the foreign sailors had been quick witted enough to drop, before the gunner corrected his aim, and the storm of lead swept harmlessly over them. The other three were cut down like corn before a newly sharpened scythe.

However, because the deck of the slowly advancing ship was below the level of the roadway, the further it moved into the bridge opening the less effective the machine gun became, hemmed in on both sides by solid stone walls.

Still thinking faster than anyone else, Corcoran scrambled backwards, away from the edge and ran, half crouching, back to the cast iron bridge control wheel. He turned and bellowed at the surviving Russian sailors to come and help him. Unused to the controls it took some moments to determine the correct direction of movement, but between them they managed to bring the machinery back to life.

The first of the two raked masts had already passed through the gap, and the ship's tall yellow funnel was moving past the end of the roadway when the two swivelling sides of the bridge jerked back into life and began to swing shut. There was an explosion of angry shouting from the ship. Then the top of a ladder appeared beside the swinging section of bridge, it was unsteady and constantly had to be pushed back into an upright position, but it was enough for at least one foolhardy man to chance his life.

His head came into view, he was clasping desperately onto the side of the ladder with one hand, and holding a revolver in the other. Before anyone could stop him, he fired a shot at the knot of men by the bridge control, it hit one of his own men, who fell to the ground shouting in pain. He lined up for another shot but never managed to take it, for once again the mystery shooter, somewhere on shore, put a bullet neatly through his head. It must have been dispiriting for the men trying to hold the ladder steady on a moving deck to have his dead body drop on top of them, and the ladder fell away to one side.

The two steel sections of the bridge continued their progress, and then with a satisfying thud they met in the middle, gave a brief tremor and settled slightly into their locked position. Seconds later the after mast met the steelwork, the bridge shuddered and a grinding noise could be heard from somewhere. The mast shook throughout its length and swung slightly to one side, some of the rigging parted with sharp twangs, but that was all. The bridge held and the mast stayed upright, Corcoran heaved a huge sigh of relief.

Had the ship been moving much faster, the after mast would have carried away, then though damaged, she would have been free to go. But now she was stuck, and had just been given an effective demonstration of what happened to any crew member foolish enough to offer resistance.

He looked around once more, hoping for some clue as to the gunman, but there was no likely candidate in sight. He shrugged slightly and strode forward to arrange for the ship's formal surrender. He wasn't entirely sure what the arrangements were for prize money when it came to capturing an enemy vessel with a swing bridge, but there would probably be some arcane precedent somewhere.

*****

The boiler was too hot to work on safely, but in order to release the last two captives, even if I didn't think much of one of them, it was worth making an effort. I was lying on top of the boiler on a couple of wooden boards, and wearing thick leather gloves, even so the temperature was close to disabling me. The two men assigned to guard me had stayed on the steel platform at the top of the ladder, the same place

302

from which Gretchen had caused the damage in the first place.

The two engineers I'd seen earlier had survived the escaping steam with no more than an nasty fright and a change of underwear, and were now helping with the repairs. Fortunately they hadn't realised that I'd been responsible for the original damage, and seemed to assume it been caused by their own men shooting through the skylight. I had managed to insert a temporary patch and was tightening the large bolt, to squash the steam packing into place, when I heard the Maxim gun. I ignored it, whatever they were shooting at couldn't be helped by anything I did. This was going to be a rough and ready business, there wasn't any way that I could replace the safety valve, the best that could be done in the circumstances was going to be like a cast on a broken leg. It wouldn't hold at anything like full pressure, but I was confident that I could get them moving again.

There were a series of bumps and nudges as we made our way between the bridge piers, moving so slowly meant that we didn't have proper steerage way and were drifting this way and that on the end of the tow lines. Then suddenly there was a furious outburst of loud outrage on deck, clearly audible through the broken skylight, and then two or three more shots.

The two sailors guarding me had left, unlike me, they could understand the shouting from on deck and would have realised the exact nature of the emergency. They obviously thought it more important than me. I tried to continue working, but then there was a heavy and very solid collision. The whole vessel shook for a moment before coming to rest. I had managed to hang on to my perch on top of the boiler, but it was time to abandon the repairs and find out what was happening, for all I knew we could be sinking.

On deck was a scene of chaos, the closed bridge holding us firmly in place like a butterfly pinned to a board, whoever thought of that was a genius, and whoever managed to execute it deserved the freedom of the town.

Scroop was standing midships, near the funnel, he was shouting at a group of sailors and waving a pistol at them in a threatening manner. I couldn't understand the language, but it was clearly some kind of unpopular instruction. Whatever order he was trying give them, they were ignoring it. It looked as if they had decided the game was up, the ship was completely without power and was held firm in the bridge, one could see their point.

They had turned and were walking away from him when he snapped. He fired his first shot in the air, to attract their attention. It worked, they stopped and looked at him, so he levelled the pistol at them and repeated his instruction. The trouble was their urge to surrender was stronger than his force of character, one of the sailors produced a gun of his own and shot Scroop straight in the stomach.

The force of the shot sent him staggering backwards into the funnel, his own gun dropping from his shocked hand. I saw the flicker of material, where the bullet had penetrated the front of his shirt. And I heard a metallic snick, as one piece of metal collided violently with another. But he didn't fall over, and he should have done. I reckoned he'd got the Captain's silver stuffed up his jumper, he'd probably been on the lookout for some sort of consolation prize.

From the looks of him, the worst damage had been caused by his head hitting the funnel. That should have rung alarm bells, it's usually the bullet that kills you – not the funnel. I can only blame the slowness of my thought process on the strain of events, in retrospect it's astonishing that it took me so long to join all the dots together.

At the time it was enough for me to know that he was both disarmed and dazed, and that an opportunity for dispensing some rough justice had just presented itself. There was an open stretch of rail, where the shore gangway had been attached; in their haste to leave harbour it hadn't been closed off. I walked over and leaned out, pointing down along the side of the ship. "I'm getting off here." I called back to him, pointing overboard at nothing in particular. He came to look - it's irresistible when someone points to something out of your line of sight, you have to go and take a look.

As he came within grabbing distance I did just that, grabbing his lapels to swing him round and reverse our positions. I was now stood inboard and he was standing with his back to the opening in the rail. I smiled at him, he was still dazed, and still wondering what I'd seen over the side.

"It isn't simply that you're a murderous little shit," I said, in friendly tones, "There's also the fact that I never liked your name. It was insulting that you couldn't even take the trouble to think up a proper disguise." With that I put the flat of my hand to his chest and pushed. Whatever stolen property he was carrying should ensure that he went straight down and stayed there.

The nature of events finally broke through his state of shock and he cried out in panic. But by that time he'd passed the point of no return and Isaac Newton had taken over. In the very second that he fell away from me, his eyes open wide like two saucers, his arms flailing out to each side, reality finally dawned in my brain as well as his.

The solid substance that I'd felt beneath his shirt, when I just pushed him, the item that had stopped a bullet, I knew what it was.

My hand had encountered at least two large ingots of metal, but not any old metal. He'd been carrying gold, that's what this whole sorry saga was all about. The train hadn't been carrying cash or Bearer Bonds, the entire Crown Prince and Antonescu performance was little more than a distraction. We'd been hauling bullion, the ultimate form of transportable currency. That was what everyone had been chasing, and Scroop's last act on earth had been to pick up a bar or two for luck – some luck. All this ran through my mind in the time it took him to reach the river.

I can never remember if gold is heavier than lead, or is it the other way round? It doesn't really matter very much, the salient point is that you can't swim with gold bars sewn into your clothing, or lead bars either, if it comes to that.

I leaned on the rail staring down at the site of his entry into the freezing brown water, and the diminishing circle of bubbles. What a sinking feeling. Always too hasty, that's my trouble, push first and ask questions later. I took my bearings from the corner of the bridge. It seemed likely that I might want to return to this spot with a grappling iron sometime in the near future.

I set off along the deck to find Pedro and the mad Major. They'd been imprisoned, along with the last two survivors of their original security team, the two that Ruth and I had managed to injure in the fight in the snow. I had warned Pedro of my certainty that these two had to be the original plotters that we had overheard at the very start of the trip. He had taken what I considered to be very casual view of this, saying only that they would be dealt with when they returned to Rumania. Still, just as long as they were kept away from me and mine, then I suppose that was alright with me.

Pedro and the Major had already been released before I got to them, so preventing me from claiming the responsibility for their freedom. They also now knew about the gold, courtesy of crew members who, seeing the ship held fast and their officers dead, had decided to change sides. They rushed to tell me of the cargo stowed below deck. As usual I was unable to resist being blasé and showing off.

"Oh, the gold, yes I know all about the gold. It was hidden on the train. Hadn't you realised?"

Despite questioning, none of the crew had any idea where Parkinson was, and it seemed that he must have escaped ashore. I left Pedro and Antonescu to take charge of the ship and its turncoat crew, having no doubt that they could cope, and hastened to follow him. Assured by two naval ratings at the top that it was safe to do so, and using a set of steel rungs set into the stone work, I climbed up onto the bridge, where I emerged to be met by Gretchen.

On seeing me emerge at the top of the ladder, she didn't say a word, but just ran over and threw her arms around me. The proceedings took me by surprise, but I'm a quick learner and hugged her

307

back. This was quite a change from the argumentative harridan who'd kept me standing in a blizzard while she shouted at me through a locked door.

But then I realised that she was sobbing, it turned out that it was less a case of her wanting to hug me in particular, than simply needing to hug somebody, anybody, who'd been there and might understand.

"You do know that we had no choice. You told me yourself that you can't simply be an onlooker to evil being done. You had a moral duty, not only to act, but to do so effectively."

"I know, I know."

"If you're lucky you could go through your whole life and never find yourself in this position, most people never do. Your luck ran out today and you had to do some unimaginable and terrible things. But we couldn't have come through without you."

As a crass and insensitive railwayman I might not have fully shared her finer feelings, but I knew all the right words

She nodded against my shoulder. Then she moved back a little to dry her eyes.

"But you didn't have to call me a mad old woman did you?"

"I'm sorry, but I only said it to downplay your importance and to encourage them to release you. If they'd realised just how successful you'd been - they'd have shot you."

Ruth limped up to join us with Magda holding one arm to steady her. Apparently after Gretchen and I had left on our borrowed horses, Stan had at last begun to make some sort of recovery. So with Ruth hobbling and Stan convalescent, Magda had managed to obtain the services of a two horse carriage, and they had been able to make their way through the snow and into town.

However, their celebrations were short lived, when I pointed out that I still had no idea where Charlie was, and that Parkinson had escaped. Ruth then insisted on taking us over to meet the officer in charge of the naval rescue party, whose firm action had closed the bridge and saved the day.

I was surprised by Ruth's degree of familiarity with the naval officer, and also somewhat surprised by his uniform, which to my practised eye looked slightly unorthodox. Whilst it's true that a certain amount of individuality is permitted on the quarterdeck, his tailor seemed to have been rather liberal with the gold braid, and there were more buttons than might have been anticipated.

He and Ruth had kissed, fulsomely, and to an extent that I considered exceeded any expression of gratitude. She repeatedly called him Rutland darling, the Rutland I could accept as his Christian name, but the darling could be seen by some as a step too far, and rather theatrical. I pushed forward to introduce myself and Gretchen, and to make my marital status clear.

"I'm Fowler, the engine driver, Ruth's husband. I'd like to thank you for your intervention, it was most timely. And this is Gretchen Schindler, without who's shooting we would have been overwhelmed at a very early stage."

Gretchen admitted that she had been the mystery shooter who had saved Captain Corcoran's life, when he was being threatened on the bridge. She had also fired the second shot which had ended further attempts to climb up from the ship's deck.

Apparently, after having been put back onto the north quay, she had seen the situation with the Royal Navy attempting to regain control of the bridge, and the danger threatening Corcoran. Astonished by the unwillingness of Corcoran's own men to fire in his defence, she had done so herself. She modestly brushed aside Corcoran's thanks, saying they had been easy shots, scarcely more than 400 yards. And this was the person that I had thought might be unwilling to pull the trigger, I hadn't appreciated just how active she'd been.

Corcoran took this information as an excuse to kiss her as well, things had clearly changed in the Royal Navy since my day. I thought it time to return his mind to his duties.

"Tell me Captain, how did you find out about our circumstances?"

"Find out my dear? Well I'd hardly say I found out. This brazen little trollop," He waved vaguely at Ruth, "Cancelled our matinee at five minute's notice, without so much as a by your leave. The she started giving me orders. I said to her, we've got a theatre full of people, all of whom have paid good money. And d'you know what she said? She said I should ring the fire alarm and throw them out, as it would be cheaper than giving them their money back." Then they both laughed.

To my growing astonishment, he continued the tale of how his day had been *totally devastated* by this turn of events. I had just seen this man in action, and he'd been brilliant - brilliant and extremely brave, but he was no more a genuine naval officer then Clarence was a Clairvoyant Pig. I put a hand out, to physically interrupt his flow of anecdote.

"What are you?"

"Well I have a wide and versatile range, but a lyric baritone normally, and an absolutely commanding presence on any stage."

"You're an actor?"

"Some have been kind enough to say so."

Then as we looked at each other, I saw a smile begin to spread across his face.

"Oh Good Lord, you actually thought that I was Captain Corcoran – oh you sweet dear boy, you've quite made my day. Hasn't he Ruthie?"

Then the two of them burst out laughing again, or to be more precise cackling, as I was still shuddering at the 'Ruthie'.

"I'm sorry to disappoint a genuine naval gentleman like yourself, but you are addressing Mr. Rutland Barrington, currently appearing in Gilbert and Sullivan's HMS Pinafore at the West Cliff Saloon Theatre, and these gentlemen are the chorus." He made a sweeping gesture, sufficient to encompass his assembled men.

"I hardly think one could go so far as to describe Ralph Rackstraw or Dick Deadeye as *chorus*." Said one of the assembled group, presumably either Ralph or Dick.

"More like Rude Mechanicals." Came a voice from the back.

"Well never mind all that. The fact is that I received a telephone call from your enchanting wife, explaining the circumstances, and so naturally we all hurried down here. The one thing she quite forgot to mention was that we'd be meeting people with real guns, that came as a very nasty surprise I can tell you."

"And *your* guns?" I queried.

"Props dear boy, stage props every one of them."

In the background the cast members were getting into their stride with an impromptu rendition of 'We Sail the Ocean Blue'. I've always liked that particular number and, were it not for the worry about Charlie, might have found myself joining in.

I looked at Ruth, despite the tragedy of Charlie's disappearance, I couldn't ignore my pride in her actions. "You organised all this by telephone from that old gentleman's house?"

"As soon as I saw the advertisement in the local paper, and saw that it was Rutland's company, it seemed like a good idea, and with my ankle strapped up there wasn't a lot else I could do. Besides Rutland and I are old friends."

I went over and kissed her, my pride in her resourcefulness mixed with a knowledge of the probable tragedy.

"You realise what it means if Charlie's not on the train and he's not on the ship, it means that I was too late. The only thing left is to organise search parties, but where do we start, he could be anywhere?"

We were interrupted by a broad, "Excuse me." From a man in a police sergeant's uniform. There was a danger of me being confused by appearances, I looked at Ruth. "Is he another one of yours?" She shook her head.

"Then you must be Sergeant Pickles, good afternoon."

Pickles was a conscientious officer, but not bright, an unfortunate combination in circumstances of limited time. After repeated misunderstandings and a certain amount of ponderous note taking, I interrupted him to explain that nothing further was going to be done until we had found Charlie. My hope was that if he had been hiding somewhere on the train when it finally arrived in Whitby, then after everyone else had left, he might have wandered off on his own. He could be roaming the streets of Whitby, alone and frightened, as we stood talking.

Despite the chill of the air, the cast of HMS Pinafore were still game for making a sweep of the town, and having been given a description of his appearance and clothing, they split into smaller groups and made their way variously into town and along the quaysides.

Meanwhile,
  the newspapers reported . . .

TO THE RED HAIRED gentleman who approached the shy ingénue on the top deck of the Charing Cross omnibus last Saturday afternoon. I now regret my intemperate response, should you wish to renew your attention you may not meet the same reply as last time. Box 656

FRIENDSHIP SOUGHT, Gentleman of refined taste and independent means, residing N. London seeks friendship of genteel lady. Your own means would be subject to scrutiny of my man of business. An interest in travel, literature and ferreting would be to your advantage. Reply in strictest confidence Box 141

SIXTEEN

When questioned, the remaining crew of the supposed Russian naval vessel, turned out to be mainly Bulgarians, and their ship was indeed an ex Ottoman fleet gunboat. None of them knew how it had been acquired, but it couldn't have been legitimately. They had been recruited in Bulgaria, and then taken to meet the ship at a small port in northern Greece. The Captain, now amongst the dead, had taken his orders from Parkinson, a man they simply referred to as Number One. It seemed that both Parkinson and Scroop had also been Bulgarian, though their English accents had been so good they must have lived and worked in England for some years.

As a final favour from Rutland Barrington, before he finished his afternoon's performance as Captain Corcoran, I asked him to speak to the Harbour Master and use his naval authority to arrange for the ship to be towed back to the North Quay, next to the train. I hadn't finished with it yet

Stan was still feeling frail and bruised, but had finally recovered his mental faculties, although anything he could tell us about Parkinson had now been overtaken by events. I was simply grateful to have him back. Our normal relationship included close friendship and a strong reliance on each other's professionalism, but never any overt display of emotion. I was rather surprised to realise just how affected I'd been by the injuries he'd suffered, and his proximity to death He did at least clear up the mystery of the missing policemen in the detached section of the train.

It seems that there had never been as many of them as was claimed in the first place, Parkinson had six locally hired thugs to help out with the donkey work, and had concealed these in the unused dining car. The deplorably low quality of his hired help having been demonstrated by their drunkenness. His ploy in detaching the last four coaches had been just one more strand in his design to make Antonescu look bad, no one would ever think to accuse Parkinson of getting rid of his own men.

A significant element of his plan had been dependant on me running true to form and reacting against Antonescu. It seemed that the Major had a track record not dissimilar to my own, and could generally be relied on to charge head first through any brick wall that stood in his way. Parkinson's plan had been one of simple genius, he had set the two of us against each other like a pair of attack dogs, and then sat back as the Major and I had chased one another round in circles, whilst nobody gave pompous old Parkinson a second glance.

It was an uncomfortable feeling to have had my behaviour predicted quite so accurately, and used quite so effectively, and all without me suspecting anything. I should get a medal for stupidity.

*****

I had been satisfied, before pushing him overboard, that Scroop genuinely knew nothing of

318

Charlie's whereabouts, but if he didn't then somebody else did, and I reckoned that had to be Parkinson. Parkinson's research had obviously uncovered the fact of my Masonic membership, it was hardly a secret. If, on the strength of that slim fact, he had been prepared to try his Illuminati password on me, then who else might he try it on?

He was on the loose in Whitby; his ship had been captured, his men had deserted, most of the roads were impassable and the railways were at a standstill. If the law caught up with him he would surely dance his way to glory at the end of a rope. He was at his wits end and desperate, even if his actions were illogical, who else might he approach for help? The answer might well be the local Lodge.

Pickles was undeniably slow, but at least he knew his own patch. He was able to tell me not only who was the secretary of the Lodge, but also that he lived only a few minute's walk away. Ruth and I followed him up the hill, I was beginning to get the picture round here, as soon as you left the harbour, everything in Whitby was uphill.

Donald Buckley, was a short and friendly man, and thankfully a lot quicker witted than the Sergeant. He welcomed us in and his wife, a homely body called Doreen, offered to make us a cup of tea. Pickles seemed inclined to accept and would have probably held out for cake, but I declined for all of us, this wasn't a social call.

"Oh what a pity, you've only just missed him. A strange man, he said that he was a Mason, but kept wanting to talk about Atlantis, as if I had any interest in some fairy tale by a dead Greek. He wouldn't have any tea either. And then it was most odd, he began to ask if we were illuminated. So I told him that the

Masonic Hall had electric light, it was installed last year by Brother Entwhistle, but he didn't seem interested."

And then upon further enquiry, he responded. "No, no, he never did say where he was going next. Surely his superiors in the police service would know that." Donald was a pleasant enough fellow and more than ready to chat with a visiting brother, but this was hardly the ideal moment for me. I made our excuses and left.

It would have been better had we caught him, but still his misdirected stumbling around was quite reassuring. It was clear, both from my own knowledge and Otto Schindler's information, that the Illuminati movement had never made any progress in Britain, we're not a conspiratorial society. Yet here was Parkinson wandering the streets of Whitby, frantically trying to tap into some non-existent secret network. It made him seem a little more vulnerable, I could already see him clutching the spikes around the dock at the Old Bailey as the judge donned his black cap.

Despite that, we still arrived back at the quay, disconsolate and unsure of our next move. Ruth and I had given this our best shot, but still come up with nothing. There had to be another angle, another way into the puzzle. But then the question answered itself.

A miniature tornado collided with my legs, with cries of 'Uncle, Uncle'. I sank to my knees, partly to hug him and partly in sheer relief. He had been cleaned up since the last time I saw him, and was magnificently unconcerned about his recent ordeal, instead he wanted to show me a toy train he was holding. Ruth came over, with tears in her eyes, but trying to control the emotion for Charlie's sake, and crouched down beside us.

"It's just like yours, but there's no Uncle Puff Puff driving it, so I'm going to do the driving." He talked nineteen to the dozen, about an icecream he'd just had, and throwing bread to the seagulls and all manner of a three and a half year old's delights. I rocked back on my heels, still holding him, but only half listening. What I wanted to know was; where had he just come from, and where had he been?

Ruth took over hugging and listening duties as I stood up to look around, a couple of respectable looking middle aged men were the only candidates. They met my enquiring glance with smiles, and stepped over. The taller of the two extended his hand.

"Good afternoon Mr. Fowler, my name is Holmes, Sherlock Holmes, and this is my companion Doctor Watson. I'm pleased to be able to assure you that young Charlie, apart from some minor bruising, is physically unharmed by his ordeal, and clearly delighted to see you again."

Ruth stood up, bristling. "You mean to say that while we've been tearing our hair out, desperately looking for a lost child, you had him all along and decided to keep quiet about it?"

Holmes made no answer, but looked surprised at our lack of gratitude. Ruth took his silence as a further provocation.

"So you've been playing trains and eating ice cream with my nephew, whilst we thought he was dead in a ditch - is that what you've been doing?" She began to jab an accusatory finger at his bony chest. "We were suffering the agonies of the damned and you were eating ice cream, how dare you treat us in this way – you . . . you fictional fraud."

Holmes had now taken an understandable step backwards.

"Madam, I can understand your emotions, but we had to ensure the child's safety. We had no way of knowing the strength of the opposition facing us, an entire ship's company of Royal Naval personnel had just made a surprise entrance. And if our intelligence on this town had omitted to mention them, then what else might have been omitted from the report? We were unwilling to gamble with a child's life."

That was a good answer, the man could think on his feet; his companion, the supposed Doctor Watson, was nodding his head in vigorous agreement. Ruth was still frowning, the pain was too fresh. Holmes thought it best to give more detail.

"You have to understand that our entire reason for being on the train was to provide en route supervision of a very valuable cargo."

I interrupted him. "We know about the gold." He looked surprised but continued.

"Well then you can appreciate our motives in disguising ourselves as the replacement Crown Prince and his secretary. Then, using expert makeup and a tincture of the South American Xinuolha tree bark, we feigned death for long enough to be convincing. Perhaps you've read my recent monograph on self administered forms of temporary suspended animation."

Ruth snorted, in exasperation. He wisely hurried on.

"Knowing of your husband's reputation, we were content to leave the protection of the genuine Crown Prince in his hands. Our principal task was to foil any attempt to steal the gold."

322

"But you failed miserably to do that," I said, "The gold was transferred to the ship without you raising a hand to stop it. It was left to Gretchen Schindler and me to stop that, along with the assembled cast of HMS Pinafore, who seem to have comprehensively pulled the wool over your eyes."

"On the contrary, we had been faced with a most serious dilemma whilst lying there, apparently dead. The two men calling themselves Parkinson and Scroop, imagining themselves to be unheard, used that carriage to discuss what they were going to do with their prisoners; your fireman and the boy Charlie. Their conclusion was that as they were of no further use it would be amusing to throw them both from the back of our train, to be run over by your own train, immediately behind us."

"And so." Demanded Ruth, by now half convinced.

"And so, after your husband had been frustrated in his bold attempt to rescue Charlie, we took a chance and ventured into the corridor, where we snatched the boy and took him back to the sleeping car with us. In the confusion it was assumed that your husband must have somehow succeeded in his removal."

"Our only regret," said Doctor Watson, now joining in, "Was that there was nothing we could do for your friend Stan."

"Which is why," continued Holmes, "That on arrival in Whitby, when they were planning to lift the carriage floor boards to reach the gold, we decided it was time to remove ourselves from the scene – taking Charlie with us."

"So you abandoned the gold altogether?"

"I'm afraid we had no choice, we couldn't safeguard the treasure without endangering Charlie, and I took a view that the Bank of England has probably got enough gold to be going on with. Then when the sailors appeared and the machine gun started firing, although Charlie was keen to watch, our only sensible move was to . . . ."

Ruth cut him short by hugging him, at this rate she would have hugged every male party on the quay by midnight. I had no idea if his story was true, but had to admit that it was a good one. I'd have been proud to produce a yarn like that myself, especially at such short notice. Charlie was still beside me, holding my hand, from the look on his face he thought this sort of stuff was better than the circus.

*****

Captain Corcoran, or Rutland to his friends, came back from giving the Harbour Master instructions to move the trapped ship and to bid us farewell, the evening performance was due to start shortly and he still had to gather his wandering chorus. I shook his hand and gave him my warmest thanks, telling him to wring every drop of publicity he could from the event. He insisted on treating Ruth, or should I say 'Ruthie', to another hug and an extensive battery of kisses before finally leaving us.

"If it hadn't been for the fact that he's so very clearly . . . well how shall we say? I'd have punched him for the way his hands were roaming."

"Oh don't be so silly, it's just his manner, and anyway he isn't."

"Isn't he?"

"No – anything but, he must have had half the girls in the cast, and if the scenery's shaking in Act Two, it's Rutland and some soubrette giving it what for behind the scenes. He'd be up my drawers faster than a ferret up a drainpipe if I let him. I must introduce you to Ellen, his wife, she's a lovely woman. She understands how things are – what happens on tour, stays on tour, it's just the way the theatre works."

A stray thought occurred to me. "Will Rutland have had your sister?"

"I would think so, everyone else has."

Not for the first time, I was relieved to be on the railways where things were more predictable.

Ruth and I were by now thoroughly exhausted, and starving, it had been a long time since breakfast and nobody had been buying us ice cream. We abandoned all our various responsibilities and wearily went into the Rope and Anchor, taking Charlie with us.

The barman seeing us with a small child, pointed his finger. "You can't bring't bairn in 'ere."

While I was still trying to work out what he'd said, Ruth had stopped in her tracks and swung to face him. "Oh no?" She said, and then simply carried on to the table by the fire, dragging Charlie unstoppably with her. The woman behind the bar, who was probably the man's wife, could be heard saying, "They're with that lot from't quay."

This was enough to resolve matters, and he came over to take our orders, in preference to finding himself shot or thrown in the river. Holmes and Watson, probably now at a loose end, had followed us in. I could well imagine they were a bit peckish, having been dead for most of the last twenty four hours.

As Charlie played with his train and the rest of us worked our way through bowls of oxtail soup and lumps of bread, Holmes gave us the benefit of his experience.

"From even a cursory examination of him, I can state with confidence that the man Parkinson was of Balkan origin, although he had recently been living in Germany, and he is also a Freemason. This would lead me to suspect that he may have confederates in the Whitby Masonic hierarchy. As soon as we have finished here, Watson and I shall search out the people involved locally and question them."

He returned to his soup. Ruth and I put down our spoons and looked at each other across the table for a long moment, both of us were wondering; should we tell him? I decided to break the habit of a lifetime and not be petty.

"He's Bulgarian in origin, not exactly Balkan, but you weren't far out. And yes, he has been recently in Germany, in Bavaria to be precise, where he was a member of an Illuminati influenced Masonic Lodge called Atlantis. And no, he doesn't have any confederates in the local Masonic hierarchy."

"How on earth can you know that?"

"Because, unlike yours, my examination of him was more than cursory, and I've already spoken to the local hierarchy, he's called Donald, and he'd sent our man away with a Masonic flea in his ear before I got there."

There was a suspicion that Doctor Watson was suppressing a smirk. I generally don't like people who smirk, but on this occasion I was prepared to make an exception. But Holmes wasn't letting go of this particular bone just yet.

"I mean how did you make contact with the local Masonic hierarchy?"

"I asked Pickles."

"You consulted pickles?"

"No not pickles – Pickles – Sergeant Pickles, Wilfred, he's the fat man in the blue uniform and the pointed helmet."

"How do you propose to track this man further?"

"I don't, I couldn't care less about him, Parkinson can go to hell in a hat box for all I care." I leaned over and picked Charlie up, to sit him on my knee. "I've got Ruth, Charlie and Stan back, all I need now is my engine. I even managed to save Pedro from a premature death. I'm a happy man."

"Pedro?"

"Oh I'm sorry, that's Crown Prince Ferdinand."

"Whom you call Pedro?"

I sighed wearily. "It's a long story."

Before we could engage in deeper conversation on this subject, there was a noise from across the bar. The two Schindler sisters, Pedro and an almost revived Stan had found us.

Pedro looked around him, like a child in a toy shop. "A real English pub, I've heard so much about these, but I've never been in one before."

"And neither have my sister nor I. "Magda said firmly, although after what Gretchen had spent her afternoon doing, I thought the pub was pretty small beer.

"After I'm married next month, I'll never have this chance again. Could someone buy me a pint of beer please, I don't have any money."

"Don't talk rubbish, you've got a ship load of gold bars out there." Hissed Ruth, leaning across the table.

"A ship load of gold bars - and Parkinson still on the loose." I couldn't resist pointing out. Acknowledging that the man still dogged our footsteps, whether I wished to admit it or not.

Holmes directed his gaze at me. "I would not presume to advise you in these matters Mr. Fowler, but for as long as Parkinson remains unaccounted for, your own, and the lives of those around you are in danger." I felt deflated, but reluctantly had to admit that he had a point, one that I had been trying to ignore.

I turned to Pedro. "Who's on guard, just Antonescu and his two men?"

"No, I wouldn't have left them alone, Sergeant Pickles and his young constable are there with them, I think it's secure."

But I shook my head. "Not with that rat still prowling round."

The barman came over to take the newcomer's orders, only to be told that apart from Pedro, and his pint of beer, the other three were devout Methodists and wouldn't touch anything he had in the house. As a method of currying favour with a publican this routine had its drawbacks. Unsurprisingly, we soon found ourselves back on the street, the winter light fading rapidly, and the temperature dropping.

Having been assisted by two steam launches produced by the Harbour master, the ship was now once more tied up against the North Quay. The two of Antonescu's men, who had been killed there, had already been taken away by the local undertaker. The bodies onboard the ship had been gathered on deck under a sheet of canvas, tomorrow would be soon enough for someone to attend to their needs. For tonight it was decided that we would spend the night in the newly vacated officer's cabins, if nothing else it would increase the level of security.

As we walked back along the quay, Stan and I caught up with our respective doings. If we organised things properly, tomorrow could see Ruth and me back in our own bed in Clerkenwell, and Stan back with Aggie. A consummation to be devoutly wished.

Meanwhile,
     the newspapers reported . . .

ERRANT PRIEST

Father O'Shaughnessy denied the charge of begging, claiming that he was collecting on behalf of the Sisters of the Holy Cross, to whom all his receipts were paid. When asked for details of the address or bank account to which such payments were made, he said that he had lost the piece of paper upon which this was written. The prosecutor, Mr. A. Dimmock, then asked to which diocese Father O'Shaughnessy was attached, he replied Cork. Mr. Dimmock then asked for the name of the Bishop of Cork. Father O'Shaughnessy replied that this had slipped his mind.

Mr. Dimmock then informed the court that his clerk had spoken to Father O'Brien at Holy Innocents who stated that he had never heard of the Sisters of the Holy Cross. The defendant replied that this was because they were very rarely seen out in daylight, as they followed the biblical injunction to do good by stealth. (Much laughter)

The Judge – It had been my intention to fine you £3. but in view of that last contribution to the seasonal spirit I shall be pleased to settle for £2.

331

SEVENTEEN

The landlord of the Rope and Anchor, when not exhibiting displeasure at our presence, had prophesied that the morning would bring more snow. On the grounds that I didn't care for the man, I had ignored him. I shouldn't have. A fresh wave of snow had now made its leisurely way across the North Sea and settled across the Yorkshire coast, or least that part of it visible to me, like a heavy blanket. This new downfall once again covered all those stretches of road and footpath that had been so painstakingly cleared yesterday.

Leaving everyone at work: the ladies to put our remaining carriages to rights, Stan to prepare the engine, and Holmes in charge of moving the gold back from the ship to the train, I made my way with Pickles up to the police station. There had been a clear, and so far unfulfilled, requirement on me to have reported these events and our subsequent whereabouts to London yesterday.

But I had been unwilling to make that report, somewhere amongst the people directing this operation was an informant. It wasn't likely to be Dolan, my general manager at King's Cross, his full cooperation was already guaranteed, there would have been no need for him to know. And anyway, although I'm not saying that the man was stupid, because that would be unfair, I was quite sure that he lacked the guile to conceal something of this magnitude.

That left Lt. Colonel the Rt. Hon. H.K. St. Aubyn-Jollie, Equerry to H.R.H. the Prince of Wales. If I had distrusted Scroop's obviously invented name, how had I ever managed to swallow that one. So if Dolan wasn't the problem and neither was Bertie, where did that leave Jollie.

I lacked the evidence to hang the man, but felt there was a question mark over the background to this whole operation. Bertie was their front man, Antonescu and I were their fall guys, and Jollie? The failure of this ambitious piece of highway robbery would hardly deter the corrupt officials responsible from trying some other stunt at some other time. The fact of the matter remained that whether Jollie was involved or not, that information was unlikely to be shared with Fowler the engine driver, and that suited me just fine. Sherlock Holmes was the man for this sort of nonsense.

I'd got what I wanted out of this: Ruth, Charlie and Stan, together with a couple of bars of gold – I have very modest expectations of life and an untraceable half hundredweight of gold bullion meets most of them.

Despite Pickles offer, I was unwilling to speak on the telephone, that could lead to demands that I would refuse to follow, so I sent the briefest possible telegram to Dolan. I gave short details of the attempted theft, leaving out all mention of the accompanying mayhem, and simply stated that in consultation with Mr. Holmes and the Crown Prince the train, with its original cargo intact, would be returning to London today – weather permitting.

He could send me any response he wanted, and I might read and act on it, or then again I might not. More probably the latter. I then sent an even briefer telegram to the York station traffic office, advising them of our plans and the fact that we would be stopping there for coal and water.

I have, in my life to date, had many and varied experiences and spent very little of my time sitting quietly in a darkened room. However, last night was unusual, even by my standards. Holmes and Watson, whom I had assumed to be somewhat ascetic in their tastes, had been happy to join Ruth, Pedro and myself in a celebration of our success to date. A celebration that included significant amounts of the late Captain's claret and cognac, if we had failed to drink it ourselves it would surely have been stolen by others.

Stan had retired early, and though the Schindlers didn't partake of anything stronger than coffee they still joined in the party atmosphere. Mind you had I, like them, faced the prospect of being snowed in on the moors for the next three months, I could well have felt the same way.

Holmes, somehow one was never tempted to call him Sherlock, regaled us with what he called the real truth behind Doctor Watson's recently published story; 'The Sign of Four'. Large parts of which were either scurrilous or ribald, but all entertaining. It was no surprise to find that emerging for the morning's six o'clock call was unusually difficult.

Despite the difficulty, Holmes had Antonescu and some of the crew at work, moving the gold, before dawn and sent others to procure cart loads of coal from the dock side supplies. For once there was another mind as active and determined as my own, labouring towards our early departure.

Holmes made no attempt to return the bullion to its original hiding place beneath the carriage floorboards, being content to simply to have the men stack it along the length of the dining car floor. I had been fascinated by the sight and feel of such an unimaginable quantity of wealth. There were 448 ingots, each, according to Homes who would know this sort of thing, weighing almost 27½ pounds. It came to a staggering five and a half tons of gold bullion.

"It's strange," mused Holmes, "That they should have chosen such a random number as 448, one might have thought they would have settled on a round number like 450."

As I agreed with Holmes at the strangeness of it, I found Scroop rising unbidden to the surface of my mind, in exactly the way that he wouldn't be rising to the surface of the river. Those two missing bars he'd had strapped to his chest had weighed as much as a bag of potatoes. It was astonishing the man had been able to stand upright, never mind swim, and him so unimpressively weedy to look at. But at least they should hold him firmly in place, until I made it back here to bring him the benefits of an early resurrection. I set my mouth firmly to avoid any hint of a smile.

The snow had eased by nine thirty, leaving another six or seven inches on top of the existing layer, the sooner we got ourselves back to London, with nothing worse than smoke, fog and grime to cope with, the better I would feel. I hate the countryside, it's boringly green with birds chirping all over the place in summer, and all that incest to

336

cope with. Then in winter it's either muddy or frozen. The only thing the countryside is good for is for laying railway lines through it, to get to somewhere more interesting.

The undertaker's men had cleared the remaining bodies, Sergeant Pickles had produced reinforcements enlisted from the citizenry to secure both the ship and its crew, and some kind soul had even found and returned my revolver. Our little party was ready for the off.

Ruth had insisted that she and Charlie would be travelling in one of the carriages, with the remnants of the rest of our party. She said that Charlie had had more than enough railway excitement and would probably sleep for most of the way back.

Donald Buckley had wrapped up warmly and come down to wish us bon voyage. I showed my appreciation of his ready information yesterday by inviting him onto the footplate and showing him how things worked. In my experience, people are generally interested in railway engines. He asked that I should extend his Lodge's fraternal greetings to my own, and I reciprocated, as one does, in the general run of polite conversation.

I casually remarked that Ruth and I had been so impressed by the beauty of his town and the warmth of its inhabitants that we were already planning a return visit, early in the new year. I did wonder, but didn't ask, if he had a rowing boat.

"That would be delightful, but you don't want to go to a hotel, Doreen and I would be happy to have you stay with us. In fact if you could be here for the twelfth you can come as my guest to the next Lodge meeting." I agreed that this would be an excellent idea, whilst simultaneously trying to picture their reaction if I managed to hack a bit off the end of one of Scroop's ingots to put in the charity plate.

Then he mentioned something else.

"I almost forget to say, but when Chief Superintendant Parkinson was round at my house yesterday he did make one very strange request. He asked if I had a pistol he could borrow. He seemed most anxious to acquire one as quickly as possible. But like I said to him; 'where on earth am I going to get one of those?' He was a very unusual police officer."

So Parkinson had no plans to hide, and the only thing he wanted a pistol for was to kill me. I delayed our departure for ten minutes to conduct a thorough search of the carriages, both inside and underneath. Nothing, there was no sign of him, it was time to leave before he showed up. I shook hands with Donald and Sergeant Pickles, sounded the whistle and began to ease us slowly into motion.

Regrettably covered by the noise of the locomotive's departure, Constable Harrowby had appeared at the far end of the quay, and was sprinting towards us waving a piece of paper in the air. No doubt it was some urgent message from London, and he was determined to get it to us. Donald and the Sergeant were unaware of this as they had their backs to the running man, to wave us off. But I was looking back past them, Harrowby knew that I'd seen him and equally knew that I was determined to ignore him. The knowledge that his chase was futile finally brought him to a standstill, helplessly looking first at the undelivered piece of paper and then at me.

I waved to them all and pulled the regulator out a little further. Whatever the message said couldn't possibly have been anything that I wanted to hear about.

The relief at leaving this madhouse was incredible, I hadn't appreciated the extent of the pressure we had all been under for the last two days. It was a pure joy to puff our way contentedly along the sparkling river valley, leaving Whitby shaken but unstirred behind us.

*****

I had arranged to leave the town on the parallel line to the one we had arrived on, so that when we came back to the Ruswarp bridge we were able to cross beside the derailed BTP engine we had so hastily abandoned last night. It was still resting at an uncomfortable angle between the track and the steel side of the bridge, not one of my better railway moments. Three small boys were stood looking at it - no workmen had arrived on site yet, but I'd mentioned it to York so they'd be here soon.

As we made our slow but unimpeded way back through the Grosmont tunnel and onto the new line over the moors, Pedro was asking me to fill in the missing areas of his knowledge about the Bavarian Illuminati, but I wasn't a great deal of use. Otto Schindler had described them as being highly dangerous political fanatics, and barking mad, which certainly summed up what I'd seen of them.

Holmes had thought them to have been involved in fomenting the unrest which had led to the French revolution at the end of the last century, and then to the Terror. He said that they would probably be working, through their contacts with the Bulgarian Brotherhood, to produce similar effects in Rumania.

He described them as mad dogs, to be put down by any means possible. All told it was a relief to be leaving their British representative further behind us with every passing mile.

Considering that we had only known them for about thirty six hours, our leave taking from the Schindlers was surprisingly emotional. Ruth, Pedro, Stan and I hugged them in turn, and thanked them for having repeatedly saved our lives. Gretchen was still subdued at the memory of what she'd had to do, but that simply indicated that she was a more caring and sensitive individual than me, something that Ruth says is no great feat. So when we promised to see them again, that was exactly what we intended to do.

Before we re-boarded the train, I decided that after his recent ordeals, Stan still wasn't looking fully fit, I'd been asking too much of him this morning. I told him to go and get some rest in the carriage with the others. If he wanted to, he could rejoin us on the footplate at York. Pedro could manage perfectly well on his own for a while.

As we ploughed our way onwards to cross the high point of the line, the view was breathtaking. The last time we crossed here had been in darkness and in danger of our lives, but now, despite my complete lack of sympathy for the natural world, I was astonished at the beauty of it.

The rolling snow covered moors stretched out all around us as far as the eye could see, apart from being in mid ocean I don't think that I've ever seen that much sky. It's a cliché to describe clouds as looking like ships under full sail, but the huge grey and white shapes speeding past above us could be described in no other way. All this scenery was beginning to turn me native, the sooner I got back to London the better,

From this point, as I remembered from making our way up here, the line performed a long continuous descent down to Pickering and so, despite the snow, the going was easy. Although seventy tons of steam locomotive is a heavy and powerful force, and at low speeds can push its way through a great many obstacles, snow on the line must still be treated with respect. On a downhill run like this it was important not to let the engine overspeed, because if you do there's a chance, even with that weight of engine and tender, of riding up onto a wedge of compressed snow and ice. And if that happens you can easily find yourself derailed. I simply couldn't face the embarrassment of that happening twice in twenty four hours.

So we were, as you might say, ambling our way along at a relaxed 25 mph, allowing the gradient to help us. We had all day. Pedro was stoking, the fire box door was open and the hinged steel driver's leg shield was swung to one side. I was stood in the driver's position, on the right of the cab, looking through my porthole, or spectacle as some drivers call it. There was a gasp behind me and a clang of metal on metal, I turned round casually, it sounded as if he'd dropped the shovel.

As it happened, he had, but only because someone had dropped him first. He was lying on his side his long handled coal shovel beside him. Above him stood an astonishing figure, black face, black hair, black hands and black clothes - but this was no colonial colleague, this was no African - this was Parkinson. In his hand he carried a butcher's cleaver and his eyes, the whitest thing about him, were staring wildly into mine.

The last time I saw this man, onboard ship, he had been a successful master criminal, a senior member of the Bavarian Illuminati and in charge of events. This change in his circumstance revealed him as he really was - a homicidal maniac.

I began to take an instinctive step towards him. In a confined space where escape is impossible, if facing a man with a knife or a cleaver the sensible move is to get close to him, deny him room to swing. If he raises his arm to use the weapon you can grab it, the last place you want to be is at arm's length, he's got an extra twelve inches of cold steel at the end of his arm.

Unfortunately, the driver's leg shield, which guarded me from the fierce blast of the open fire box door, was not only open, but wedged into position. Between Parkinson and me the folding driver's seat had been let down from the bulkhead and was fixed onto its support leg. I would have to step over something to get at him, strangely he felt no urge to wait for this and came to me instead. I flattened my back against the side of the cab, but the movement was no more than my mind's natural reaction, rather than anything truly helpful.

His arm swung upwards and even more rapidly down again, the steel cleaver shone in the air. My hands came up to guard my head, but he was a man possessed, his movements smooth, rapid and fluent; and I was swimming through treacle. My last sight was of the broad flashing blade.

*****

Consciousness returned, it seemed unwillingly, many parts of me hurt, but mainly my head. The side of my face was flat against the steel of the footplate floor, I could taste coal dust in my mouth. Even before I tried to move them, I realised that my arms were in an unnatural position and probably tied together. Then I actually did try to move them, and found that I was right. My legs were similarly bound. I must have been unconscious for several minutes for him to have done that without me knowing.

"Do you know Fowler, the true pleasure in this isn't going to lie in killing you. It's in the fact that you're fully aware of your impending death, and of the fact that bold brave Lieutenant Fowler R.N. can't do a single thing to save himself. You and those silly women thought you were so clever, and now look at you."

I twisted my head up from the floor to see him sitting on the driver's chair, arms folded across his chest, sneering down at me, lying at his feet. He was still black, but now I realised the cause. Having known that we would have checked the storage locker in which Ruth and Charlie had hidden, he had literally buried himself under some of the coal in the tender. That displayed a level of single minded determination that was both rare and chilling. But he hadn't finished gloating.

"That's why I hit you with the side of the cleaver and not the blade. I wanted you in this position, and that's where I've got you. I wanted to kill that weakling you call Pedro, and that's what I'm going to do next. His uncle, the King will find himself isolated once people hear that his brilliant young nephew and heir is dead. The knowledge that the Crown Prince is waiting in the wings is the only

343

reason people still tolerate the King. With Ferdinand dead there'll be rioting in the streets demanding the King's replacement, and my people will be the only ones to produce an answer."

"You do realise that you're mad, utterly insane, don't you?"

"If that's what you want to call success, then I'm happy to agree with you. But first I would suggest you watch this."

He stood up and stepped over me, quite calmly, secure that there was nothing I could do to harm him. I couldn't turn my head far enough to see, but could feel that he was manhandling a body behind me. He dragged it round and held the head up by its hair, so that I could see the face, it was Pedro. There was blood covering one side of his face and his eyes were shut - it wasn't obvious if he was alive or dead.

Crouching over the comatose figure he slapped its face, repeatedly. Pedro moaned and began to come round, he slapped him again. This time he opened his eyes. Parkinson dragged him to his feet, holding him quite easily against the cab wall with one hand. I'd already experienced him half strangling me with one hand. He turned to me and smiled.

"Do you know, after I left the ship I was wondering where I could find a gun, but then I remembered there were guns lying about all over the train, so I just went and picked one up before I buried myself." He smiled blackly to himself at the oddity of the expression, then reached into his pocket and took out a pistol. He swung Pedro into the cab doorway, pointed the pistol at his belly and pulled the trigger. There was a bang and a flash, then, with a small grunt of exertion he sent the body flying from the train.

He turned back to me. "This is an impressive sort of madness, wouldn't you say. The Brotherhood want the Crown Prince dead, and now he is. The Brotherhood want five and half tons of gold, and I shall give it to them. In fact I shall probably also have your woman as well, she looks as if she might provide me with a short but entertaining final ride. Final for her you understand, not me."

He laughed, but it wasn't a properly mad laugh, just a brief perfectly normal sort of laugh, a bit of a disappointment in the circumstances. This sounded like a man who was going to do exactly what he said.

He walked around me, relishing his complete control of the engine, as well as its doomed driver.

"So much for your overblown reputation as a hero, what did that lead to? First you had to be rescued by a pair of German hausfraus, and then you needed the cast of some musical pantomime to help you out. Is this the best the British Navy can produce – a bunch of prancing young men? I had hoped for more from you. But tell me how did you know about the Friends of Adam, that you mentioned on the ship? Who told you that, do we have a traitor in our ranks?"

"I don't think so, it's just a normal part of our Lodge announcements, it comes under the heading of Health Warnings. You know the sort of thing: if you drink dirty water you'll get cholera, if you sleep with cheap whores you'll get pox, and if you mix with the Illuminati you'll end up having sex with your mother. Now that I've met you I can see what they mean."

He smiled tolerantly at me, I wasn't even reaching him, let alone bothering him. "We should be in Pickering in another ten minutes or so, and just before we get there I shall slit your throat." Leaning down he patted the side of my face in a friendly sort of way. Then he began to shovel some more coal into the roaring firebox, he seemed to be familiar with our basic routines, which I found worrying.

Any spare time I'd ever had to review the situation was long gone, what was left? I was lying sideways across the footplate, my head close to the right side of the cab. By moving slightly each time his back was to me I managed to move the top of my head against the steel plate of the cab side, then I bent my knees slightly to draw my legs up. I was conscious of my limited time in this position, the heat from the open fire box door was blistering, it was almost enough to singe your clothes. That was why the driver had a steel shield to protect his legs.

The next time he stepped by me, with his shovel of coal, I put every ounce of effort I had into a wild, vicious, two legged lunge, jabbing my tied feet at his, my head against the cab side giving me the necessary fixed point to thrust against. I made contact and caught him by surprise, he staggered, the shovelful of coal went flying, then he collapsed helplessly to the floor.

I rolled urgently towards him, being jolted and shaken by the shifting motion of the footplate floor. I collided with his fallen body, twisting round in an attempt to use my feet again, this time against his head. He was dazed by his unexpected and heavy fall and I caught him, not quite as hard as I might have hoped – but hard enough to bang his head backwards into the bulkhead. The trouble was that left me in the wrong position for a second, killing blow. I squirmed backwards to try and regroup, but as I did so he recovered sufficiently to scrabble beyond the range of my bound feet.

He stood up, leaning against the wall for a moment, to take stock of what damage I might have done him. Not enough, was the answer. He looked at me, as if he were mildly surprised at what I'd been able to do, but mild surprise won no prizes. He was upright and ready for action, while I was trussed like a turkey, and ready for stuffing.

"Can I relax now? Was that it – your last major effort? Your trouble is that you're out of your depth and out of condition – you're an amateur. But now it's time you joined your friend." He laughed again, but this time he didn't sound so sincere.

He took a knife from his pocket, it looked every bit as nasty as the one I had taken from one of my earlier assailants, there had been so many it was beginning to be difficult to keep track. He swung the blade out and it clicked into position. I felt cold and tired, losing does that to you. It's not the exertion that exhausts you half as much as the losing, and this time I was going to lose permanently.

He squatted down beside me, in the middle of my own cab floor. He grasped a handful of my shirt front to steady himself and put the point of the knife to the side of my throat.

There was a sudden and hideous squealing, his eyes widened in alarm and confusion, and as the engine slowed, my helpless body began to move forwards along the floor. I realised immediately what had happened, someone had applied the emergency brakes.

Unfortunately for him, whilst I was flat on my back and unable to accomplish much more than slide into the base of the boiler, he was squatting beside me on his haunches, a very unstable position in which to cope with emergency braking. This was just like me standing on the outside of the engine and telling Ruth to put the brakes on. He shot forwards, head first, the knife still in his hand. With the difference in our relative movements his forward motion removed him from my field of vision, all that I heard was a thud, followed by the most hideous, but strangely muffled scream. Then as the engine ground and squealed its way to a halt, I finally recovered enough control of my bound body to turn myself in his direction.

He had been propelled head first into the open firebox, his shoulders were wedged tight into the frame of its open door. As I looked, his arms and legs were thrashing violently, but pointlessly about. At that temperature his brain would have boiled within seconds, in fact his whole head would be no more than a charred horror by now, the movements I saw were the uncontrolled spasms of a dead man.

The air was filled with the smell of burnt hair and burnt clothing. I am one of the least squeamish people imaginable, and yet even I was revolted by the gothic nature of his going. However, one benefit from being trussed like a turkey was that it was going to keep me from the hideous task of wrenching the still twitching corpse from the firebox door, to reveal its blackened cinder of a head.

Having finally come to a halt, there came a rush of interested parties, all desperate to discover the cause of the problem. Antonescu was helpful enough to undertake Parkinson's extraction. It was just regrettable that as the body was dragged free, there came a new sensation; the unmistakeable smell of Sunday lunch - of freshly roasted meat. That with the memory of Pedro's brutal end made for a very unhappy mix of emotions.

The passenger's knowledge that there was a problem to be concerned about, came from having seen Pedro's limp body tumbling to the ground beside the train. By a stroke of either great good luck, or great presence of mind, before we left Whitby Stan had removed the wedges he inserted in London, which had disabled the automatic braking system. Pulling the communication cord had thus brought down the curtain on Parkinson's deranged performance, and incidentally saved my life.

Now all that was left to us was the sad and mournful task of retrieving Pedro's body, Antonescu's fears for his safety on the footplate having been fully justified. I closed the now unoccupied fire box door and pulled the reverser lever fully backwards, then let some steam into the cylinders to take us back to look for him. This was a cruel turn of fate for our affairs, we had been so close to a successful conclusion, only to have such a vital part dashed from us at this late stage.

We hadn't travelled far since the shooting and so it was only two or three minutes later that we came across the body. The surprising thing when we found it, was the body's position, it was standing upright. He had not only survived but managed to climb to his feet, and was now leaning against a track side fence. He was dazed, and had no idea how he came to be where he found himself, but otherwise was not seriously injured. Apparently landing face first in deep snow is an effective pick me up for those who have recently been assassinated. I wondered if word of this new and exciting treatment should be circulated around hospitals.

I jumped down and rushed to grab him before he fell over again, and also to check for the bullet wound. He was the second person in twenty four hours to have taken a bullet in the belly without fatal consequences. They weren't all carrying gold bullion, were they?

The front of his shirt showed the mark of the gun shot, but only the scorched blast mark, there was no bullet hole. I went back to the engine and found the pistol lying on the floor, it was Ruth's blank firer. The stupid man had picked up the wrong gun – thank God for that.

As part of my scheme for rotating injured firemen, Stan returned to the footplate and Pedro went back to be tended by Ruth. The Major insisted on staying up front with me, to help with the shovelling, in a weird sort of way I could almost imagine growing to like the man. I shook my head to try and clear the thought.

Having quite run out of replacement drivers, I stayed where I was, with a rather attractive bandage setting of my dark good looks. Or at least that's what Ruth said as she finished tying it, but then she's always been such a bloody awful liar. After which we had only to collect the four detached carriages and the missing constables before it was full steam ahead for London. I felt we'd all probably had enough excitement for a day or two.

*****

Our arrival in King's Cross, later that afternoon, was a scene of carefully muted panic, it had been determined that there should be no publicity, but a

350

million people seemed desperate to know what had happened.

During our cross country progress, the night before last, a stream of messages had been arriving back at the King's Cross traffic office. Our refusal to make the scheduled stop at York, our unscheduled diversion to Whitby for which, mysteriously, no responsibility had yet been allocated. All swiftly followed by the apparent disappearance, somewhere in the night, of a complete train, all its personnel, five and a half tons of gold and the Crown Prince of Rumania. There had been a considerable amount of knicker wetting hysteria, with various officials desperately trying to allocate blame to anyone other than themselves.

On our arrival back in London, Pedro had once more reverted to being Crown Prince Ferdinand and, along with the faithful but now coal stained Antonescu, had been removed to a nearby hospital to confirm his state of health. It seemed that my own health was of less immediately pressing concern.

Then, to complete the panic, Scotland Yard had finally woken up to the fact that a detachment of their detectives had been commandeered by two officers who were presently on sick leave, and whose movements could be accounted for with sufficient reliability to guarantee that they weren't on the train. To my astonishment it transpired that there really were two genuine police officers called Parkinson and Scroop, they just didn't happen to be the ones I'd met.

Police reports of the massacre on Whitby docks had increased the confusion, with the Lord Lieutenant of Yorkshire having been instructed yesterday to call out the militia. But before any of this could take effect, the unusual combination of Gretchen Schindler, Driver Fowler and the cast of H.M.S. Pinafore had taken the requisite actions to bring this spectacular grand larceny to a halt. The only serious amendment to the truth that I felt impelled to make was when asked the whereabouts of the bogus Scroop. I pleaded ignorance, thinking that any mention of shallow water, gold bars and a grappling iron would only serve to confuse matters.

As I gave my account to a senior and apparently genuine police officer, the multi titled St. Aubyn-Jollie being unaccountably absent, Holmes and Watson were with me, corroborating my statements. Their presence simplified the whole process, if Sherlock Holmes said that something was so, then officialdom tended to accept the fact. Without their supporting evidence I would probably still be explaining matters.

After the questions and explanations had finally run their course, and all parties were told that they were, for the time being, free to go; Holmes, Watson and myself were having a word.

"As you might imagine, my good friend here," he placed a hand on Doctor Watson's shoulder, "Will no doubt be putting pen to paper in the near future, to detail our adventures. I would esteem it a personal favour if you were not to mention our recent cooperation to anyone. It really is most advantageous for me to have my very existence doubted by the general populace. And although the good Doctor is always anxious to play up my own role in these events, sometimes unfairly, you have my word that your contribution will not be ignored."

Watson seemed uncomfortable with this dissection of his methods. "I really don't think

352

there's any need to cast me as such an irresponsible chronicler. At least I manage to produce a record of your cases, and usually one that people will pay money to read. Lord knows what would happen if the paperwork was ever to be left to you."

"Gentlemen," I said, "You may take as much or as little credit as you wish, and I will still read the story with interest. I have no desire to claim any sort of credit or glory, having already been down that path once before. I have a loving wife, a nice home and satisfying employment, that should be enough for any man."

"Ah, but do you also have a grappling iron, or would you like to borrow mine?" Asked Holmes, with what could only be described as a Knowing Look. He must have somehow discovered Scroop's end, but said nothing, he was clearly having some amusement at my expense. Perhaps he really was as clever as they said. But I felt no embarrassment in my actions and so accepted his offer of the loan of the item. With a deep feeling of relief I finally went to find Ruth and Charlie and we made our weary way home.

*****

The simple suburban pleasures of Clerkenwell welcomed us back; the familiar streets, the friendly hellos as we passed people we knew, and at last our own front door – with not so much as a solitary Crown Prince in sight.

We had been uncertain what sort of worried or panic stricken message might await us from Charlie's ma, Hannah, but strangely there was nothing. Despite the haste of our departure, we had taken the time to post a brief note to her, explaining that we would be taking Charlie away for the night, and would send word as soon as we were back. That was supposed to have been yesterday, but we had been otherwise engaged at the time. She should have been beside herself with worry by now.

As neither of us felt like cooking, Ruth had been round the corner to Guarini's for some plated meat pie, which she'd put to warm in the gas oven. I busied myself with lighting the fire in the snug, after we'd eaten I would walk over to Hannah's, taking Charlie with me.

But whilst the three of us were still finishing our meal, Hannah appeared - bursting in with her usual 'Anybody Home?' as she marched in without knocking. Charlie was delighted and rushed to hug her, weak and feckless as she undoubtedly was, her children still loved her.

"Look I know how upset you must be, and I'm so sorry, I wouldn't have done it for the world. It was just that a spot came free at the Gaiety in West Ham, and Harold said that I couldn't afford to turn it down." She gabbled on, apparently determined to produce the maximum number of words in the minimum amount of time, to forestall the objections she clearly expected us to make.

"I knew you wouldn't mind, it was only for a couple of nights. And honestly I couldn't get back yesterday, I wasn't feeling too well."

I felt the need to interrupt. "Never mind that, did you get our letter?"

"Letter? Oh yes there was a letter waiting when I got home, but I haven't opened it yet. I know you won't believe me but I haven't had a single minute to myself, it's just been rush, rush, rush. It's been like a madhouse." She tailed off, realising that Ruth and I had stopped looking at her, and were now looking at each other. There were so many things to say to this deeply foolish woman that neither of us were quite sure where to begin.

But there was something even more pressing than our disapproval, Charlie wanted to share his adventures, he had a lot to say and his mother was the one to say it to.

"We all went on the train together, and Auntie Ruth and me hid in this coal hole, and then some men came and there were guns and shooting. Then the bad men kidnapped me and kept me prisoner."

Hannah scooped him up, with a beaming smile all over her face, this was exactly the sort of diversion she needed, anything to take the spotlight off her. When Hannah said that she *hadn't been feeling well,* it meant she'd been so hungover she couldn't stand up straight.

Charlie was unstoppable, he had to tell someone what had been going on. "Then Uncle Puff Puff came looking for me with his gun, but then the two men that everyone said were dead, came out and picked me up and took me back into their cabin with them. Then later on one of them bought me this train." He held up the bright red engine to be admired. "Then there were all these sailors, who werc friends of Aunty Ruth, and they shut the bridge on top of this ship. Then the men on the ship got very angry . . . ."

IIannah looked at us proudly, as Charlie pressed on with his slightly jumbled but essentially accurate version of events. "Have you ever heard anything like it? He's a proper little comedian this one, and no mistake." She looked fondly down at him.

"You're going to be on the boards – just like your ma – aren't you Charlie?" Then she hugged him tighter and kissed the top of his head, but even that didn't stop him pressing on with the story.

I began to see why Holmes and Watson could feel so secure with their balancing act of presenting the truth to a disbelieving public. As for Charlie ever going on the boards – he'd need to be steered away from that one, he was far too bright for such a hopeless trade. I might even get him a job on the railways.

Meanwhile,
the newspapers reported . . .

AN APOLOGY ISSUED
Following a spate of alarming, and at times downright hair raising, reports arriving recently from northern parts, light has finally been shed on the mystery.

It seems that a theatre manager in that well known resort of Whitby, Yorks, desiring to increase ticket sales, hit on the novel approach of transferring a part of his performance to the great outdoors.

Following a ceremonial march through the streets of the town, complete with drawn swords and stage rifles, the cast of Gilbert and Sullivan's HMS Pinafore held a mock battle at the fish quay, during which numerous participants were 'despatched' with great gusto, complete with stage blood and 'gunfire'. They then performed an al fresco medley of songs from the show, before repairing to more normal surroundings for their evening performance.

Unaware of the theatrical nature of these proceedings, many residents and bystanders were completely taken in by the apparent seriousness of events, some even summoning the assistance of the constabulary.

A penitent theatre manager has now issued a formal apology to all those who were unaware of the true nature of this performance. Reliable reports from Whitby state that all remaining tickets were rapidly sold out.

A spokesman for the producer, Mr. Richard D'Oyly Carte, said that he strongly deprecated all such tricks and thought them quite unnecessary.

If you enjoyed reading about
Charlie Chaplin's Uncle,
then you might enjoy
a couple of other books
by the same author . . .

RUDE AWAKENING
Ian Okell

'Tangled and dangerous relationships in a sweeping saga of conflict, betrayal and discovery. As seen through the eyes of an entertaining and extremely devious observer.'

'They were either going to install me as the Arch Druid, or they had something of a sacrificial nature in mind. Perhaps I should tell them I wasn't a virgin.'

He already knew his cancer was terminal and lying in hospital, finally surrendering to the morphine, Michael accepts that he is dying. But suddenly it's all gone wrong - he's awake when he should be dead, and in a place he's never seen before.

Is this just the random sparking of failing brain cells before the last goodbye? Is this what death feels like? Out of place and out of time - even realising that he is still alive doesn't do him any good. He is at the wrong end of an impossible journey, in a society untouched by civilisation.

Sample five star Amazon Reviews *more onsite*

A Magical Mystery Tour – It's so gripping I was concerned the pace might fall off but I needn't have worried. Now I've finished, I don't know if I have been reading an adventure, a history, a travelogue or a very moving love story, I am going to have to read it again. (RB)

Classic Storytelling - treads a delicate line between witty observation and tense action. (JK)

Published by - youwriteon.com
**Available from all good book shops
and from Amazon - in book or Kindle version**

LOOSE CANNON
Ian Okell

It isn't paranoid to think they're trying to kill you - not if it's true. Loose Cannon takes up where The 39 Steps and Rogue Male left off, but this time with a regular supply of sharp one liners to go with the mayhem.

Harry Lyndon is a civilised and happy man, his world organised just the way he likes it. But then, out of the blue, someone tries to kill him - and he has no idea who or why.

The trouble is that when he tells the police it turns out they also want him dead. Something is horribly wrong, He's forced to run, with nothing but the clothes on his back. It isn't mistaken identity. His credit cards have been cancelled, his flat watched and his girlfriend disappeared. He is the named subject of a full scale terrorist alert - and they're going to shoot him on sight.

Only one thing might help - without his anti psychotic tablets he's getting more than a little unstable himself - dangerously so. Somebody, somewhere, thought he'd be a pushover . . . .

Sample five star Amazon Reviews *more onsite*
An Impressive Performance: The pace relentless and the narrator both ruthless and witty (N.C.)

Just What I Needed: It grabs and involves you and makes you genuinely care what happens to the participants (T.H.)

Published by - youwriteon.com
Available from all good book shops
and from Amazon - in book or Kindle version

Lightning Source UK Ltd.
Milton Keynes UK
UKOW041847290313

208422UK00001B/1/P